W9-BUZ-362

Advance Praise for *What's Never Said*

"Susan Shapiro exuberantly limns love among the ruins (of writing programs!) in her glimmering new page-turner. She gets it all exactly right—the flashing egos, the yearning for connection crossed by the hunger for achievement—and it's written with sly wit and razor-keen intelligence. It's sexy and hilarious, but also as haunting as the perfect poem."
—Caroline Leavitt, bestselling author of *Is This Tomorrow*

"*What's Never Said* is the work of a master—a fun, charming master. Brilliant dialogue, quick and expert prose, unforgettable characters. If there's any justice in publishing this will be the hit of the season."
—Darin Straus, award-winning author of *Half a Life*.

"Shapiro writes about the romantic and creative lives of New York writers the way only a true insider can, nailing all the longings, petty rivalries and genuine passion. *What's Never Said* is a fizzy, delicious drink of a novel."
—Teddy Wayne, bestselling author of
The Love Song of Johnny Valentine

"Mining the downtown literary scene, Shapiro strikes comedic gold in this rollicking story of poets behaving badly. It's all here, the searing verse and sultry trysts, brutal betrayals and enduring friendships. And something else too: a deep, abiding love of the ink-smeared world she so deftly sends up."
—David Goodwillie, author of *American Subversive*

"Susan Shapiro is the Nora Ephron of a new generation. *What's Never Said* is poignant, charming and heartbreaking."
—Susan Jane Gilman, bestselling author of
The Ice Cream Queen of Orchard Street

WHAT'S NEVER SAID

SUSAN SHAPIRO

Heliotrope Books

NEW YORK

WHAT'S NEVER SAID

This is a work of fiction. All the characters, places, and events portrayed in this novel are either products of the author's imagination or are used fictitiously. Any resemblance to actual events or persons, living or dead, is coincidental.

Heliotrope Books LLC
heliotropebooks@gmail.com

Cover by Judy Tipton-Katzman

Designed and typeset by Naomi Rosenblatt with AJJ Design

Dedicated to Danielle Perez and Naomi Rosenblatt,
my great Greenwich Village editors

Also by Susan Shapiro

Five Men Who Broke My Heart
Lighting Up
Only As Good as Your Word
Secrets of a Fix-Up Fanatic
Speed Shrinking
Overexposed
Food for the Soul (with Elizabeth Maxwell)
Unhooked (with Frederick Woolverton)
The Bosnia List (with Kenan Trebinecevic)

PART ONE: 2010

1

April 2010

LILA

Lila knew it was dangerous to show up at Daniel's reading. She should take off right now, disappear out the back door before anything happened. Her eyes darted nervously at the six books cradled in her arms, Daniel's new one on top, already adorned with the circular golden sticker: "Winner of the Pulitzer Prize." Giving him the envelope in her purse felt too risky. Her hand was sweating.

"He's only signing his new collection." A nerdy bespectacled Barnes & Noble salesman pointed to the hardcovers Lila held as she stood at the end of the long queue.

She didn't understand what he wanted.

"You have to leave the others at the register," he scolded, as if she was scheming to take something that wasn't hers. Or was that just her paranoia?

Lila's husband, in Los Angeles on business, would be livid to learn she'd lied to him by coming. Daniel had surely brought his Israeli wife and children along. Lila was fine now, stable, happily married. She should leave her romantic past lost and buried, where it belonged. But she couldn't let Daniel go without telling him tonight.

She gave the clerk back the other books. She already owned *My Father's*

Secret—which Lila herself had titled one long-ago winter evening at Daniel's old Horatio Street hovel. In fact, she possessed the collection in galleys, hardcover *and* paperback. She finally felt ready to share the secret that *she'd* concealed all these years. It would be her last chance to slip him the page she'd hidden in her pocketbook and watch his reaction. Would he be upset? She pictured him enraged, demanding she leave. Or maybe he'd be moved to whisper, "Let's sneak out for a drink later." She already regretted coming. She didn't belong here.

"Thank you," the clerk snapped, reclaiming the contraband.

"What an idiotic rule," mumbled a dark-haired teenager behind Lila, rolling her eyes. White iPod buds dangled from her ears. She had a pirate tattoo on her arm, rectangular glasses, a metal ring piercing her lower lip.

"Right. You'd think they'd figure out the more he signs, the more books they sell," Lila said, trying not to stare at the girl's lip piercing, wondering if it hurt when she kissed.

As the line crawled forward, Lila clung to Daniel's latest, smiling as if in on a private joke: His Jewish anti-hero failure shtick had paid off at last. Forty years after Portnoy, *Losers Like Me* made him a winner. She turned to the page titled *Hard To Recall* that chronicled how Daniel's dad had displayed affection for him only after he was diagnosed with Alzheimer's. "Are you forgetting your disappointment, Father, or remembering you forgot me?"

"Any good?" asked Lip Ring.

"He's so fucking intense," Lila said. Was she swearing to sound hip?

If she turned around and went home now, nobody would notice. Why was she so afraid to stay? It had been almost three decades since she'd been Daniel's naïve nineteen-year-old student. She tried deep yoga breaths, inhaling for stress release, quietly taking in air, blowing it out through her mouth in steps. It wasn't working.

The girl caught Lila in the middle of an exhale. "You okay?"

"Yeah." Her badass style reminded Lila of the way her best friend Sari had looked when they'd lived together in the grad school dorm. "You're in college?"

"Parsons Design. My mom studied with Daniel Wildman at New City University."

"Me too," Lila admitted, realizing she saw herself as closer to the girl's age than her mother's. Just being in Daniel's proximity made her regress to the age when they'd first met. "What's your mom's name?"

"Her maiden name was Mary Jonas," Lip Ring said. "It was, like, way back in the eighties."

"Sounds familiar."

"She had the hots for this famous Irish poet, Cormick."

"Like everyone. Except me. I had a thing with Wildman," Lila blurted out.

"You did?" Lip Ring removed her ear buds.

Lila raised her eyebrows a little.

This girl who looked like Sari inched closer. "Was it serious?"

Lila nodded yes.

"What happened?" Lip Ring asked.

Lila flashed to the first holiday party Daniel threw for their class. After everyone else left, they'd sat on the wooden floor of his dusty West Village one-bedroom, drinking cheap Chardonnay from paper cups, as she anxiously chattered about a rewrite. "You talk too much, too loud, too fast," he'd said, cutting her off. Noticing her blush, he'd added, "Don't be nervous, we're not having an affair or anything."

Lip Ring's inquisitive gaze made Lila self-conscious. "Graduate writing programs are notorious hotbeds," she backpedaled a bit.

"Man, why did I pick design? All my teachers are, like, totally gay." She laughed. "Well, cool you guys stayed friends."

"Yeah, cool."

Except Lila had not had any contact with Daniel since 1983.

She'd only heard about the Pulitzer at the magazine that morning, from Sari's email with the subject heading "Can You Believe Wildman Nailed the Big Kahuna?" that linked the *nytimes.com* article. Sari was one of only three living people in the world who knew the whole story. Daniel didn't.

Neither did her husband—who'd emailed from California "did you see who won the pulitzer," in all small letters; the news had turned him into e.e.cummings.

"Good for him." Lila had pretended this new honor for Daniel didn't stir up alarm.

"You're not going to his reading, are you?" he'd called to ask.

"No," she'd answered, debating—as she said it—whether she would defy him. After hanging up, she'd slid off her iPhone. Then she'd locked the door to her office and Googled "Daniel Wildman." Within seconds she was listening to an audio clip of him reciting his verse about their split decades earlier: "She revises her resume nightly / making the choice between love and ambition, / as if her heart is a prism in which each pleasure must be fractured."

It was a visceral shock to hear his deep, lilting, familiar voice. Had he always been so accessible? She clicked the blue icon and listened again, recognizing Daniel's self-deprecating wit, which Lila, a near-sighted Wisconsin girl with thin skin and size ten shoes, had over-identified with from the start. His stanza on the art of losing love, with its nod to Elizabeth Bishop, could refer to *any* torrid affair from his past. But *she* had inspired *To An Ambitious Young Woman*. When he'd told her she was the sole student he'd ever touched, she believed him.

Lila had gazed at the rugged face pictured on his website, his brown oval eyes so penetrating they'd rendered her transparent. His wife, standing next to him, looked petite, a better fit for Daniel, who stood Lila's height, five foot nine. "You're trying to tower over me," he'd argued once, when Lila had worn her favorite spiky heels.

Hungry to find out more about him, she'd uncovered an old post on the charity camp his wife founded, where Israeli and Palestinian kids could play in peace, when Daniel's sons were young. At this point, they were finishing college and his daughter was Lila's age when she'd studied with him. Although Lila had found a good husband and top publishing house for her book, she couldn't compete with Daniel's award or his wife, the International *Tzedakah* Queen and Mom of the Year. She was oddly gratified that his work was being recognized, but it was a selfish glee, as if his prize validated her literary taste. And her pain. If you sacrificed everything for a poet, he should at least turn out to be a major leaguer, right?

Now she scanned the crowd to get a peek at his mate. There she was—with her makeup-free face, chestnut hair streaked with gray. Daniel preferred the natural type. He never had liked the way Lila dressed; he'd once told her not to bother shaving her legs or underarms. "If I wanted to be a hillbilly, I'd go back to Baraboo," she'd replied. Then he'd stolen Lila's hometown for *Jewess From Baraboo*, despite her protest that the suffix "ess" was sexist.

Within minutes of the Pulitzer news conference this morning, she'd noted, Daniel's website bio had been updated to include the prize. And *he* had once chided Lila for *her* youthful ambition. She wasn't young anymore; she was turning fifty. When she'd heard Daniel would be a block away, she'd sneaked to her files and found the page from that horrible, haunting night, so ancient it was typed on an IBM Selectric. She was sick of keeping quiet. She was ready to give Daniel her only copy to read, hoping the gesture alone would be liberating.

Jittery all day, she'd left the magazine early to get her hair done, having her highlights frosted ash blond, her original color. She'd put on the black silk dress and Prada high heels she'd bought at Bergdorf's for her Charlie Rose interview. As the line crept closer, she scanned all the collegiate kids in jeans and sweatshirts, feeling overdressed. She should have worn Levi's and loafers, to look like seeing Daniel again was no big deal.

Even half-obscured by a pillar, his chiseled face was regal. He was powerful before the grand audience, more self-assured than he used to be. Lila was relieved she'd relinquished his other books so she didn't seem like a groupie. As she reached the head of the line, the clerk, who'd been marking names on Post-Its to show the author what to sign, had disappeared. Lila stood before Daniel, separated only by the thin table. Her hand sweated as she held out his slender book, feeling elated, a grad student again, younger, completely unveiled.

"Thanks for coming." Unlike the last time they'd been this close, he was serene, sober.

"My pleasure. You killed," tumbled out of her mouth, as if she were still his coed.

"Thanks." He looked up at her. "Who should I inscribe it to?"

"To me," Lila said.

He tilted his pen on the page, glanced up sideways and asked, "Your name?"

What? He didn't know? Her breath stuck in her throat as he stared at her blankly. He was near seventy now. Was his eyesight failing?

"Sign it to Lila Penn." She stared at him, waiting for her name and face to jar his recollection.

"One *N* or two?" he asked in a monotone.

"Two *N's*," she answered, dumbfounded, pushing her hair behind her ear. He didn't know how to spell her married moniker? That meant he'd never seen her byline. She felt flushed and frazzled. Maybe he'd inherited "the forgetting disease" that had afflicted his father.

"With that last name, I hope you're not a writer," he said, looking pleased with his quip, the same cheesy joke every other idiot made.

"No, I'm a teacher." She inverted their connection, trying to trick him into a reaction. But it was a lie. She'd recently been asked to teach a class, but she hadn't responded.

"Okay, thanks for buying my book," he said by rote.

Her eyes fell on his inscription: "To Lila Penn, All the Best. Daniel Wildman." As if she were any stranger. Her forehead was hot, her heart knotting up in her chest.

Had he seduced so many students he couldn't even recall who she was? She must have overblown their relationship in her head. Could she be the one whose memory was addled? Sari had insisted she'd had a distorted self-image. Lip Ring hovered right behind her, staring. She felt so ashamed, as if she'd just been exposed as a pathetic hanger-on, an imposter.

"My maiden name is Lerner." She blinked back tears, not believing he'd erased her. The whole room blurred.

"My wife Ronit kept hers," he said smoothly, no recognition in his eyes. Then he reached his hand out for Lip Ring's book and opened it. "Who am I signing it to?" he asked the youthful interloper, flashing the same polite grin, finished with Lila.

"To my mother, Mary Jonas. She studied with you a million years ago."

"I know Mary! You look like her. She still work at Little Brown?" He laughed aloud, the big, hearty full-bodied laugh Lila used to love. "Must have been at least two million. Do you have a name too?"

Lila caught her reflection in the framed store poster, focusing on the faint marionette lines around her mouth, mortified to suddenly realize she'd lost her youth and beauty. She usually still saw herself as attractive. Yet she was obviously no longer a head-turner, the woman Daniel had called "his luscious muse." Had she changed *that* much? The older suitor who'd adored her, exalted her looks more than any other male she'd known, had no idea who she was. *But Daniel, you were the one who accepted me, discovered me, drew stars in the margins of my rough drafts.*

She should have listened to her husband. Lila could not handle seeing Daniel. She slinked to the register, fumbling for her wallet, so flustered his book fell to the floor. The rule: *If you drop a book, kiss it, sacred like the Torah"* echoed from her childhood. She crouched down and quickly scooped it up, humiliated, invisible. As she went to pay, Lila spied the envelope she brought in the pocket of her purse, but it was too late. She had obviously overestimated her effect on him, her place in his romantic lexicon.

Out of all the conflicting scenarios she'd envisioned for almost thirty years, Lila had never once even imagined that Daniel Wildman wouldn't remember.

PART TWO: 1980

2

September 1980

DANIEL

He took the long way tonight, strolling down the West Village's uneven cobblestone streets, sucking in deep breaths of the brisk air. Daniel hoped it would calm his anxiety before the orientation party for new creative writing graduates he was stuck co-hosting. He loved being in the classroom, but he found these superficial Cormick-fests exhausting. He wished everyone could see the truth: he did all the work while his boss was a lecherous figurehead who would arrive late, get soused and charm the fifty newbies into believing their parents' exorbitant tuition would make them the next Adrienne Rich, John Updike or Ashbery. He swore to himself this would be the term he'd blast out of Cormick's shadow and break the humiliating monster block that had kept him from finishing his second book for the last decade.

Daniel planned to stash his coat and briefcase in his office and down a shot of the secret Suntory whiskey Howard brought him from Japan before launching into his dancing monkey routine—for one hour. Then he could rush home to nail the end of his poem on the shallow nature of ambition. Stepping off the elevator on the third floor, an impossibly tall dirty blonde in a plaid dress ambushed him before he could get to his office.

"You're Professor Wildman? Oh good. You're my teacher—and my adviser. I'm Lila Lerner. I just moved here from Wisconsin."

Ah, so this was the Lerner girl, the scholarship kid he almost rejected after he discovered she'd finished her undergraduate degree in two years. He hadn't pictured a big, blond, blue-eyed Jew, let alone one so gawky. Her pale, freckled skin was free of makeup. Her beige sweater seemed hand crocheted. Talk about right off the bus. No wonder she was always racing for diplomas and rewards. Daniel glanced at his watch—she was twenty minutes early. He flashed to the stanza he'd been honing, on strivers whose entire self-worth revolved around stacking up external accomplishments, "as if achievement were redemption."

"It's an honor to meet you," she said, thrusting out her hand.

Her grip was robust—and endless.

"So you're only 19? Planning to finish your Ph.D. by the end of the mixer?" he teased, wrestling his limb free.

"Why? Are you threatened by fast women?" she blurted.

Indeed he was. But she looked more like an awkward teenager, with her lopsided ponytail, thick eyebrows, and gangly arms bouncing around like a marionette. He realized, with amusement, she probably hadn't even caught her own double entendre.

"According to my schedule our class starts on Monday," she said, smiling cheerfully, fishing out the printed page from her knapsack to show him, along with her school I.D., as if he wouldn't believe who she was without proof, adding, "I'm a poetry concentrate."

"I know, Lila," he said. "I'm the one who accepted you."

"You are? Wow. How amazing, the first person I meet is the one who took me."

How amazing, I'm in the place where I teach, he thought. "Must be fate." He smiled.

"Right. Total poetry kismet." She giggled.

"Let me just put away my stuff," he said.

She mistook this as an invitation to trail him into the cluttered, windowless cave where he'd kept office hours for the last ten years. He hid his briefcase under the oversized oak desk and grabbed his favorite silver Cross pen and clipboard.

"What a mess. How d'ya find anything?" Surveying his notebooks, supplies, antique ashtray and knickknacks on the window ledge, she picked up his old magnifying glass with the mermaid etched on the handle. "Seriously cool kitsch," Lila said, holding it up close to her eye and staring at him through it, as if she were Inspector Clouseau.

His late mother had won it for him at the Coney Island arcade. Interesting that Lila had zeroed right in on the most treasured relic in the room, like she had X-ray vision. It unnerved him. He gently returned the last present his mom had given him to its place and escorted Lila out.

In the main room, the table was set up with wine, beer, soda cans and cheese, no utensils. He reached under the cabinets for paper cups, napkins, plastic knives and a corkscrew. Where were the crackers? He found a box of Saltines he opened quickly.

"Listen, I wanted you to know that I really appreciate the financial aid. Otherwise I'd be stuck in Madison. They're good for fiction, but confessional poetry's my passion. I know Auden said 'Poetry makes nothing happen,'" she shared breathlessly, "but I think he was being facetious. Don't you?"

Thankfully a group of coeds poured out of the elevator. "Come on in, come in," Daniel greeted three girls—all with oval glasses—followed by two tall foreign-looking boys. "I know you're just here for the free booze." He pointed to the drinks. "I'm Professor Wildman, co-chair of the MFA's poetry division."

"Mary Jonas," said the short, bespectacled nerd in a corduroy skirt.

"I am Lenu, from Nigeria. I'm working on a novel," said a tall, thin black kid, putting out his hand.

"Like Chinua Achebe," Daniel said, giving him a firm shake.

"Yes, yes." Lenu smiled. "*Things Fall Apart.*"

"I heard it was a response to the racism of Conrad's *Heart of Darkness,*" Lila jumped in. "The title's from Yeats' poem *The Second Coming.* Though I'm sure you already know that."

Actually he hadn't. Daniel recited to himself: "Things fall apart; the center cannot hold." How had he missed it all these years? He did a double take, glancing over again at Lila. He had to admit she seemed well-read.

"Where's Conor Cormick?" asked an elegant brunette in a wool dress. "I'm Judith Bay. I was accepted at Iowa and Columbia University. But when I showed Cormick the work I published at MacDowell, he called my poems enthralling. So I decided to attend NCU just to study with Cormick."

Can you use his name in a sentence four more times, Daniel wondered. "Maybe he's in his office?" he suggested, pointing down the hall. She took off, sashaying her ass in her tight dress, her high heels clicking. Yeah, I'll bet it was your poems he was enthralled with.

"I heard Cormick read *The Second Coming* at the Irish Festival in Dublin," Lenu said. "As an internationally exiled author myself, it spoke to me. That's what convinced me I would be an asset to New City's program."

Graduate students were such poseurs. They drained him. Daniel opened a can of Bud, turning to find Lila staring at him.

"Well, *I* came here just to study with you," she countered. "I can't wait for your Intro to Post-Modernism. I was glad to see your syllabus is all confessionals, my favorite. Too bad eighty percent are male. And it's odd you're holding class on Yom Kippur."

This one didn't come up for air. "What's it like being one of the three Jews in Cheese Land?" he asked, hoping to lighten her up.

"My mom's famous in our town for getting kosher sharp cheddar by the crate. I'll get her to send you a chunk. Though it's fattening." She grinned, revealing dimples on each cheek. Maybe there was something refreshing about this motor-mouth's lack of filter. "She wants to know why NCU didn't cancel classes on the holiest day of the year."

They met twelve minutes ago and she had already managed to put him on a guilt trip, make him fear her mother and give him a headache. "The class ends at six, before the holiday starts at sundown," he told her. "It's not a yeshiva or public school. Just leave early if you need to."

"I didn't move cross country to miss a second of your very first class," Lila said. "Do you know if the housing and student loan offices are still open? They assigned me a double in the dorm, but my roommate didn't show up. I can't afford a single by myself."

"You need to ask your resident advisor," he said, now worried she'd wind up homeless and that he had to reschedule his class for the holiday. As Lila hovered, standing too close, he wondered how many Jewish students would prefer meeting earlier. Where was his roster?

A raven-haired troublemaker in a black leather miniskirt, halter, torn fishnet hose and combat boots marched up, held out a long brown cigarette that looked like an anorexic cigar and asked, "Got a light?"

"No. I don't smoke," Lila said. "It's bad for you."

"I'm Professor Wildman. And who might you be?" Daniel went into the pocket of his beige corduroy jacket to handed a pack of matches to Motorcycle Mama.

"Thanks, man. I'm in your Monday Intro. Sari Dare."

"That'll make a great byline," he said.

"In Armavir it was Sarpuhi Derohannessian," she deadpanned, blowing smoke in his face. "You shorten Wildman? Bet you started out Wildmanoffsky."

Daniel laughed, recalling Sarpuhi's file—edgy Armenian comic with clever pain, a female Bukowski. He had selected her, too. He liked her bravado and dark, risky sarcasm about "Jews getting better PR for their Holocaust." She wore too much eyeliner and he wasn't a fan of her ripped black clothes, as if she'd invented Nihilism. He bet she was the one the dean complained had stunk up the dormitory with her candle-lighting Goth routine and pot smoking the first day the dorm opened, before classes had even started.

"Do you live in student housing?" he asked.

"Weinstein dorm. Scared the Ohio chick I was supposed to room with right back to Dayton." Sari looked pleased with herself.

Another handful. "This is Lila Lerner," he pointed. "She has a double with no roommate. You two should consider living together."

With a horrified expression Sari said, "No. I want a single."

"I requested a non-smoking floor." Lila sounded equally freaked out at the thought.

Daniel leaned on the table, looking at them. Superficially they were opposites. Yet their work was the most ambitious and animated of the new batch. Despite external humor, their literary landscapes were filled with old souls and sadness. He sensed they could help each other, but dorm issues -which were not his domain—stole precious hours away from his poetry. This wouldn't be his problem if Cormick, the damn director, took care of the female students instead of taking them to bed. Daniel checked his watch. Figured Cormick would be late to his own event.

A hand touched his shoulder. Daniel turned. "Howard. You sneaked up on me there," he said. Daniel introduced his shy colleague to the dozen pupils standing around. "Professor Fell teaches Craft of Poetry. He has a blue belt in karate, so don't fuck with him."

"Brown in Tae Kwon Do," Howard mumbled, staring at the floor.

"He seems mild-mannered, but he's hiding superpowers. In Iowa they called him PoetryMan," Daniel said, glad to illicit a half-smile from Howard.

"Sari doesn't like me," Lila said, gluing herself to Daniel's side as Sari mingled with a hip looking group by the makeshift bar. "Maybe we're not each other's type," she said.

"People are like poetry. You can't tell anything at first glance," he offered.

"You can't judge a book by its cover?" Lila decimated his metaphor into cliché. "You're really the one who accepted me? You liked my poetry? Think it shows promise?"

"No, it means I thought you were a talent-less poseur," Daniel kidded.

He had actually felt tricked six months earlier, when he put her writing sample in his "maybe" pile. She had left off her birth year. Calling the records office for clarification, he found out she wasn't even twenty. He preferred older grad students. Lila was too young. But then he reread the forty poems she submitted –twenty more than requested—overstuffed with biblical references and kooky inverted Kabbalah prayers conjuring up an Alice in Latkeland. Every stanza led back to her father's suicide when she was six, and her crazy Jewish mother overcompensating with too much food. Daniel's mother had taken her own life. He felt stirred by Lila's desperate search for another father, God, or rabbi to protect her. Her pages were too long, unpolished, veering from smart to trite in every other line. Still, her tone struck him as more raw and heartfelt than anything he'd read by an applicant in a long time.

Despite her good grades and test scores he decided: not emotionally ready for grad school or New York. Lila had hardly any life experience. The only work listed on her resume was babysitting, part-time waitressing, and a summer spent as a typist at her local Jewish community center. Her personal essay was on her mother's penchant for bright plaids and loud patterns. He should have advised her to get a job and reapply a year later—with an autobiographical piece about herself, not her mother, as if she didn't know where she started and her mother left off. She could use a friend here, he bet, as Sari returned, smoking her skinny cigar.

"So is this as exciting as it gets?" Sari asked.

"Oh, you lovely lasses need a drink," sang Conor Cormick, barging in between Daniel and the girls, forty minutes late, handing plastic cups to Sari, Lila, Mary Jonas and Judith, the high-heeled show off who was gaping at her hero.

"When we met at the Writer's Colony…" Judith cooed.

"Ah yes, those blustery evenings at Bread Loaf…"

"MacDowell," Judith corrected, fluttering before Cormick, who stood six foot four—six inches taller than Daniel. In his sixties, he remained ruggedly handsome, still sporting his thick brown mane. Cormick poured the cheap Chardonnay, saying "I have hard stuff in my office if you'd prefer something else."

"I want the harder stuff," Judith cooed, all googly-eyed.

"Got any Johnnie Walker Black?" Sari asked him.

"Indeed, I do. Classy taste, my lady," Cormick fawned.

"Don't overdo it," Daniel warned. Last year Cormick got the cutest girl so blitzed she puked down the stairwell. Cormick found it amusing while

Daniel sat up with her until three in the morning, feeding her coffee and bread to absorb the booze and make sure she didn't have alcohol poisoning.

"Don't mind Wildman, he's famous for scaring off pretty first years, dipping their pigtails in the inkwell," Cormick said, winking at Lila. "Meanwhile I'll be reading with the *Atlantic* poetry editor at PEN next week. You ladies should meet him. I hope you'll all come."

Daniel glared as Cormick's eyes lingered over Lila's substantial breasts beneath her loose potato sack of a dress and hausfrau sweater. She noticed and blushed. Cormick had nerve drooling over Daniel's youngest student. She was only nineteen, for God's sakes! He wanted to warn Lila that Cormick had rejected her application, implying they had already accepted too many Jews. The flowery Irish twit—who'd won last year's Pulitzer and everything else Daniel ever wanted—had said, "We've taken enough ethnic feminists for one term, don't you think?" At that point Daniel had lied, insisting Lila Lerner was already in the "accepted and notified" pile.

He would never take a student *only* to spite his boss. What finally swayed him was her last poem about how, as a little girl, she would feign nightmares so her mother would "rush in with Yiddish songs and never leave./*Rojinkes mit mandlen*, I tricked you to save me." Daniel had played the same game until he was six, when his mom did leave, never to return.

"To you, my dear, and your upcoming adventures in this gorgeous mosaic of a city you're about to conquer," Cormick was now telling Lila, clicking his paper cup against hers.

She couldn't possibly be buying that crap, could she? Cormick only popped into these meet and greets to pour drinks and check out what he called "the new crop." How many would the married egomaniac seduce this year? Daniel counted five last semester. He wanted to report him to the dean, but the university needed Cormick's international prestige as a draw to its expensive program. They'd even started a Cormick-run Dublin branch. The only place they sent Daniel was an MLA conference in Newark. They wouldn't even pay for a car service; he had to take the PATH train. He was twenty years younger than the old lothario. Women here flirted with him too; he just didn't abuse his power.

"Why does Cormick have a stunning wife and four kids while screwing all the hot chicks in the program?" Daniel often complained to his yarmulke-wearing therapist, Dr. Zalman.

"Why don't you screw some hot chicks too?" Zalman asked. "And stop making every man into your abusive father."

"Because I'm not taking advantage of girls half my age."

"What would happen if you did?" Zalman asked. "She'll kill herself like your mom and it'll be your fault?"

"I want his hands off of my kids!" Daniel shouted.

"They'll be your only kids if you don't take some woman to bed soon," Zalman said.

Daniel was hot for Roxanne, a gorgeous actress he'd met at NCU's theater wing. After spending a few romantic weekends in bed together, he was completely smitten. But when he confided he couldn't finish his book, she'd suggested he call her cousin—who was hiring a copywriter at his medical advertising firm. He felt demoralized. He needed someone who could comprehend the depth of his literary passion. Students, however, were off limits. It was deeper than a legal or practical matter for Daniel, as if being immoral had the power to mar his poetry.

"Have you beauties met the whole cast of characters or can I keep you all to myself?" Cormick asked, before introducing Sari, Lila and Judith around, playing the master host. "We can continue the party at my place across the street later if you want."

"You live in a carriage house in Washington Square Mews?" Judith fawned. "I've always wondered what they look like inside."

"I'll be happy to show you the landmark that houses this landmark," Cormick quipped.

Daniel was disgusted. On his $25,000 a year salary, he could barely afford the exorbitant $800 a monthly rent on his one-bedroom while Cormick—who earned five times that—was given a free duplex in the regal luxury townhouse, which he used for his tacky trysts while his family lived in Connecticut. It was bad enough that he was taller, richer and better connected. But the poetry Cormick created was dripping with genius, the sweeping, effortless, Gentile kind. He'd filled six fat, acclaimed collections in the decade Daniel had been struggling to complete his slim second book. As if Cormick was hoarding the muse away from Daniel.

"Success comes easy to him. He had a mother who adored him and didn't abandon him, like yours," Zalman said. "You'll always have to work harder. At everything."

It was true. Daniel could barely hide his dismay, watching Cormick play around.

"Come on, help me out here, Danny Boy," said Cormick.

Daniel leaned against the wall, watching the scene, feeling claustrophobic and inferior to his boss, who knew Daniel despised that ridiculously condescending nickname.

"This is Howard Fell, whose stunning series *Lithium Lullaby* ran in this month's *American Poetry Review*," Cormick bragged.

Howard bowed his head. Of course Cormick preferred the quieter, compliant Fell.

"And the majestic Faith Powell, contributing editor to *Ploughshares*, honoring us with her divine aura," Cormick went on.

Daniel watched as Lila looked up at the even taller six-foot Powell, checking out her salt and pepper hair, denim skirt and turquoise Indian blouse. She and Lila could star in "Attack of the White Amazon Writer Women."

"Our lovely Faith is in charge of fiction," Cormick added.

"That makes me sound like a liar who perpetuates falsehoods, doesn't it?" she asked.

"Oh, I loved *Isis, She of the Throne*," Lila told her.

"Why thank you, dear," Faith lit up. "That was my first novel, I started it at Yaddo."

"What's Yaddo?"

Would Lila next ask if *The Paris Review* was a French burlesque show? Then again, Daniel found it heartening that she'd memorized poetry but never heard of the famous writer's colony. She wasn't as calculating as half of the students here, who'd sacrifice their unborn for a byline.

"It's a brothel disguised as an artist colony," Faith answered.

Despite the outfit, Daniel found Faith good-looking, as well as brilliant. She and Daniel were an item the year she'd separated from her husband. She had five books out and now ran PEN American Center's reading series. Daniel was glad *she* had broken *his* heart—not the other way around—and that he'd stayed on her good side. She'd become a prestige player like Cormick, the kind Daniel aspired to be. If only he wasn't such an obsessive perfectionist, still rethinking line breaks and punctuation on poems years after they were published. He wished he were less sensitive and more prolific and politic. But he'd always flunked faking it.

Escaping to the men's room, Daniel pondered the saying about academia: so petty because so little was at stake. As he washed his hands, he looked in the mirror, the gray specks in his receding hair line mocking him. He was forty. His mother was already dead by his age, by her own hand. His father was a rich, overworked investment banking analyst at a firm he hated, who criticized Daniel constantly. He'd never remarried, or even dated anyone else. Some legacy he'd left Daniel for work and love.

That was probably why, when Cormick had first taken Daniel to dinner, got him drunk on Irish whiskey, quoted Daniel's own poetry back to him and offered him a job, he'd been sucked in so quickly. In Cormick, he'd finally found a poet father who understood and admired him. So a year later, when Cormick bypassed him for a promotion and started ignoring Daniel and belittling him in public, the betrayal felt swift and sadistic.

Swinging by his office, Daniel grabbed his coat and briefcase, scanning the *Times*. The Ayatollah issued inane demands to secure the release of

Americans hostages; Daniel felt personally let down by the President's indecisiveness. He'd had hopes for Carter ever since he'd read that, as a boy, he'd get bored on the peanut farm and read Dylan Thomas. But lately Daniel saw him like Cormick– a self-righteous show off, brilliant at everything but running the country. He also loathed Reagan who, like Cormick, was a good looking, vapid, charming fake. Daniel considered backing Ted Kennedy in the primary. But the story of that poor girl in Chappaquiddick was too troubling. Kennedy also became Cormick in his mind. Despite his liberalism, Daniel just couldn't respect a married man who couldn't keep it in his pants.

Turning to sports, he saw the Mets, his favorite, were in fifth place. Every headline made him feel weaker, like he was personally losing the game, the Middle East peace, the world to stronger, better men. He felt left behind, unable to catch up. Daniel just wanted to break though his ambition poem, alone, at his home. He was about to slip out the side door when he heard Cormick bellowing Yeats. "Never shall a young man/Thrown into despair/By those great honey-coloured/Ramparts at your ear,/Love you for yourself alone/And not your yellow hair…"

Daniel crept out to catch a glimpse and caught him standing on the refreshment table, reaching out for Lila to dance. She looked uncomfortable, shaking her head and putting her hands deep in the pockets of her sweater. The Gaelic hound persisted, swigging a gulp from the Johnny Walker he'd managed to fetch, then handing it to her. She took the scotch whiskey with her right hand and slowly brought it to her mouth. Oh God, the sight of his advisee about to sip from the same bottle that Cormick's lips had touched made Daniel wince. He couldn't afford to alienate his boss but he had to get her away from Cormick now. He quickly grabbed a memo pad and leapt between them.

"Here's the housing form you requested, Lila," he said, staring in her eyes, willing her to understand she did not have to accept Cormick's offering.

"Oh good, I better hurry and fill it out." She put down the bottle, nodding to show she appreciated his ploy, then hurriedly followed Daniel out. On her way, she swept up her coat, knapsack, books and bags from the Strand Bookstore. She looked like a bag lady about to topple over. Her lumpishness touched him. He reached out to help her carry her stuff to the elevator.

"Thanks for saving me," she said, impatiently pressing the down button several times.

"So Yeats isn't your favorite?" He tossed the memo pad atop the hallway shelf.

"Mad Ireland hurt him into poetry." She paraphrased Auden.

"Ah, you prefer Wystan Hugh to William Butler?" he asked.

"Truthfully I prefer your brilliant, brash, raw post-modern honesty."

He recognized the line as the blurb from Gerald Stern on his own book jacket. What a sponge.

"Really, *Beyond Despair* blew me away," she gushed. "Especially Uncle Sidney screaming '*Gonif* where's my check? When I was a kid in Poland, you didn't do that to a friend' and Grandpa Nadie, 'whose lies held us together like bandages.' It's Isaac Singer set to verse."

Quoting a poet back to himself. She wasn't so naïve after all.

"Will you sign mine?" She put her bags down, unzipped her backpack, and pulled out his book.

The sight of his first paperback—published in the fall of 1970—filled him with a mix of nostalgia and dread. Back then, such luminaries as Richard Howard and Maxine Kumin hailed him as the new young voice in American poetry. The kiss of death; he had hardly had anything in print since. He took out his pen, fearing it could be his final collection.

"This means so much," she said, reading his inscription aloud: "To my discovery, Lila Lerner –Don't be afraid to believe your pain. Yours, Daniel Wildman."

"From Auden's *The Sea and the Mirror*! I totally love that poem. How did ya know?" She held his book close.

How shocking—her poetry professor knew a famous poem. But Daniel didn't answer, he was too busy regretting that he'd written "my discovery" instead of "my student" and "Yours" instead of "All the Best," as usual. Why had he sounded so proprietary—because he'd wrestled her away from Cormick and won? When the creaky elevator finally came, they stepped into the small cage together.

"My mom loved your book too," Lila said. "She only let me come here so I could study with you."

"Most people are drawn to the program because of Cormick, the big award winner."

"How old is he anyway, ninety?" Her hungry blue eyes sparkled up at him. "And who judges all of those prizes he wins? I bet a bunch of trust fund Ivy League WASPs bestow them on other trust fund Ivy League WASPs."

Convulsing in laughter, he wondered where she'd heard that. Cormick was Irish Catholic. But still, how long had it been since he'd really laughed? Clearly he had underestimated this Lila Lerner– she certainly knew all she needed to know about the New York poetry world.

"Don't worry. You'll get your due. I'm sure it'll all come out in the wash," she added in sing-song tone, unaware she was speaking in Hallmark adages that he was deleting in his head, already editing her. But there was something very sweet and perceptive about her attempt to console him, like she understood.

"A motherless boy needs endless love," Zalman always warned.

"So what was your big rush to finish undergrad so early?" Daniel wanted to know. It had taken him seven years at three different schools to get his undergraduate diploma.

"I love your poems about all your screwed-up relatives," she said. "But you think your Ohio clan's soul-crushing? My mom, step-dad and his *mish-pucha* put the Wildmans to shame. You gotta visit Baraboo to believe it."

"Baraboo is a real place?" he asked. "It has a good sound to it, three syllables; I like the alliteration. You should use it in a poem."

"You can have it," she offered.

"Be careful. You don't want to give away your best stuff."

When the door opened, they walked out toward the exit together. He held her bags and lifted her tattered teal coat as she fumbled to fit her arms through.

"Really, it's all yours," she said. "Help yourself to my whole life."

3

December 1980

LILA

Lila had read all about legendary New York book parties—where drunk writers were discovered or fell in love or got stabbed. She couldn't wait. She'd never been to a professor's home—or a real literary soiree—before. Tonight was the most important event she was ever invited to, launching her new big city life, the one she was destined to live, far away from Baraboo. She revised her mother poem in her head, waiting for Sari on lower Broadway, in front of Unique. They were meeting at the clothing warehouse at two, though Sari was always late and Lila eternally early. She shivered in the freezing air but feared that putting on the hood of her parka would ruin her bangs. She needed good hair for later—and a perfect rewrite of her mother poem. She should start in the middle, throw you into the scene, "show, don't tell," as Professor Wildman instructed. "Passover morning I find you in your yellow kitchen/ where you're making matzo brei…" A brilliant revision would prove to him she was special. Sari said the serious literati dressed down, which was fine since Lila only had seven dollars anyway, just enough for a new scarf or lipstick or glitter nail polish to make her stand out.

"Got it," Sari said, suddenly by her side, looking tough in her motorcycle jacket and miniskirt with tights. She didn't even seem cold. She showed off two nickel bags of weed.

"I can't wait to tell my brother there's a store you can just walk in to buy pot," Lila mused.

"Here." Sari slipped one bag into Lila's purse.

"I can't take it." Lila was embarrassed she didn't have the five dollars to spare. Her scholarship and loans didn't cover the $800 a month dorm fees for the 200 square foot room they were sharing. Her waitressing gig barely paid her phone and electric bill. She worried everyone in her whole program was richer, classier and higher brow than she was.

"You have no choice," said Sari. She lit a joint right there in the street, sucking in smoke.

"Won't we get into trouble?"

"Cops don't care unless it's coke," Sari handed it to her and she took a hit.

At first their roommate experiment had been a disaster. Then, mid-September, Judith Bay, across the hall, reported Sari to the resident adviser for smoking marijuana. Lila—who'd hated Judith since she'd hurt Professor Wildman's feelings at the mixer by going on about Cormick—ran out to get lavender incense sticks that she burned for 24 hours straight. Then Lila informed the R.A. that her snobby neighbor was too drunk to tell the difference between pot and incense. Lila envied Judith—a slim, sophisticated, soft-spoken intellectual from an upper-class family who'd already been published in *Ploughshares*; she was everything Lila wasn't. When Judith wound up moving in a huff to a nearby apartment, Sari celebrated by lighting Lila's first joint in New York.

"I'll pay you back later," Lila mumbled now. Actually though there was no way she could ever keep up with Sari—an affluent, confident, sophisticated only child of two Park Avenue psychiatrists.

"The ganja boutique switches locations all the time and you need the password, so I'll have to take you," Sari told her. "Or we can get some delivered to the dorm."

"Man, I love this city," Lila said. "The only thing we could get door-to-door in my home state was Dominos. My brother's driving to New York for the holidays. This'll kill him."

"His first time here?" Sari sucked in more smoke, then handed the joint back.

Lila nodded. "He wants to go to Times Square on New Year's Eve. Will you come?"

"Only hicks do that," Sari said.

"I am a hick," Lila reminded her.

"Don't be so proud of it."

When a police car drove by, Lila flinched, hiding the joint behind her back. She pictured missing Wildman's party because she was thrown in jail for drugs and shipped back to her mother in the Midwest in shame. Members of her temple already thought she was a deviant for getting a graduate degree instead of a husband. Jeff—a sweet law student, the first and only guy Lila had slept with—acted like Manhattan was a phase she'd get over, then rush back to him.

"Don't worry." Sari took the weed and put it out with her fingers, then slipped the rest back in her long cigarette packet. "Now we're ready for vintage clothes." She led Lila into the huge loft-like space. Lila gaped at the red painted murals on the walls and the rows of pink, green and striped afros rested on the checkout lines. Gloria Gayner's *I Will Survive* was blasting.

"You can get something for Wildman's party here," Sari said.

It had to be sophisticated. Since junior high, Lila wore her mom's hand-me-downs—bright patterns, high-buttoned shirts with bows, skirts below the knee. She'd thrown most of them out when she got to the city and avoided stuff anybody had worn before. "I don't know, buying used clothes seems dirty."

"Most of the stuff they sell is brand new," Sari reassured.

Breezing through racks of Spandex and Lycra, Lila felt stoned and dizzy. She wished she was beautiful like Judith or Sari—skinny and sexy in her little skirt showing off tiny thighs. Even at her thinnest, Lila's were twice as big, and freckles marred her ghost-like skin. Jeff once said she resembled Cybill Shepherd in *Taxi Driver*. But then again, he thought he was the Jewish De Niro, muttering "Ya talkin' to me?" and "The city is filled with filth and scum."

"I wouldn't be seen dead with anybody in that hideous thing." Sari yanked away the striped jumpsuit Lila held up, pulling out a slinky black dress instead. "Time to ditch the pigtails and jumpers, you're not Cindy on the *Brady Bunch*." She loosened Lila's hair from its elastic band. Lila shook her head at the sequin number. Totally not her.

"Just try it," she said, pushing Lila towards the cramped dressing room, surprising her by coming inside.

"Too small. I need a large."

"Why do you always wear oversized clothes? Your bod is hot. Why do you hide it? Afraid of male attention?"

"With the religious crew I grew up with, tight clothes meant you were a slut," Lila said. "Orthodox women can't show bare arms or legs. My mother's family practically disowned her for being seen with her own hair in public. She's supposed to wear wigs."

"That's some prehistoric shit," Sari said.

Sari had no clue. When Professor Wildman told the ROTC recruiter not to give out fliers in the NCU building, he'd joked to their class that they could get thrown out of Greenwich Village for being Republicans. Lila had blanched; her small clique of Midwest Jews loathed Carter's Christian evangelism and his criticism of Israel. Her Uncle Ezra called him "the Peanut Brain Baptist" and convinced her to vote for Reagan. It was something Lila could never tell her roommate—or her professor –or they'd see she'd never fit in here.

Sari left, then came back with a size medium. "So this sophomore, Phoebe, told me after she blew Cormick, he sent her poems to *American Poetry Review* and they took one."

"That's immoral and gross," Lila said, thinking she would never do anything sexual to get published. She tried not to feel self-conscious with Sari standing so close. She left her jeans on while pulling the frock over her head.

Interesting, but it didn't fit right. Lila took it off.

"At least the old man can still get it up," Sari said, handing her more black frocks to try.

"*APR* did Professor Fell's series, right?" Lila asked. "He seems smart. Don't you think?"

"What a mouse. I prefer macho men who aren't afraid to take control. At least Wildman runs our class with an iron fist," Sari said. "Though in his poems he's like Portnoy incarnate."

"Like a poetic Woody Allen." Lila nodded, holding up a sleeveless mini.

"Know why you like *Manhattan*? Cause you're his Mariel Hemingway," Sari teased.

"I am not! No way. She's a pathetic kid mooning over him. I'm not like that." Lila felt herself blushing. She'd hoped nobody had noticed she'd been *crunching* out on him, as Sari called it. Not like someone as important and brilliant as Professor Wildman would ever even notice a hayseed student like her.

"'If I fall asleep in your clothes/I won't dream of you,'" Sari said.

She was flattered to hear her roommate recite lines from Lila's anti-love poem "Below Zero." Especially since Sari's minimalist fiction was so impressive, filled with ethnic references undercut with slang, about "the Hays and Gor-gors with their razors and Rabiz," always prowling for "Armo Armor."

"Kind of cool Wildman's inviting us to his apartment." Lila pictured floor-to-ceiling book shelves, a king-sized bed with a regal brown spread. "What are book parties like?"

"Publisher is Copper Canyon, so this one will be pretty low-rent," Sari said. "But nice that Wildman wants to celebrate Fell's little book."

Lila didn't know why Copper Canyon wasn't high rent or Fell's book was little. But she trusted Sari's judgment. "Wildman and Fell are like Mutt and Jeff." Lila pulled a knit number over her head that got stuck.

"Who?" Sari asked, pulling the dress off.

"An old comic strip my dad used to like," Lila explained.

"Is your dad really a plumber?"

Lila hesitated, ashamed of her broke and broken family. "That's my step-dad, Pete." He was nice enough, though her brother lamented that their mom had found the only Jewish plumber in the whole state. "My real father was a newspaper editor," she added.

"That's a hip gig," Sari said.

"Well, he was a copyeditor at the *Baraboo News Republic*," Lila clarified.

"Try this Betsey Johnson. The label says punk rock bombshell."

Lila laughed at the thought—but not the price tag: 42 bucks, too much. The hundred a week she made waitressing was gone. Her mom had sent thirty dollars for the holidays, but that barely covered the Hanukah presents Lila had sent to her family. "It's too much."

"I want to see how you'd look as a rock star," Sari said. "Just try it on."

Lila put on the dress, running her hands over the soft fabric. The crushed velvet material was really soft. She liked the long sleeves, flared skirt and corseted style that tied in the back. But Lila worried how low cut the top was; you could see her cleavage. "My Uncle Ezra thinks New York is a dirty, scummy place filled with pimps, drugs dealers and whores. My dad would hate that I moved to New York."

"How old were you when he died?" Sari asked, scrunching the sleeves.

"I was six," Lila said.

"What happened?"

Lila wrote about it but rarely told anybody how he'd died. "Suicide," she mumbled.

"Wow. I'm sorry." Sari touched her shoulder. "How'd he off himself?"

Man, New Yorkers were relentless. Maybe it was because both of Sari's parents were psychologists? "Pills," Lila said quietly.

"Why'd he do it?" Sari asked.

Nobody had asked her that before. "He injured his back in an accident. Mom thought the steroids they prescribed made him crazy. There was depression on his side of the family." Lila sometimes suspected she had it too. "Mom met Pete a year later. He showed up to fix a leak."

"My father the shrink would say your mom needed someone to fix *her*,"

Sari threw out.

Lila couldn't fix her mom. Growing up, she felt guilty her mother was so sad after her dad was gone. The only time she ever smiled was when Lila recited her funny rhyming stories about their insane family, doing all the different Yiddish-accented voices.

"Why does everybody here call therapists *shrinks*, anyway?"

"Thomas Pynchon coined it in *The Crying of Lot 49*," Sari said.

"That's right! Dr. Hilarius," Lila recalled. "Oedipa's psychiatrist."

"It's short for headshrinker," Sari filled her in. "Pynchon was alluding to a savage headhunter."

"He meant it sardonically?"

"Hilarius went crazy and admitted to being a former Nazi doctor. Some shrink," Sari told her.

"Oh, I always thought shrink was more of an earnest term—like someone who shrinks your problems away." Lila felt like a dolt.

"Man, you really are fresh off the turnip truck," Sari said.

"You're an elitist Manhattan snob," Lila retorted, staring at the pretty dress.

"Thanks, I'm trying," Sari said, smirking, pulling the material down. "This one makes you look hot. But it's hard to tell with your jeans on. Get rid of them."

Lila didn't want her friend to notice the high-waisted underwear her mom bought her. Sari—who walked around their dorm room in tiny lace bikinis—called them "granny panties." Lila slipped her Levi's off carefully, making sure the velvet dress covered her. Sari inspected the outfit, pushing Lila's hair in front of her shoulders.

"Get rid of those ripped knee socks."

Lila took them off, then looked in the mirror. Black did make her sultry. She'd lost weight from walking everywhere. At five foot nine and 130, she was down 17 pounds in her first 4 months in New York. Brushing her mane in front made her face seem angular; she looked more like Sari now. But the dress was too tight and showy. "It's not really me."

"That's the whole idea," her roommate said.

Lila brushed her hand against the fabric, still staring. She loved it. Too bad she didn't even have enough to put it on layaway. "Too expensive," Lila said, not wanting to take it off.

"I'm buying it for your birthday. And I'm taking you to get your eyebrows waxed."

"My birthday's not till next month," Lila said. "What's wrong with my eyebrows?"

"Look how thin mine are." Sari pointed to the slim lines over her eyes. "You're lucky you're light haired. If you were Armenian like me, you'd be a gorilla."

When Sari left, Lila glanced at her reflection, hair down, in the daring dress. She looked older, urban, glamorous. Her mom said women in tight clothes were "asking for it." Was she? Lila winked at the vamp in the mirror. What would her professor say? As she reluctantly changed back into her frumpy self, Sari snatched the garment, heading to the register. Lila didn't stop her. She felt bad to let Sari buy it for her. But Lila wanted to be the crushed velvet punk rock bombshell at Wildman's party tonight. She promised herself she'd pay Sari back one day. When Lila was a rich writer having her own book party.

On their way back to the dorm, Sari bought a six pack of Rolling Rock bottles from the bodega and handed Lila one of her cigarettes. She'd never smoked before but Sari was teaching her how to French inhale her More Menthols.

"These look like cigars," Lila said, coughing.

"Like long, skinny, brown dicks," Sari said.

Beer, cigs, joints in public, penis similes. Sari was the most exciting girl she'd ever hung out with. How did Prof Wildman know they'd make a good match the first day of school? Sometimes he knew Lila so well it freaked her out.

That night Sari helped blow-dry her hair and put on black eyeliner and pencil on her now much slimmer eyebrows. Lila's face felt naked without half her usual brow hair. She checked herself in the mirror, sucking her cheeks in, pretending she was Christie Brinkley on the cover of *Sports Illustrated*. Then Lila stuffed her revised mother poem in her purse before she put on the velvet dress with a glittery silver scarf she borrowed from Sari and chunky heels she wobbled in. Lila shared her mom's rule to never show up empty-handed and picked up $1.99 Entenmann's cookies on sale at Gristedes. Her heart was pounding as they knocked on the door.

"You baked these just for me?" Wildman asked as he let them inside.

"We bought them at the supermarket," Lila said.

"I know." He pointed at the box and cracked up.

Why was he always teasing her? She felt so embarrassed and stupid as she took off her backpack and coat. "Great dress," he said. She knew he'd notice! But then he greeted the next girl "Wow, you look terrific," and told the boy who followed "You sure clean up nice."

Lila turned away from him, rearranging her scarf to cover her pale cleavage. She looked around. Professor Fell stood by a table with his new paperback, and all fifty students from the program seemed crammed inside. Wildman darted about, showing his guests around, pouring drinks, a hyper, buoyant, proud host. He was more comfortable now than at the orientation party. Lila noticed that Cormick wasn't there, surmising that was why. She was shocked by how small Wildman's place was: one gray couch, three chairs, a mini-kitchenette—only a little bigger than her double in the dorm. Someone said you were supposed to put your stuff in the other room, but she didn't see it.

"Where's your bedroom?"

"You always ask men that?" Wildman asked, grinning as Lila turned red. "Over there."

Holding her backpack and coat, she walked into a room that was 100 square feet. The walls seemed musty, the paint on the radiator chipped. Major professors with published books lived in places this old and tiny? She folded her green parka as two other girls rushed in, taking off their jackets. Lila smiled, tucking her green parka carefully on his bed, right up against the window.On the small dresser, she spotted a picture of a pretty woman with hair the color of black bread, twisted in a bun. Another old-fashioned photo showed the same woman holding a child's hand. She saw the boy was Professor Wildman, with the beloved lost mother of his poems. Lila had a similar picture, one of her and her father pushing her on the swing set when she was a little girl but she'd hidden it in her bottom desk drawer. How could anybody get it on with pictures of a dead parent so close to their bed?

She fumbled with her stuff until the other guests left his bedroom. She stayed. Snooping around, she found a Hallmark card with a cartoon elephant. Underneath she spied a head shot of a beautiful red-haired lady with made-up brown eyes and a turned-up nose. A resume was stapled to the back, topped with the name "Roxanne McDowell." Aha! No wonder he'd said *Portnoy's Complaint* was brilliant. He had his own Monkey, a gorgeous *shiksa* goddess. She wanted to know whether the redhead was an ex-girlfriend or his current flame. On the way out, Lila caught her profile in the mirror and vamped sideways. She was wearing the control-top black nylons her mom had sent, which flattened her stomach. Sari called them "old hag's hose," but Lila was sure they made the dress look sultry and romantic.

Joining the party, Lila drank a rum and Tab, getting tipsy, pushing her hair across her face, sucking her stomach in, sure this was the best she'd ever looked. But across the room she caught Professor Wildman handing Judith a book. Why would he give one to Judith? She was thinner than Lila, even at her most svelte, and that show-off sprinkled references in her poems—in three languages. She wore a black dress too, but hers looked fancier, like silk.

"Gimme a smoke," Lila told Sari, interrupting her flirtation with Kosta, the foreign fiction grad who penned pretentious two paragraph short stories about murdered pets.

"I'm not giving my last fag to a fake smoker," Sari snapped. "Why the mope?"

Lila glared at her nemesis, standing in the middle of the living room with Wildman. "I want to be his assistant next term, but I bet Judith will get it."

"She's probably diddling him to stay on the honor roll," Sari joked.

Lila was sure Professor Wildman wasn't like that. He was the type her mom called "a *mensch*." When James Brown's *I Feel Good* came on, Lila watched everybody dance. Wildman looked surprisingly smooth as he fast-danced with Faith, lighter and looser, his hair messy, like a real person having fun. Professor Fell slipped between Judith and Sari—even the sweet mouse could boogie when he was blitzed. Lila, an awkward dancer until she was totally drunk or stoned, was not going to humiliate herself in front of her most important professor. Instead she kept drinking, checking out his *tchotchkes*, touching each book, tape and kitschy ashtray, as if the secret to being a great poet was hidden here.

At midnight, Sari took her coat. "Come on, we're going clubbing uptown."

Lila knew that meant dance dives with $20 cover charges. "I think I'll hang here."

"Come on, I'll treat," Sari offered.

"That's okay. I'm kind of tired. I'm going home soon," Lila lied. She was really just waiting for Judith and the rest of the gang to get their wraps too. Good, this could be her chance to get Wildman alone. But after the last group of rowdy guests left, Professor Fell stayed. He was talking to Wildman. Lila took a long time in the bathroom, waiting Professor Fell out. When she came out of the john to find him still there, she began cleaning up like she did at home, bringing the half-finished chips and peanuts to his mini-kitchen. "Jewish parties have more food than booze," her mother had said. Wildman was a Yid but maybe he needed a woman around to host. Why hadn't he invited the hotsy-totsy redhead in the photo? She bet his actress wasn't intellectual enough for him. Was Lila?

"Aren't you leaving too?" he asked after Fell left.

"In a few minutes," she told him, psyched she was finally the last one there, standing with Wildman in his kitchen. She was scared he didn't want her here. "I could tell you need help cleaning up." She flitted around, putting glasses and bowls in his sink. "At the end of the parties I'm always the cleaner-upper. I usually help my mom fit everything back into the refrigerator, that's my job." He was always surrounded by students before and after class who'd line up for his office hours. But now that she had him to herself, she was babbling incoherently. Why couldn't she shut up?

"Oh good, free maid service," he slurred. "So for an old man I can still throw a pretty cool bash. Right?"

"Very cool," she agreed. "The coolest. Totally awesome. Much better than the club scene. Which I can't really afford anyway." Damn, why did she just say that? She sounded like a Valley Girl who'd only come to his party for the free booze.

"More vino?" He poured the last of the bottle into a blue glass and handed it to her.

Did that mean he wanted her to stay? "Sure." She tossed the wine back, though she'd been drinking rum and Tab.

"Want to take the brownies? And there's a leftover bottle of that diet soda you drink."

She liked that he'd paid attention to what she drank. She didn't want to be rude but she was on Sari's diet of salad, dope and More cigarettes. She brought the glass to the sink where they hand-washed them together. Weird that nobody she knew in New York seemed to have a dishwasher or a disposal. "You didn't invite Cormick tonight?"

"He's usually with his wife and kids on weekends," he said, rinsing the blue glass.

"Is Professor Powell married with kids? None of the faculty brought dates."

Lila was dying to know why he hadn't invited his redhead girlfriend. She handed him dishes, carefully squirting dishwashing liquid into the sink so it didn't splash her dress. He turned on the faucet higher and sponged the saucer. Standing so close, she could smell his cologne—Old Spice, the kind she loved, that her ex Jeff used to wear. When Professor Wildman handed her a dish to dry, his hand touched hers.

"I find school parties easier to navigate alone," he said cryptically, worming out of revealing how tight he was with the redhead. At least he wasn't diddling Judith tonight. Lila was so thrilled to get him to herself. She had him exactly where she wanted him—now she could pick his poetry brain.

"Professor Fell said Charles Wentworth, poetry editor of *Urban Review*, has a precious, phony, postmodern bent. You agree?" she asked.

"Yes, he prefers pretty air," he said. "Well-crafted, didactic, academic."

"You're not into pretty air?" She washed the blue glass.

"I prefer ruthless," he said.

"Like when Philip Larkin started with 'they fuck you up, your mum and dad?'" she asked.

He nodded, turning the water higher. The soap bubbled up. "Sari says the school literary magazine needs reviewers. Do you think I should try?"

"No. Don't waste your time," he snapped. "You're a poet. Book critics are like eunuchs at an orgy. They wish they could to do it but can't."

"Professor Powell writes for *The New Criterion*," Lila argued. He rinsed another plate, then handed it to her. She was pleased; he'd called her a poet. She pulled a towel from the cabinet handle and dried her hands.

"Not well. Real poets and novelists can't craft decent criticism."

Lila loved his strong opinions on everything. "Professor Powell invited me to hear the Israeli poet Ari Halev read next week. You know him?"

"Another prestige player. At least he's got balls. Have you read *War Tastes Good*?" he asked, going to the living room shelf to look for it. She followed. Good, she was getting a book—like Judith. But there was a special one she wanted more. "Professor Wildman, you said I could look at the first draft of *Beyond Despair* that you used for your thesis?"

"Call me Daniel," he said, pulling out the slim, typed copy bound in a blue folder that he'd slid between the hardcovers.

"Thanks, Daniel." She tried his name on, standing there, paging through his book, wishing she could ask him to sign it. But then he'd know she planned to keep it. "Wow, this is where it all started. It's, like, really historic."

"What are you, twelve years old?" he asked. " If you don't stop using the words 'like' 'really,' and 'gonna' I won't be seen with you."

Where did he want to be seen with her?

"You're getting a master's degree in literature at a literary program, for god's sakes."

Maybe *Pygmalion* was his thing, seeing himself as Henry Higgins to her Cockney flower girl Eliza. "I revised *To My Mother*. Will you read my new draft now?"

"It's two a.m.," he said. "You had too much to drink. You should go home."

"But I incorporated all your notes." She'd been pulverizing her poem obsessively all week for him. "Just for a minute?"

"Okay, okay," he relented. "Quickly."

She rushed to his bedroom, carefully slipped his books into her backpack. Her palms were jittery as she pulled out the folder from her purse. This was what she'd been desperately craving all day and night: his hands on her poem.

She rushed back and gave him the page. He led her to the couch and put a book underneath it to lean on. She sat next to him, watching excitedly as he took a blue Flair from his desk. His eyes scanned her lines. Then his pen jumped in, circling words, crossing out others, messily marking up her page with stars, squiggles and symbols. She found this process enthralling yet torturous, as if a cardiac surgeon was stitching her heart with no anesthetic. The first time he'd cut out two stanzas of "juvenile throat clearing," Lila couldn't believe how painful it felt. She ran out of workshop crying, ready to quit. But Sari said everybody freaked at first critiques. Soon, as Lila was typing her first drafts, she would envision what his pen was going to do, already addicted to getting killed by him.

"Your mother's a good cook? Whose mom isn't?" he asked. "Too common, one-dimensional, on the surface. Where's the brewing rage and pain?" He shook his head as if she'd disappointed him. "You're writing about Pesach. So tell me, why is this night different from all other nights? You're the big Jew. The first Passover plague is *Dam*," he used the Hebrew word. "So where's the blood here?"

Lila loved being so close to him on the couch, but it was confusing. She felt excited yet safe, like she could sit here with him forever. She didn't want to destroy the electric vibes by disagreeing. But she couldn't help arguing. "Every line doesn't need multiple meanings and subtexts," she challenged. "Even your hero Freud said 'Sometimes a cigar is just a cigar.'"

"I read that his actual translated quote was 'Sometimes a cigar just wants to be a cigar.'"

"Right. So what if I want to be funny or rhyming and not so bloody?" she asked.

"If your goal is light verse like Ogden Nash, try another teacher."

Was that a threat? Dorothy Parker was more her style but she didn't want him to stop fixing her poem. When he came to her mother's pulpy brisket, he bellowed, "Now here's the blood! What took so long?" He cut out more. "Okay, read your first two lines out loud."

She obeyed. "Passover morning I find you in your yellow kitchen/where you're passionately making us matzo brei for the holiday."

To her frustration, he crossed out half of the words. "Okay, now listen to my version," he said. Then, in a deep voice that sounded like Cantor Rubin at her old synagogue, he intoned:"'Your kitchen, your passion/for matzo brei...'"

"Shit, yours is better," she had to concede.

"Read your original next line," he ordered.

"'No wonder I dreamt of setting your house on fire/destroying your flowered apron, your thick red hair engulfed in flames,'" she recited. There was the blood and rage he'd demanded. Right?

"In dreams I set fire to your/apron and thick hair,'" he read.

"Wow, that is good. How the hell did you do that?"

"Editing actually works," he told her.

"Who edits you?" she asked.

"Usually Howard. But he's doing some readings out of state. So we're getting together the end of January."

"How can you bear waiting that long?" Lila could barely wait for his class each week.

"Well, maybe now I don't have to." He rushed to the other room, then came out holding a single sheet of paper. "Here, read my latest poem. Tell me what you think."

He was asking *her* opinion of *his* creation? Oh, my God! She'd never critiqued a poem by a professor before.

"It took me four years to finish," he added.

Four years! That was longer than her whole undergraduate and graduate career so far. She'd never heard of anyone taking that long to finish a poem. Knowing it took him that much time made her freeze. It was too much pressure. "Why do you want my take?"

"I'm curious about your opinion."

Was it a test? "Why do you care what I think?"

"I like your comments and notes on everyone's work in class."

"You do? You like how I edit? You never said that before." Lila bet he never showed Judith or the actress any of his poems. "Do you think I'm the best editor in our class?"

"Shut up and read."

Her eyes devoured his thirty-line, full-page chronicle of visiting Ernest Hemingway's house in Key West. She waited for poignant, intense and revealing truths to shock her, transport her, make her laugh and cry, like his other work did. But it read like a boring visit to a Florida tourist attraction. There was no blood here. Instead there was just a male author who revered Hemingway. Who didn't? This poem just wasn't happening. But she didn't want to hurt his feelings since he'd spent four whole years on what he obviously thought was a masterpiece.

"There's potential for heaviness here." She pointed to the third stanza.

"Potential for heaviness. That's all you have to say?" he asked.

She didn't want to add anything else, afraid she was ruining the night. "I'm sorry. The booze made my brain fuzzy." Lila stood up. "Listen, it's late. I should head home."

"Wait, sit back down. I want to hear your take. Tell me more. What's the pretext and subtext?" he asked as he did in class.

"Pretext—you're going to see the museum on Whitehead Street where a famous author you admire used to work." Lila took a breath and then said exactly what she thought. "Subtext is why your father lied to you about your mother's suicide."

"What? Where did you get that?"

"Well, you wrote about never getting to say goodbye to your mom in *Beyond Despair*.""And here," She pointed. "At the end of third stanza, you say 'Papa, tell me the secret.'"

"It's not about my father!" He raised his voice, snatching his poem back. "Papa is Hemingway's nickname. I was asking why *he* committed suicide."

"I know his nickname," Lila said. "But it's the only direct address in six stanzas and it sounds like you're asking your father to reveal the secret of your mother's death."

Lila's mother had lied to her, saying her daddy was sick and had died of pneumonia. She didn't find out the truth until she was in junior high, and that was from her Aunt Francine.

"That's ridiculous. Hemingway shot himself in the head." Daniel jabbed at the lines.

He was freaking her out. As somebody who'd lost her dad by his own hand, Lila knew it had to be dealt with delicately. But she so wanted to be his muse, to unlock him the way he'd been unlocking her. He'd said crafting confessional poetry was like peeling away all the layers of lies you tell yourself until you get to your most naked honesty.

"You were a little vague about her suicide before," she tried, in a quiet voice. "So when you said that…" This was a bad idea. She should have figured out that he did not want the critical assessment—and intrusive personal analysis—of his worst trauma from a lowly student, even one who'd gone through the same tragedy herself.

"What? Say it," he insisted.

"Was your father there when it happened? Did he lie to you? Keep you from saying goodbye to her? It's not about Hemingway. It's about *your* papa's secret."

"No. That's not it. My mom was sick. He thought I was too young to see her at the hospital. He was afraid it would traumatize me."

His eyes darted from her to the page. He suddenly seemed sad, confused. Oh no, Lila feared she'd hurt him. Projected her parents' story onto his poem. He was her professor, not her friend or fellow student. She should not have criticized him.

"I didn't mean to overstep. I should go home." She went for her coat in the other room.

"It's late. Here, let me give you money for a cab," he told her at the door.

He handed her a five, avoiding her eyes. She hoped he'd stop her. Or walk her home. Or offer to help her hail a cab. But he didn't.

Rushing outside, she pocketed the money, deciding to trek it alone though it had started snowing and her heels were too high to go fast. She started crying in the snow, mortified she'd offended him, botching the critique of his rueful—albeit misguided—elegy. How could she flunk the most important test she'd ever taken? He could kick her out of the program, never speak to her again, hate her forever. She needed Sari, but back at the dorm there was a message that her roommate was staying at her folks' uptown. She couldn't call her mother after sundown.

Lila slipped on sweats and a Badgers T-shirt but couldn't calm down, head-tripping. She worried she'd screwed up her first book party and the magic with Daniel and she'd never get another chance. She pulled out her mother poem, staring at the swirls and arrows he'd drawn on her page, running her fingers over his scrawls. Reading it again, she spotted an extra comma and semi-colon and extra words everywhere. She fiddled with the punctuation and line breaks the rest of the night. She didn't even notice the sky turning light outside. When the phone rang at nine a.m., she thought it was her mom, the early bird, calling to get the scoop on the party. But then she remembered it was Sabbath when her mom never used the phone.

"Good morning, Lila," Professor Wildman said. "How are you?"

She was shocked. He'd called her before—to pick up Xeroxing or course packets for him—but never on a Saturday morning.

"Couldn't sleep," she mumbled, lighting a cigarette, sipping the warm diet soda on her end table, wanting to know why he was he phoning. To demand an apology? Throw her out?

"You forgot to take the bottle of Tab," he said. "Why don't you come over and get it?"

"Now?" She took a breath.

"Yes."

She stabbed out her cigarette, her hand shaking. What was the subtext of that?

"I want to show you the new version of my poem," he said, his voice earnest. Desperate.

Oh. Now she got it. She pictured him up all night, obsessively revising his lines over and over, just like she'd done. She was scared to go back but couldn't say no. "Be right there."

She threw on jeans, gym shoes and a coat, applied makeup, taking her hair out of its ponytail, clutching her poem, running twelve blocks back to his place. He opened the door in the same gray slacks and shirt he had on the night before. He hadn't slept either! Without a word, he let her in and handed her his revision with the new title *My Father's Secret*.

Standing up and catching her breath, she read it, devouring all the changes he'd made. Overnight his last stanza had become a potent direct address to his dad, demanding answers to what had really happened during his mother's final moments. "Wow, it's fantastic. Knocks my socks of," she blurted out, then hated that she'd used that dumb Midwest kid's expression. But she was psyched out of her mind he'd taken her suggestions. "You nailed it."

He smiled, nodding his head, his dark hair falling over his eyes, looking like a mad professor, even more hyped up than she was. "Yeah, I nailed it." He went to his desk, pulled out a manila folder. "Here." He handed her a typed manuscript, *Ugly and Sad* on the cover.

Sleep-deprived and hungover, it took her a few moments to understand. He was trusting her with the early draft of his next book! "The world is ugly and the people are sad," she quoted the Wallace Stevens poem he'd mined for his title. This was the best book party in the universe—and it was still going on.

"Tell me what you think." He was casual, no big deal. But she knew it was monumental.

" I wouldn't buy anything called *Ugly and Sad*. Call your collection *My Father's Secret*," she suggested, feeling bolder about her opinions.

"Interesting." But he seemed weirded out, something invisible shifting between them.

"I couldn't sleep all night because I was so worried I'd botched your poem," she admitted. "Like I was dumb and misread it and you hated me."

"You're the opposite of dumb, Lila. You're sharp and intuitive. It just took me a while to process your comments," he said. "Don't worry, I could never, ever hate you. Promise."

Lila pulled out the revision of *To My Mother*. "Check it out."

Wildman read it, nodding. His verdict: "Definitely tighter and more rhythmic."

"I took all your changes," she said. "Can't believe how much better you made it."

It was miraculous. Plunging into each other's verse and revising together was the most fun she'd ever had, better than sex. Just as intimate but you'd get a more lyrical poem out of the deal. She could do it forever and never get tired. In the sunlight, his place looked warmer and cozy. She felt protected here, like she never wanted to leave. "I think I'm falling in love with you" spilled from her lips before she could stop it.

He laughed, as if she were joking. Lila was stunned by his reaction, immediately regretting her words. She could tell her face was getting red and tears were welling up.

"I'm sorry. I didn't mean to laugh." His voice became softer. "Listen, it's just that everybody always thinks they're in love with the person who fixes their work."

She shook her head. "I'm not everybody. You're not just the person who fixes my work." She felt hurt that he'd reduced her to such a grad student stereotype. "You get who I really am more than anyone else I've ever met."

"Lila, I know it can be exhilarating to connect with someone who shares your artistic vision and pushes you further than you can take yourself," he said slowly, measuring his words. "But you'll find others, especially editors, who'll inspire and publish you."

"You're the only one who makes me better," she said.

"Look, it's an intense connection. That's what bonded Howard and me when we studied together in Iowa. In our first workshop, he suggested bold changes to my poem. Made it much deeper and more musical."

"Really? Fell's *that* good an editor?" She was intrigued.

"Spectacular, almost visionary. That's our link. If we were gay, he'd be my husband."

He laughed again but this time it seemed kind. She loved his loud, full-bodied, bubbly laughter that filled the whole room, making it warmer. When he abruptly swept closer, she thought he was about to kiss her. She flinched back, her hand shaking.

But he was just reaching for the picture of a young Daniel and Howard in graduation gowns on his end table, to show her. "Relax, Lila, we're not having an affair or anything."

4

January 1981

DANIEL

"Thanks for the great weekend, baby," Roxy whispered Monday morning. She kissed his neck, then slipped into the bathroom. Daniel tried to go back to sleep but his ears were assaulted by the song her mezzo-soprano pipes belted out in the shower. "Good times and bum times, I've seen them all/And, my dear, I'm still here./Plush velvet sometimes/Sometimes just pretzels and beer, but I'm here."

He put the pillow over his head to muffle out Ethel Merman. Roxy was a happy, hyper morning person, but seven a.m. was too early for a downtown poet to function. The water stopped, but she was soon clanging around his kitchen—making her usual coffee and toast. As he heard her come out, he peeked. She was wrapped in the luxury blue terrycloth towel he'd bought at Macy's after she'd started staying over at his place, the other one twisted into a turban over her auburn hair. She threw off the towel and picked up her pantyhose from his dresser. It was worth sitting up to watch her slowly slip them on her long, slender legs. He enjoyed the way she robed and disrobed theatrically, as if she were Rita Hayworth and the cameras were rolling. She knew he was an avid audience.

"I've slept in shanties, guest of the W.P.A./Danced in my scanties/Three bucks a night was the pay, but I'm here…" Funny to hear a luscious 29-year-old croon the *Follies* swan song of a 75-year-old decrepit showgirl. The nylon slid up Roxy's thigh, erasing the freckles from her pale limb. She put on her beige high heels, stepped into her retro brown pencil skirt and shimmied before hooking the bra over her big, gorgeous breasts. "I've stood in bread lines with the best… /In the Depression was I depressed?/Nowhere near, I met a big financier and I'm here…"

A disjointed post-modernist, Daniel found rhymes low rent (even Sondheim's). He'd never been a musical theater guy. On their first date last January, he decided that her decision to shorten her name from Roxanne to Roxy after seeing *Chicago* was a deal breaker. But when he'd reported to Zalman she was a sweet beauty who sizzled in his bed—where she'd fallen that first night—his shrink advised him to keep his sardonic mouth shut and his lonely arms open.

Daniel was drained from spending the whole weekend together, but now he felt rejected that she was rushing away. "Glad you liked *True West*." He'd feared the two-act they saw at the Public Theater was too dark for her. But if she found the production too angry, she didn't let on.

"So thoughtful of you to get tickets, honey. You know, I had a cameo in *Chorus Line* when it opened at The Public," she said, retrieving her white silk blouse from his closet.

"I wish I could have seen you on stage." He wondered if he'd be jealous looking up at her in a risqué costume with all the men panting after her. The thought turned him on. Or maybe it was how she was buttoning her top so slowly.

"You will. When Katy's with her dad this summer, I'll be able to audition again." She took the towel off of her head, swung down her shoulder-length hair and brushed it vigorously. Then she painted her thick lips with ruby liner.

For all Roxy's dramatic flourishes, he admired her practicality. After her marriage ended, she took a full-time job as a secretary in NCU's theater department –where they'd met at last year's big Christmas party. That night a drunk Roxy revealed that Evan, her thespian ex and father of her daughter, fell for a male director—which explained why he'd been resisting her exquisite body since he'd made her pregnant on their honeymoon. Daniel had the good fortune to be the first straight man to ask her out post-divorce.

She seemed like a great mother, though he could never imagine giving up—or even deferring—his poetry dream to be at an office 9 to 5. Especially now that his creativity was finally flowing again. She'd calmed him down, smoothed out his jagged edges. Was she the muse who'd brought his poetry back?

"Roxy, I want you to read something."

"How about I take it with me, hon? Gotta get Katy to day care," she said. "You want coffee and toast? I left you jam and hard-boiled eggs in the fridge from yesterday."

"You have to read it here. This is important." He jumped out of bed, put on his flannel robe and rushed to his desk to grab the latest draft of his poem *My Father's Secret*, the best work he'd done in years. Lila said it was the best he'd ever done. He handed Roxy the revision he'd carefully retyped ten times until he got it right. She'd read his book but he'd never shown her anything rough before. He imagined it would move her, shock her, impress her back to bed.

"I wish I had more time today, but Evan has to leave at eight," she reminded him.

"It's only fifteen lines," Daniel begged. Roxy sat down on the bed and read it while he paced. He'd told Roxy that his mother had killed herself, but not that his dad had kept the cause of her death from him for decades. He sat down next to her. "So what do you think?"

She looked up at him, bit her lip, then looked down at the page again. "It's intense. Really deep," she said. "Can I take it with me to read more carefully later?"

He couldn't tell if she understood what he was revealing. "Does it surprise you?"

"Aw, baby. I didn't know you were so sad." She put her arms around him and ran her hands over his hair, adding, "You didn't deserve this. Life isn't fair." Then she got up and put on her ivory coat with fur around the collar that made her look like Snow White.

"A surface reaction followed by clichés and Hallmark sentiment," he reported to Dr. Zalman at his session late that afternoon.

"Stop the presses: your hot tamale isn't a brain surgeon," Zalman said.

"Maybe she's just too busy with her daughter."

"You chose her because she's capable of nurturing a real human being and now you're competing with her three-year-old?" Zalman asked, though it wasn't a question.

"My work is essential to me. I have to be with someone who understands that."

"Why show her your poem when she's rushing out the door?" Zalman wanted to know. "You had all weekend together."

"I was feeling close to her," Daniel insisted.

"You were sabotaging your closeness, giving her a last minute test she'd fail so you could end the most nurturing relationship you've ever had. Fear of Intimacy 101."

"Lila saw what a breakthrough this poem was," Daniel pointed out.

"Lila, your 20-year-old protégée?" Zalman squinted. "The puppet you trained to mirror your *mishegas*."

The insult to Lila pissed him off. "She is nobody's puppet. She's already as sharp a reader as Howard. And you can certainly understand a poet wanting to be with someone like-minded," Daniel argued. "That's why Ted Hughes was so drawn to Sylvia Plath."

"And why her head was so drawn to the oven," Zalman told him.

"What about Robert Lowell and Jean Stafford?"

"He almost killed her in a car accident. Before they divorced."

"I was just reading Lowell's searing letters to Elizabeth Bishop," Daniel tried.

"She's gay and he died from a heart attack going to see his other ex-wife. The one he didn't almost kill in a car accident."

"How do you know about these scandals?" Zalman must have been putting his kids through college by treating a slew of crazy Manhattan poets as patients.

"You confessionals can't keep a secret." Zalman smiled.

"There are no writing duets who lasted?" Daniel suddenly realized why he was asking.

"Robert and Elizabeth Browning in 1846," Zalman deadpanned.

"So my chances aren't good?"

"Stay with your showgirl. Or find a doctor," Zalman suggested. "Or a dental hygienist. A lawyer. A kindergarten teacher."

"Because it would be inappropriate…"

"Idiotic and inane," Zalman cut him off. "Anyone but your poetry protégé."

Walking home, Daniel knew Zalman was right. Roxy was older than Lila, ripe, ready for love. She adored him. Turning onto Greenwich Avenue, he was reminding himself of his oath to never touch a student when he saw Howard coming out of the martial arts studio.

"Hey, buddy, how was judo?"

"Tae kwon do," Howard corrected.

"That was a nice little book party we had." Daniel patted his pal on the shoulder, surprised that Howard had never really thanked him, or left a note or bottle of wine. Daniel rarely gave parties for anyone.

"Yes. Yes," Howard said.

Wasn't he cold with no coat on? Daniel sometimes felt his friend was so depressed and inside his own head he didn't feel the weather. "So have you had time to look at my manuscript yet?" He couldn't not ask. "You got the revised version in your box at school?" Daniel knew the answer since he'd checked twice until it was gone. Did he hate it and not want to tell him?

Howard nodded but the proverbial man of few words didn't answer. It had been three months. How long did it take to read fifty short poems? "You noticed I changed the title?"

"*Ugly and Sad* is better," Howard said.

"Lila thought it was too derivative," Daniel admitted.

"Lila Lerner?" Howard's eyes perked up. "Your student?"

"She's working as my assistant now."

"What does she assist you with?" Howard's lips upturned into a little smirk.

"Nothing like that," Daniel said. "I'd never touch a student. That's Cormick's racket," he assured himself. He would never emulate his sleaze-ball boss.

"She's been looking good lately," Howard said. He seemed to be mulling her over in his head. "Lost weight. Ditched the plaid jumpsuits. Different hair."

That was a lot of words all at once for Howard. Had he been scrutinizing Lila? Daniel had been too. It was hard to stop staring at that low-cut velvety dress she'd worn to his party. Was his fellow professor hot for Daniel's star protégée?

"She seeing that foreign student?" Howard asked. "Tarik?"

Tarik? "I doubt it. They're always arguing in my workshop."

"How's Roxy?" Howard asked.

"She's good. How's your hot blond shutter-babe?" Daniel reached for her name—Bette? Bunny? "Betsy," he remembered in time.

"Betsy's fine." He smiled. "You and I—both happy in love. Never happened before."

"You know, she's not a bad editor," Daniel told him. Could she really be seeing Tarik?

"Roxy?"

"No, Lila," Daniel said. At least Lila read his pages and gave him notes quickly. What she didn't have in experience, she made up for in manic energy. She was becoming Howard's main competition for his best reader.

"If you want to trust students with your work," Howard mumbled.

"Well, I'd much rather trust you. If you can find the time," Daniel added, then regretted sounding so needy.

"I'm in the middle. Truthfully, hard to read you when I'm writing," Howard admitted. "You're too good. Don't want to get you in my head and steal anything."

"Hey, thanks, man." Daniel smiled. So he was liking the manuscript, after all.

❧

"Lenu's short story blows," Lila declared that night, after Daniel's workshop. "Like that mailman would really stab his mother and cat in iambic pentameter. Just what the world of literature needs, a rhyming mix of Oedipus and Stephen King. Totally sucks the big one."

"What does that even mean?" Daniel asked. "His sonnet is performing oral sex?"

"And you accuse me of being too literal-minded, Professor Higgins." She hit his arm. "You know it was pretentious. He came to the typewriter wearing a suit instead of being naked."

Daniel enjoyed when Lila stayed after the private fiction and poetry group he ran for students who wanted more one-to-one help. The fee was $200 for twelve sessions, but he didn't charge her. Each Tuesday night she helped him clean up while dissecting the evening. As she poured leftover Coke into the sink, he noticed that Howard was right. She did look prettier and thinner lately—her hair now cut in Cleopatra-style bangs. She was wearing tight dark jeans and a low cut black V-neck sweater. Who was motivating her makeover?

"So what did you think of Tarik's Istanbul story?" Daniel tested.

"Like I told him, I hated the sexist undertones," she said.

"I know." Daniel nodded. She didn't like Tarik—Howard's sexual radar was way off.

"Though Mailer, Roth and Bellow's machismo doesn't mar *their* vision," she said.

She wasn't comparing Tarik's work to the masters, was she? "It's hard to decipher his vision with his mixed-up verb tenses and misused prepositions," Daniel added.

"English clearly isn't his native tongue. And the fact that Islam sanctions polygamy doesn't mean it's not disgusting," she said. "Though it did seem heartfelt and authentic. And the mystical undertones hooked me. It reminded me of the novel you gave me, *Midnight's Children*."

He was taken aback by Lila's high praise, usually reserved for him. So she was falling for a handsome 26-year-old foreigner who stood six feet four. He couldn't compete with Tarik's height or exotic background. Daniel knew he was a dime a dozen neurotic American Jew, retracing literary territory Philip Roth already over-trod. He wished he could flash back to his graduate school days—when he was younger, dabbling in magical realism, showing so much promise he hadn't fulfilled. Lila would have been more attracted to the guy he used to be.

He could see why she'd prefer Tarik—a Jewish girl with a Muslim-born lover could be spicy; it would certainly inspire better poems than her mother's matzo brei.

"Tarik's scene at the shrine of Baba Rishi blew my mind," Lila was saying. "Though I wish his narrator would trash that third wife shit." She picked up an empty beer bottle from the floor.

She was swearing and using too much slang. Maybe throwing her with Sari wasn't so brilliant. He bet Tarik had made a move on her. Daniel told himself it was better that Lila's crush on him was waning. He was with Roxy—and that relationship was easier, healthier and more appropriate.

"Yes, one wife would be more than enough," Daniel said. He didn't want to be the mentor to a young mixed-up girl who only loved his mind. But now he feared he'd lost his shot to be more than just a father-figure to Lila, who threw her black leather coat over her shoulder winked and said, "See ya, teach."

5

February 1981

LILA

Lila ripped open the Valentine's Day card accompanying the lilies in her dorm room that Saturday morning, excited. Finally Daniel figured out they couldn't live without each other!

Alas, the long-stemmed pink and white present, in a Plexiglas vase, was from Jeff, Lila's first—and last—boyfriend in Wisconsin. She regretted stumbling back into bed with him over her holiday visit. When she'd called to ask Sari's opinion long-distance, her roommate's advice was: "He won't add a number to your long list of one lover, so I'd screw the hell out of him." Damn, Lila now realized that Sari—the proud slut—should not be her carnal conscience.

Jeff, a college football player, was still buff, with those big shoulders, his aggressive arms and legs all over her like an octopus. The distance hadn't dulled their chemistry—they did it four times that Saturday night. But Jeff had no idea Lila had faked it. It wasn't his fault; the only way she'd ever "reached nirvana," as Sari called it, was by herself. She'd fantasize that Jeff was making love with another woman, someone hotter than she was, one of *Charlie's Angels* private eyes, in the kind of tiny white bikini Lila wouldn't dare wear in public.

"Can't wait for you to come home, Li," Jeff had scrawled messily on the card. She hated the nickname "Li," pronounced "lie," as if he was calling her deceptive. ("Every word matters. Even a comma changes the meaning of a whole sentence," Daniel had said.) She'd just been back to the Midwest and didn't plan to visit again for another year.

"Hey Jeff, thanks for the lilies. They're lovely," she said into the pink princess phone her mother let her bring from her old bedroom. Sitting on the bed in her dorm, Lila lit a half-cigarette left by Sari, who—typically—hadn't returned from her hot date the night before.

"They're stargazers," Jeff told her. "Just like you."

Was that a compliment or a swipe? "You do know that I'm committed to my work here."

"Of course, Li. I think it's great that you're doing something creative. And I want to help you finish your degree." He paused. "I was thinking I could supplement your scholarship, so you can quit waitressing."

"That's really sweet," she said. "But you're only working part-time. You have law school loans to pay off." She was desperate to be just a writer, not a waitress, but didn't want this kind of support from a man. She needed to do it on her own.

"It's not like I don't have my own pipe dreams. Sometimes I want to be a senator…"

"Pipe dreams?"

"Well, nobody makes a living as a poet. You said that even your poet professor has to teach to pay his bills and lives in a shithole."

"I never said that about his apartment. And my other poetry professor lives in a huge fancy brownstone and won the Pulitzer Prize."

"When he was eighty," Jeff argued. "Come on, sweetie, how are you going to pay for your thirty thousand dollar degree? You gonna sell your poems on the sidewalk?"

Lila slammed the phone down. Fuming, she flung his flowers in the garbage bin down the hall. Ten minutes later she heard her mother's voice guilting her and went to retrieve them but they were gone. She rushed downstairs and asked the woman at the front desk in her dorm lobby, "Do you know where garbage from the sixth floor is taken?"

"Do you live here?" she asked.

"Lila Lerner, Room #609." She took out her I.D.

"Someone left this for you," the woman said, handing her one red rose with her name on a card. It was a sign! Lila threw out the present from the wrong man to accept this more poetic love offering from the right man: Daniel. But on the way up the elevator she saw the card was signed by Tarik. Her mom had flipped out in high school when she'd started dating Jeff because he was from a reform family –not Jewish enough. What would she think of a Muslim from Turkey? Not that Lila would ever let her family, or anybody else, dictate who she would love.

Why did the wrong men always send flowers?

On the card he'd carefully written a line from Rumi, an ancient poet:"The rose's rarest essence lives in its thorns." What a classy way of ending the polygamy argument they'd had at Wildman's workshop. At the bottom he added "Dinner tonight?" It was last minute. But Lila liked his minimalism and his handwriting. She heard Sari's voice saying, "What do you have to lose that you haven't lost already?" She agreed to meet Tarik at the Cookery, a restaurant with jazz down the street, at 8 p.m.. She threw on her crushed velvet punk rock bombshell dress with her chunky black heels and was putting on makeup when her roommate came home.

"Ooo la la," Sari said. She was in her black jeans from the night before. She looked hung over, with messy hair and smudged mascara under both eyes, like a raccoon.

"You okay?" Lila handed her the heart-shaped box of chocolates that were on sale at the supermarket, the same kind she'd sent her mother. The only people she'd bought Valentine's Day presents for this year were women.

Sari handed her a thick joint rolled in red paper.

"Cool biz!" Lila said. "How'd ya do that?"

"Henna dye," Sari said, then took the joint back, lit it and inhaled a few long hits. "Lenu and I are going to the 'Love Sucks' reading at the Nuyorican. Want to meet us there?"

Aha! Her new lover was their classmate Lenu! Sari's parents couldn't bear her dating non-Armenian men; Lila wondered what they'd make of a Nigerian. Sari was so brave.

"I have a dinner date too," Lila told her, taking the joint and inhaling.

"Don't tell me—Professor Portnoy is finally going for it?" Sari opened the candy, took a tiny bite out of one, put it back. "Hate caramel." She tried another. "Yuck. Marzipan." She returned it to the box.

Sari's candy exploration grossed Lila out. "You'll be happy to know Tarik asked me to dinner tonight!" Lila wanted to become a Manhattan sophisticate like Sari, and multi-cultural too.

Sari's mouth fell open. "You're not going, are you?"

"I thought you'd be proud of me." Sari was always pushing her to try new things, be "less Wisconsin hick" and get over her "pathetic unrequited crunch" on Daniel.

"You know what he is." Sari sneered.

"Ms. card-carrying left winger thinks a Jew can't date a Muslim?" Lila was stunned.

"It's not about you. He's a Turk!" Sari stubbed out the joint and handed what was left to Lila, who slipped it in her wallet.

"Why are you being racist?"

"Racist means you hate someone because of their race," Sari insisted.

"Then xenophobic and anti-religious," Lila tried.

"Anti-murderer," Sari said. "They killed one and a half million of my people and never even apologized. My Grandpa Duddy watched the Ottoman soldiers slaughter his whole family."

"I'm sorry," Lila said. "But you don't want me to share a meal with a Turkish guy because his grandparents might have been anti-Armenian 65 years ago?"

"They also treated Jews like second-class citizens," Sari told her. "How would you feel if I went out with a Nazi?"

"There's a difference between a young German guy in New York and a

Nazi." But now Lila felt guilty she was going out to dinner with the wrong flavor guy wearing the dress Sari bought her.

"Fine! Ignore my genocide! Everybody else does!" Sari yelled and slammed the door on the way out. Then she came back, grabbed the chocolates and left again.

"You wore that dress to Professor Wildman's party," Tarik said at the restaurant.

"I don't have many dresses." Lila was embarrassed to be wearing the same outfit.

"You look pretty."

"You do too," she said, staring at his slim physique in his fitted jacket and black pants. "I mean, handsome." He was so much younger, taller and easier than Daniel.

As they were seated in a booth, Lila surveyed the dimly-lit, spacious, casually arty eatery. "I didn't mean to insult your story at Daniel's workshop." Lila should have called him Professor Wildman, wondering if that would tip Tarik off that there was something special between them.

"You are passionate woman," Tarik said. She was intrigued by his accent and the way he sometimes left out articles and connectives. "'I've never been good at secrets/unbutton myself heedlessly,' Tarik recited, and 'In dreams, I set fire to your apron/and thick hair.'"

"Quoting a poet back to herself. Good ploy," Lila told him, thinking that last line only worked because of Daniel's edit. Was her professor reading poems to his redhead tonight? Lila tried to guess what Village restaurant Daniel would take his actress girlfriend to. For a second she feared running into them at this place and eyed the room suspiciously. Feeling stoned from Sari's strong weed, she imagined Daniel here, spying on her date. She hoped he'd be furiously jealous to catch her out with another man, a dashing foreign poet at that.

"I loved that line from Rumi on your card." She pretended she was with someone she was falling in love with, for Daniel's benefit, in case he was watching. "Tell me another," she cooed.

"The fire of Love cooks us to perfection," he recited. "Every night it drags us to the tavern./It makes us sit with the drunkards there,/Where we're safe from the eyes of outsiders."

"How divine." She sipped water. "Rumi is Turkish?" She scanned the crowd. No Daniel.

"Persian. Sufi mystic. We like spirituality," Tarik said. "I show you Turkish poets? You know Orhan Veli Kanik?"

"Tell me a line." Daniel wasn't the only man who could turn her on to new poetry.

"I buy old clothes and cut them into stars," Tarik said.

"That's elegant." Lila applauded.

When the waiter came, Tarik ordered veal and a bottle of red wine from 1970.

"I'll have a Diet Coke. And the chicken cacciatore," Lila said. "Tell me another."

"You made me wait so long, so long that/I got used to missing you/You came back after a long time/I now love longing for you…"

"Sublime!" She nodded. "I once wrote an autobiographical poem about a woman who was better at longing for love than getting it."

"You?" he smiled.

"Probably. Like your man of longing. Who is he?"

"Aziz Nesin," Tarik said. "Political activist with fifty aliases."

"Imagine so many different identities." Lila wished she could have more herself.

When their drinks came, Tarik instructed the waiter to pour two glasses. "Have wine with me," he insisted.

"Why did you get a bottle from ten years ago?" she asked, wondering if it was still good a decade later, and if you got a discount for old stuff.

"A friend and wine are best when old," he said, clicking her glasses.

The kind she was used to from home was *Manischewitz*. This was more sour.

"After you get graduate degree, will you move home?" Tarik asked.

"No. I'll get a job and stay in New York," Lila told him, drinking more. The taste was growing on her.

"Your family will let you do this?" Tarik poured more wine.

Lila shrugged. "Why not?"

"Dangerous alone. Before you marry…"

Lila finished her glass. Emboldened, she said, "I might never get married."

"Woman writer needs husband," he insisted.

"Tell that to Sylvia Plath." Now she poured herself a tall glass, finishing the bottle.

He looked confused. "She had husband and two babies young."

"Yeah, then her husband's affairs ruined their family," Lila said. "She would have been better off unmarried and childless. Like Emily Dickinson. Jane Austen. Elizabeth Bishop."

"You don't mean." Tarik shook his head.

"Of course I do." Did she?

"Something wrong with woman who doesn't want to be wife and mother," Tarik said.

"What do you mean by *wrong*?"

"Broken. Damaged. Not normal. Crazy," he listed. "How do you say—disturbed."

Lila was so stunned she couldn't speak. Daniel would never say anything so close-minded. Jeff, a staid Wisconsin lawyer, wouldn't even think it. She couldn't believe something so prehistoric had come out of Tarik's mouth.

"Why the fuck would you say something so ignorant?" she asked.

"Speak quietly," he said. "Not attractive for ladies to swear."

"Fuck you!" she said louder, standing up.

He stood up too, his eyes jumpy and horrified. "Sit down," he whispered through clenched teeth, like it was an order.

She did not sit down. Lila marched out the door. She had never walked out on a guy at dinner before. It felt totally cool, like she was the poet version of Gloria Steinem. Until she realized that she was overdressed, high and alone at 9 p.m. on the Saturday night of Valentine's Day, with the city full of couples on dates. How humiliating. What if Daniel caught her now? Tarik would tell him she was a mean jerk and they'd both hate her. Lila started to cry, planning to head back to her dorm to hide under the covers. Instead she kept going, to Washington Square Park. Sitting on a bench, she lit the remnants of Sari's red joint. Nobody noticed her amid the transvestites, hippies and students who, despite the freezing cold, were all gathered around the fire eater. A homeless guy she always saw there asked, "Hey pretty clothes, what ya doin' back here?" She laughed. "Dumped my date," she said, handing him the joint. They shared it as a guitar player sang Joni Mitchell's *Free Man in Paris*. These were her people. She hummed along, tingly, dizzy, starving.

Then she remembered she had in her purse the $20 her mother sent her for Valentine's Day with a card that said "For the love of my life, my beautiful daughter." She decided to take herself out to dinner at Dojo's—her favorite dive. She changed into the flats she'd hidden in her purse and waded through the hordes of bohemians and homeless men hanging out on decrepit St. Mark's Place. It smelled of burning incense and the falafel food truck on the corner.

Lila forged on, passed the seedy bodega, the dive bar, the graffiti-lined record shop and the tattoo parlor. More crazy characters were strolling at this jam-packed East Village intersection than she'd seen in nineteen years of Baraboo, population 10,000. In the past when she'd craved crowds, Lila drove her rusty 1975 blue Honda forty miles to the mall at Madison and to University of Wisconsin football games with Jeff, but that was the jeans-and-flannel-shirt brigade. Here she was awed by the New York graffiti artists and foreign women selling used blouses and coffeemakers on the sidewalk—not even noticing it was twenty degrees out. All the oddballs were decked out as if Valentine's Day was Halloween—girls in gowns with vampire capes, and men in dresses, high heels and makeup. Everybody carried bizarre objects:

antique chairs, bagpipes, a boa constrictor. She felt like she was floating, escaping from prison to live in this exciting drug-filled carnival.

At St. Marks Bookshop, she treated herself to a poetry paperback: Louise Glück's *Descending Figure* on sale for $2. Then she sat inside at DoJo's and read the angry female Jewish poet's words, craving chicken yakimeshi. Sari had turned her on to this dive restaurant and its awesome four dollar meal. Every other week when Lila got her paycheck, she'd treat herself to this special dish. The only thing Lila didn't like about it was the sliced onions. She'd pick them out one by one, building a pile on the side.

Right after ordering, she had a revelation. She stopped the waitress and said, "Excuse me, Miss. I have a question. Can I get my yakimeshi without onions?"

"Sure, hon. No problem," the waitress said.

Lila was amazed. Forget Jeff, Tarik and Daniel and all her male Svengalis trying to teach her all their wisdom. She'd just learned the most important lesson on her own: you could order the world without onions! Just as it came, she saw Sari walking by through the window. She was alone too. What happened to her date? Lila ran outside and called out to her. "I left Tarik at the Cookery and smoked your joint alone in the park."

"Lenu bangs me four times last night, then blows me off Valentine's Day. It's a stupid motherfucking Hallmark holiday," Sari muttered, then started crying.

"You were really into him?" Lila asked, surprised.

Sari nodded, sniffling. Lila held out her arms, which Sari fell into. "I'm so glad you're here. Come hang out with me." Lila rubbed her back, then led her inside.

Sari sat down at her table, blowing her nose with Lila's napkin. Then she stuck her fingers in the yakimeshi, picking out chicken and some carrots, plunking them in her mouth.

"Tastes different," Sari said.

"I special ordered it," Lila told her. "You can just order life without the onions!"

"Nice metaphor," Sari said.

"Right? I know!" Lila cracked up, then asked the waitress for another fork, thinking she wound up with the exact right person she loved most on Valentine's Day after all.

6

November 1981

DANIEL

This year he was determined to break his New York holiday curse.

He stared at Roxy, in her blue-and-white polka-dot Doris Day dress, marveling how she managed to look so lovely this early in the morning. Daniel pictured how sweet it would be, waking up to her every day. He was sick of being alone, depressed, over-thinking everything. Zalman was right, you could be ambivalent and make a decision. He was turning 40, it was time. He'd just ended a stanza: "I march down the avenue searching for my bride." Maybe he'd be like Stephen Crane, who'd imagined being a soldier in *Red Badge of Courage*, only to later live out his fiction in real life by joining the Marines. Yes, Daniel would write his own future too. But why did the thought of marriage always conjure up battle metaphors?

"Let's have Thanksgiving here," he proposed to Roxy over breakfast. He pictured them cooking together, then falling into bed with champagne and leftovers.

"Well, Katy and I…"

"With Katy too, of course," he jumped in. He was actually relieved when Roxy finally introduced him to her adorable daughter over the summer. He knew that meant she was testing him out—as a spouse and a father. He'd struggled to play the part of "Mommy's friend Daniel," trying funny faces that made Katy giggle, pushing her on the swings in Central Park. He bought her a special book for her fourth birthday, a first edition of Robert Louis Stevenson's *A Child's Garden of Verses* he found at the Strand's Rare Book Room. But when he tried reading Katy *My Shadow,* the first poem he'd loved as a kid, she began reciting *Horton Hears a Who.*

"The picture of the gray shadow looks like Horton the elephant," Roxy explained. "Evan reads it to her every night before bed, it's her favorite."

He was there *every* night? She'd often praised Daniel, telling him he was the smartest man she'd ever dated, and the sex was always beyond hot. But he sometimes worried that he couldn't compete with Roxy's ex—the elephant in every room. When his colleague and former lover Faith, the feminist, mentioned (despairingly) that her own daughter adored pink ballerina Barbie, Daniel rushed out to Toys "R" Us to get one for Katy the next day. The first one he found was College Coed Barbie—a gift he thought ingeniously pro higher education—until Katy almost choked on the doll's tiny plastic shoe. ("She'll be old enough next year," Roxy said, banishing the blond toy, with mini-accessories, to a high shelf.)

"I'll get Katy a booster seat and make her favorite mac and cheese," Daniel now offered. "I usually cook a big dinner with my writer friends, but we'll tell everyone to bring their kids." Did other friends of his even have kids? Faith's daughter was in third grade. Did that make her too old to play with a four-year-old?

"That's so sweet," Roxy said. "But babe, listen, we already have plans to spend the holiday with my folks in Texas."

"Oh. You didn't tell me." Daniel pretended it was no biggie, rustling through the *Times* Sports Section, disappointed with the Knicks again. He flashed to the last line from a poem by Howard about male sports team over-identification: "When *they* win, *I* win. When they lose, they lose." Howard could sure cough up a kicker, even if it was just spinning a cliché around; Daniel had to give him that.

"We planned it months ago." Roxy sipped her coffee, turning the page of *The Post* she'd picked up on her morning jog. "Good article about Mayor Koch pushing for more arts funding."

Daniel couldn't stand Koch. "You should have mentioned your trip, is all."

"You should have said something earlier," she snapped, putting her cup down, leaving fuchsia lipstick on the rim. "I'm not Co-Ed Barbie. I can't make last-minute plans on a whim. I have a child to take care of."

It was his fault. Ten days in advance wasn't enough time. He'd waited too long to ask. But she hadn't brought up anything about the holiday either. He feared he'd never come first in Roxy's life. And she didn't have to make fun of the backup present he'd picked out for her daughter. But Zalman would tell him to stop being a victim and ask for what he wanted.

"Maybe I can come with you?" he tried.

"Evan's meeting us there." She took her plate to the sink. "The divorce counselor wants us to normalize things for Katy. She's having a tough time understanding why Daddy doesn't live with us anymore."

"No problem," he said, rejected and replaced. Daniel couldn't actually be jealous of Roxy's gay ex-husband. Could he? More like edged out. She already had a family; there was no room for him. All the details about Evan and their dysfunctional mélange made him claustrophobic. But he heard Zalman's voice warning him not to screw it up with Roxy, who was sweet and nurturing and liked to cook for him.

"You make the best omelets," he coughed up, finishing the last bite even though she'd fried it with an onion. He hated onions.

"We'll do Christmas together, hon." She sat down, reaching for his hand across the table. "We'll go to Midnight Mass and you can open presents with us. I love the holidays. I'll get you a Santa suit for this sing-a-long that me, Katy and Evan do at a Harlem nursery."

She wanted him to go a hundred blocks uptown to entertain a bunch of kids in a Christian costume with her gay ex-husband. Didn't she know him at all? "Listen, I'm not really the type of Jew to decorate a tree or play Santa," he said.

"Oh, you poets are so serious and intense all the time." She grasped her hands around her neck in an exaggerated choking motion. "I'll never understand what goes on in your head."

He now saw this was true, she never would. Forget Christmas with her tree, kid and ex-husband. Daniel didn't think he could marry someone who actually read the *New York Post*—no matter how hot she was.

"What did you think of that essay on Plath and Sexton in the *New York Review*?" Lila asked Tuesday night after his private workshop.

"I haven't seen it yet," he admitted. "Anything new?"

"Rehash of Alvarez's theme that they weren't victims and the metaphysical aspects of their suicides speak louder than psychological limitations," Lila said. Gathering the abandoned pages left on the floor, she picked up all the copies of her poetry, lest she miss one single star or squiggle anybody had scrawled in her margins. When there wasn't too much work, he'd let her bring in her poems to read aloud too. "Of course a male critic has to cite a male author to reiterate what Joan Didion said better in 1970," she added. "Hey, I have another rewrite we didn't have time for tonight. Can you check it out?"

Between her endless revisions and Gloria Steinem lectures, she was the most taxing student he'd ever had. But whenever she wasn't around, he missed her. She plopped down on his couch, pulled a folder from her backpack and took out a new page. He assumed "Early Stages" was from the Jewish food-laden series of poems she'd been obsessed with.

"Drunk on my mother's hidden sherry," she read aloud. "I peel off my sheer pantyhose like a snakeskin on the carpet/turning on bright lights and scratching your pale back/with long red nails I still grow/because that long ago night you said you liked them."

Pretty provocative. She was chronicling the night she'd lost her virginity at sixteen. She'd never shared it with his workshop or class, as if she'd saved it just for him. She was in black jeans and black top as usual. Wasn't a snake a penis metaphor? He'd never seen her in pantyhose.

"Too many words," he said, crossing out her throat clearing, extra adjectives, redundancies. "'I turned on lights and scratched your back/with long nails I still grow/because that night you liked them,'" he read, uncomfortable to realize he was editing her first seduction.

This poem was a letter to a man she was missing, and it wasn't him. She was addressing her first lover back home. Daniel didn't like the present tense. He crossed it out too and put it all in the past. She leaned over to watch him. He could feel the sweat on the back of his neck. She touched the edge of the page. He glanced at her nails, now longer, manicured in clear gloss. So it wasn't Tarik inspiring her makeover. That flirtation must have been over. The tall football player from her past was back in her verse. Was she seeing him again?

"Why cut the eye shadow double entendre showing a shadowy layer in her inner vision?" she asked. "You said we should add idiosyncratic details. It might fit in the third stanza. What do you think?"

"I think you talk too much, too loud, too fast," he said. "The same way you write."

"I should be Emily Dickinson, a quiet little mouse, so you men can do all the talking?"

This again! As if she was the original suffragette. But how passionate she looked when she stood up for herself—her angry blue eyes flaring, soft cheeks becoming red. "Dickinson knew poetry isn't only what's on the page. It's about feelings hidden between the lines, what's never said." He stood up to get away from her, grabbing Plath's Ariel, Lila's bible. "Plath doesn't write 'I hate my mother and since my father died, I think of offing myself to ease the pain I'm in.' She says, 'Dying is an art. I do it exceptionally well.'"

He stared at her, thinking he could never be like Cormick, screwing around with young co-eds on the sly. Daniel didn't want to screw around; he wanted someone to settle him down. But would Lila seriously consider a guy his age? He put Plath on the table and picked up a Hefty trash bag to finish cleaning. "Hey, are you and Sari going home for Thanksgiving?" he asked, not looking at her.

"Nope. I'm only going back to Baraboo for Hanukah. Sari's folks are in Armenia. We're thinking of trying Wo-Hop, this fun dive in Chinatown with the meanest waiters. They yell at you." She picked up the empty soda cans and beer bottles.

"Want to come to a little Thanksgiving party I'm hosting?" he asked, accidentally tossing the clean stack of plastic cups into the garbage.

"Really? You mean it? I'd love to. Wow. Cool biz." She looked up at him, her eager eyes like sparklers. "I'm totally there."

Now *this* was the reaction he wanted. Lila was so much easier to make plans with than Roxy. She was unencumbered, no full-time job, husbands, exes or kids, all her relatives out of the way in another state. Daniel didn't come with the baggage of an ex-wife and child and lousy divorce, so why should he date someone who did? He didn't want to be a woman's second priority. "Good. We're on then. Howard will be here. Come over early. We can all cook together." He fished out the clean cup package, hoping she didn't notice.

"But I don't know how to make turkey or anything," she said. "I usually hate formal holiday celebrations."

"Me too!" His mother had died in the middle of November when he was 12. So for the rest of his childhood, Thanksgiving was bleak and depressing. But then, when he was 20, in his sophomore year at Iowa, he and Howard cooked an impromptu meal at the funky railroad flat they shared, inviting their classmates. It was the sixties, so everyone got drunk and stoned while roasting the turkey and making stuffing, dancing to The Dead and Dylan, turning their little celebration into a legendary 10-hour party-fest. Daniel had wound up in bed with Gabrielle, a comely British blonde lit major who fell for him—hard—making him the envy of all his male classmates. Thus the ritual was born and carried with them to Manhattan. Every year a bunch of downtown artists and writers popped in for free food and booze. But he'd never figured out how to make Turkey Day cool again and special. Until now.

His friends would go nuts over Lila and Sari. They were beautiful and sharp as hell. But Lila was his protégé, he reminded himself, a student. Getting a headcount, he remembered that Howard was on the outs with Betsy, thus she wasn't coming. Faith and her family hadn't responded to his invitation yet. Neither had his Brooklyn poet pals Bob and Davie or Stanley, his rickety retired biographer friend who lived on Christopher Street. Howard was the only other confirmed guest so far, as well as Lila and Sari. Damn, he'd just inadvertently arranged a double date. To avoid impropriety, he'd leave a message to nudge Stanley. He recalled that even Stanley had managed to find a steady companion, a guy from the senior center. If Daniel invited Stanley and his boyfriend, it would be all couples.

"Let's invite Lenu and Tarik too," Daniel said, to show Lila it was a big friendly gathering. "The more cooks, the better the stew." Oh God, what kind of clichés was he mangling?

"My mom's a great cook," Lila said. "Last time I tried to make tea, I burned the water."

She was the anti-Roxy. "You know, you can be female, smart and a good cook," he taunted.

"Or I can be female, smart, and never serve any man food." She stuck out her tongue.

Should he be worried about her drinking, drugging and sarcasm? It wasn't average neurosis that plagued people like him and Lila. It went back deeper, to their early loss. Zalman warned that losing a parent young increased your risk of committing suicide later in life.

"Some children develop a pathological link to the lost parent," Zalman said. "It plants a romantic notion that killing yourself is choosing to join the loved one you long for most."

"It's not just my Mom," she said. "Grandma Yetta stuffed my face and made me serve my brother, stepdad, male cousins. They invented eighteen Jewish holidays to promote starch—latkes, humantash, matzo, knishes. No wonder my *mishpucha's* all zaftig."

He led her back to the living room couch, where they sat down. "Feeding someone can be sweet and caring." He'd spent half his life wishing he'd come home to find his mother in the kitchen again, baking her challah with raisins, the delicious aroma filling their house.

"Look, I adore my mom," Lila said. "But she's stuck in Baraboo without a job, dependent on a man cause she got hitched at nineteen and had babies too young."

"You're just trying to be the opposite of your mother," he told her.

"I need you to critique my poems, not my life." She stood up and emptied a dirty ashtray. "And who are you to talk? Your father's a Republican Cleveland banker and you're a Greenwich Village poet who can't tie your shoelaces without your shrink's approval."

Ouch. Good line. But he already had Zalman. He didn't need any more analysis—especially from this unanalyzed Wisconsin ball of fire. "Well, you can marry, have kids and still write and cook," he said, trying to convince her. "Many women do."

"Not at the same time. Sari says it's the Sylvia Plath syndrome, trying to have a Type-A mate, babies, and big career before thirty would make anyone stick their head in the oven."

He was getting sick of the silent advisory board of Plath and Sexton that his crowd injected into every argument. "It isn't healthy for men to live alone either," he said.

"You and Howard are pretty old and *you* guys aren't married with kids."

"You want to be as pathetic as me and Howard, broke, living alone in a 500 square-foot apartment in your forties?" he asked and sent her home, bathing in the sound of her light-hearted laughter. For the first time in decades he was excited about Thanksgiving.

"Lila, you need to get over here," Daniel said on the phone early Thursday morning.

"What's up?" She sounded groggy. "What time is it?"

When she arrived, in torn jeans and a different black top, she looked half asleep, her spiky bangs sticking up, making her look 12. He led her to his small kitchen and pointed to the food overtaking his counter: a huge 20-pound cooked turkey, cranberry sauce, cardboard containers of vegetables, stuffing, gravy, potatoes, a loaf of challah bread, and three fruit pies.

She glanced at the counter, then back at him, looking confused. "What'd ya wake me up for? I'm, like, still stoned from last night."

"Well, stop frying your brain," he grumbled. "This was just delivered from Ben's Kosher Deli on the Lower East Side." He crossed his arms.

"I didn't know you were ordering in."

"I didn't order this," he said.

"So who did?" She leaned against the cabinet.

He went to the monster turkey box to show her the long receipt taped atop, paid for by the credit card of Hannah Lerner.

She examined the bill. "My *mom* sent you all this? Damn. All the way from Wisconsin." Lila's cheeks and neck became crimson.

"I called the deli. They said your mother phoned in the order. They usually don't take credit cards from out-of-towners, but she convinced the owner —in Yiddish!—that her poor suffering daughter and her poet friends would starve without her food, that it had to be delivered this morning. If you didn't know about it, how did she get my name and address?"

"I guess she had it from when she sent you that thank-you note after your party," Lila said quietly, looking down at the parquet tiles on his floor.

Every year, when he'd help kids in his classes get published and jobs and internships, his star students and their grateful parents sent him gifts: a knitted scarf, homemade brownies, wine. Nobody had sent him a kosher Thanksgiving meal for a dozen people before.

"Oh, I know what happened. I told Mom I was freaked out about the cooking dinner part, afraid I'd look stupid." Lila smiled sheepishly. "Jeez. She must have spent a hundred bucks on this." She bit her lip. "I've lost weight since I've been here. She's worried I don't eat enough."

"But I already defrosted my own turkey."

"What's wrong with having two birds?" Lila tried, clearly not getting it. As if the food didn't matter at all.

"I was hoping to serve the one I'm cooking," he explained.

"Okay. Who cares? I'll bring Mom's to the dorm." She put her hands in her pockets, seeming annoyed, not looking at him.

Yet he wanted her to understand, to take his side, to see how intrusive her mother was being. She was mangling his holiday plan. What if the administration found out a students' mother had sent him this food? It would look like a lover's feast. "Don't you find it bizarre that she did this?"

"You don't have to embarrass me. It's just food. You're having a neurotic overreaction!" She was defensive. Or was it hurt? Damn, he never meant to hurt her feelings.

Now he felt mortified. These Lerner women were bringing out all his Jewish guilt. "You don't find it odd? I mean, if your mother is so omnipresent in your life, how are you ever going to get close to a man?"

"Why do you care who I get close to?" she asked. "And I've been close to lots of guys who aren't threatened by my mom's love. She's an over-feeder. Stop the presses," Lila raised her voice. "She grew up a poor orphan, she lost her husband. She misses me. I write about it all the time. You told me she's my most vivid character."

He felt as if Hannah Lerner had sprung from Lila's poems to crash his holiday party. He liked her better on the page. He tried not to let his day be wrecked by the blonde Wisconsin *balabusta* he'd never met.

"But she didn't send a care package to your dorm. She had it delivered to your male professor's home. Picture how that looks." He was miffed Lila couldn't see it was inappropriate. "Dr. Zalman would say it was controlling your holiday and usurping your female power."

"Why don't you ask your male shrink about your jealousy of anybody who has a mother?" she shot back, planting her hands on her hips and twisting her torso towards him.

That was mean. But for some reason her nastiness was turning him on. He wanted to grab her hard and kiss her to shut her up.

He took a breath and stepped back. "Did you call the therapist I recommended?"

"No. And I never will," she yelled. "I can't even afford real doctors. Though I did find this nice female gyno at Planned Parenthood who gave me a year's worth of the pill for free."

Why would she tell him that? Was she flirting? He looked for clues in her huge aqua eyes, partially covered by the uneven bangs he wasn't used to. He kind of liked her looking unfinished. "Does that mean you have a clandestine beau? A secret lover who sneaks into your dorm?"

"Who uses the words *lover* and *beau* anymore?" she asked.

"What do you call it?"

"Having a fuck buddy."

"Now that's poetic."

"Why are you so interested in my sex life?"

"I just want you to be careful. Dr. Zalman gave me the number of a female psychologist, Dr. Ness, who has a sliding scale, if you ever want anyone to talk to.

"Just because you need a head doctor doesn't mean I do."

"Look, I'm sorry if I overreacted," he said, moving her mother's fat poultry so there was room for him to sit on the counter. He felt sad and stupid that he'd lost it in front of her. "Everything is too important to you," Zalman often told him.

"Don't worry about it," she said.

"When I was a kid…my mother died in November." He wanted her to know the old wound she'd inadvertently opened. "So, you see, I miss her most this time of year. Thanksgiving is really loaded for me. My few friends are the only family I have left."

She was quiet, then said, "I'm honored you invited me. You're the most important person I have here. I'll bring the extra stuff back to the dorm."

He nodded, realizing that he didn't really want to win the argument; he wanted to win her. "You don't have to. Don't worry. We'll eat Hannah's food too," he relented. "We'll just have a lot of choices this year."

"I can invite other friends if you want," Lila offered. "Though it might be nicer if it's small."

"Yes. Let's keep it more intimate." He lifted the tin foil covering the turkey. He cut off a slice of breast meat from the side and took a bite. "Not bad."

"Let me taste." She leaned in closer.

On impulse he tore off another sliver and fed it to her, his finger grazing her soft lips. He inhaled her tangy perfume. Unsteady, he leaned back against the cabinet, deciding that he didn't want Lila around other guys. "We don't need anyone else," he said, suddenly dying to know what she meant by her most important person *here*. Who was more important somewhere else?

7

January 1982

LILA

As they followed the crowd pouring from Cooper Union's Great Hall after the reading, Lila was mortified by her mother's bright turquoise suit, flowered blouse, matching purse and shoes. Her dyed blond hair was puffed up from the Baraboo beauty shop.

"My favorite was that handsome Irishman," her mom said. "No kvetching, no depression, no victim shtick."

"Sshhh, Mom don't be so loud," Lila whispered.

Growing up, she was proud to have a warm, pretty mother who liked to gossip and hang out with her. But now, seeing her in Manhattan for the first time, her bright tacky clothes and Midwestern chattiness didn't fit in. She should be more subtle. The New York literati spoke quieter, wore darker colors and less lipstick than the ladies at their Madison Temple. Lila saw that her mother would never get anything about this world and worried she'd be a bad reflection, like a "hick" stamp on Lila's forehead.

"Another female charmed by the Gaelic bard," Sari said. "He does have a macho aura."

"Oh please," Lila sneered, pissed they were praising Cormick, Daniel's enemy. She wanted her mom to be wowed by her professor. That was why she'd nixed celebrating her 21st birthday with discount tickets for *A Chorus Line,* insisting instead on the protest reading for Irina Ratushinskaya, a Russian dissident poet jailed in a Siberian labor camp for "the dissemination of slanderous documents in poetic form." All the important poets had read. How could her mother not tell Daniel was the deepest? What if he overheard her exalting Cormick? Daniel had already overanalyzed her mom from the Thanksgiving food fiasco. Lila was afraid what would happen when they met in person.

"Wildman was the best reader and it's the most important event I've been to," Lila said.

"It's the only reading I've ever been to," her mom proclaimed, with a chuckle.

Lila flinched. Was she proud of not being literary? "You know, Abraham Lincoln gave his first anti-slavery speech in the Great Hall in 1860," she said, identifying with the theme of liberation on her big day. "Louise Glück was amazing."

"Yeah, Glück blew me away," Sari conceded.

"She's the angry one who looks like Morticia on the *Addams Family*?" her mom asked.

"She does not," Lila said, though she actually did a little. Her mom should turn off the boob tube in Baraboo and attend more literary events. "Can't you tell how smart Wildman is?"

"He reminds me of your Uncle Izzy."

"He's nothing like Izzy!" Lila told her mother, offended. "He's much more handsome."

"You like Izzy," Sari said. "You wrote two poems about him."

"I should get royalties for the use of my family members," her mother joked.

"I love how when you'd come to see him he'd say '*Vhy* von't you ever visit me?'" Sari imitated Izzy's Yiddish accent.

"If we brought him a gift, he'd say *Vhy* don't you never brink me nothing?" her Mom jumped in. "His favorite line was 'Nothing's so bad it can't be vorse.'"

"This brave Russian woman is thrown in jail for the crime of expressing herself and you're parodying my poem," Lila said. "And Wildman's *much* younger than Izzy."

"Yeah, he's your age, Mrs. Lerner," Sari said.

Lila shot her a scowl. She hadn't realized Daniel was her mom's age. Thinking about it creeped her out. She used to like having the youngest parent of all her friends. But Lila couldn't imagine getting pregnant at 21, like her mom did.

"Injustice is what great poems should be about. Not Hallmark bull on how lovely your homeland is." She took a swipe at Cormick. "Good writing starts with drama, conflict, tension," she quoted Daniel as they headed upstairs. "Let's get out of here."

"Let's go to the wine and cheese reception," Sari said, giving Lila no choice.

In the side room were slices of cheddar with Ritz Crackers, plastic cups and jugs of cheap vino. "Boy, when they say wine and cheese, they really mean that's all they serve." Her mother shook her head. Lots of people, little food—Hannah Lerner's vision of hell. "We should have brought some cold cuts or something."

"Remember how Daniel freaked from all that Thanksgiving food?" Sari asked Lila.

What the fuck was wrong with her big-mouthed roommate? Lila grabbed some wine for them and downed hers.

"He didn't like the food I sent?" Hannah looked devastated. "It wasn't good?"

"It was delicious," Lila reassured.

"Was the turkey overcooked?" her mom wouldn't let the Thanksgiving food go.

"No. It was excellent," Sari echoed, getting how she'd put her foot in it.

" I should have ordered the fancier caramelized onion stuffing but I know you hate onions."

"It was fine, mom. Everything tasted great. Daniel had just already planned to cook the meal himself. So we had a lot to choose from," Lila said. "That's all."

"But serving too much is always better than not enough." Sari lamely tried to recover.

"People's relationship with food tells you a lot about them emotionally," Hannah said.

"You should have heard Mark trashing poets and their pathetic wine and cheese galas," Sari added. "He said, 'No wonder these guys are so wimpy. They need hamburgers.'"

"You took your brother to a poetry reading?" Hannah asked Lila.

"After he dragged us to the Empire State Building, Statue of Liberty, and Carnegie Deli. How much tourist crap can you stuff into three days?" Lila went for another glass.

"Mark liked the Village best," Sari piped in.

Lila spotted Daniel in the corner. Embarrassed by her mom's Hawaiian color scheme and not wanting a weird confrontation, she nervously turned in the other direction.

"Oh you must be Lila's mother from Wisconsin," said Judith Bay, ambushing them. "I read about you in Lila's poem 'Overbearance.'" She thrust out her slender hand. "So lovely to meet you. I'm Lila's classmate, Judith."

"Yes, we're working out a royalty payment schedule," Hannah said, shaking Judith's hand, then touching the pin on her lapel. "What a pretty brooch."

"Cartier," Judith sniffed.

Lila scrutinized her classmate. She wore an ash-colored mid-length skirt with white blouse, nude hose and flat shoes, holding a gray coat. Her dark hair was in a bun. She clutched a notebook. Lila touched the hem of her own velvet black frock—which she'd worn because Daniel preferred dresses. She hoped she didn't look like she was trying too hard.

"What did you think of the reading?" Lila quizzed her.

"It would have had greater impact if everyone read Ratushinskaya's work in its original tongue and not their own poetry," said Judith, never one to miss a chance to show off.

"Everyone would have fallen asleep," Sari countered.

Two cute Norman Mailer wannabes from the program walked by. Judith lodged herself between the fiction dudes, quoting Ratushinskaya in Russian, pseudo-intellectual flirting.

"You've made so many new friends here," Hannah commented.

"Competitive bitch from Boston," Lila whispered. "She's writing epic verse on her rich great-grandfather Bartholomew so everybody knows her family came over on the Mayflower."

"My daughter never did mince words," Hannah said. "*Tucchos affen tisch.*"

"Rear end on the table," Lila told Sari. "Mom, tell her that big Yiddish insult I love."

"*Zolst vaksn vi a tsibele mitn kop in dr'erd*—May your head grow in the ground, like an onion," Hannah said, and Sari cracked up.

As if pulled by the sound of laughter rising from the one woman in the joint he'd not yet come on to, Cormick rushed over. "Girls, so lovely to see you. And this beauty I've never had the honor of meeting must be Lila's mother. I see the resemblance—gorgeous midnight blue eyes and the high sculpted cheek bones of a great Russian princess."

Lila was grossed out. "Mom, this is Professor Cormick, head of our grad division."

"Please, call me Conor ." He kissed her mom's hand, playing the gallant knight. "My close friends call me Con."

With good reason, Lila was sure.

"My close friends call me Hanny," her mother answered.

They did not. Lila had never heard her mother called that in her life. This was getting creepier by the second. Even her mother's fuchsia nail polish made Lila blanch. Judith had a French manicure—a slim line of white on the tips.

"What a lovely outfit, Hanny. This hue lights up your oval orbs and golden tresses."

Lila waited for him to break into his song and dance to Yeats' yellow-haired girl. She assumed her mom would be appalled by his silly display, but she seemed jazzed.

"I'm visiting from Baraboo. I haven't been in New York in twenty years, but I love the big city. My late husband and I spent our honeymoon here," Hannah confided, blushing.

When Lila was a kid, she'd loved the story. In 1959, before she was born, when her parents "didn't have two pennies to rub together," her dad—the *Baraboo News Republic's* assistant editor—surprised his fiancée with a plane ticket, ring, and proposal for a 28-hour trip since he had to be back to meet a deadline by 9 a.m. Monday.

"Ah, yes. Manhattan is the most ripe city for romance," Cormick said.

"Your poem made Dublin sound so enchanting," she answered. "With the swans on the balustraded stream and the gentle veils of rain."

Since when did conservative Jewish Hannah Lerner memorize Irish Catholic poetry? Lila stared at her mother. Basking in Cormick's gaze, she appeared younger and sexier. Uh oh. Lila never liked her stepfather Pete but she hoped their marriage wasn't fraying.

"I stole that from Yeats," Cormick told her, smirking.

"T. S. Eliot said mediocre writers borrow while great writers steal," Hannah shot back.

Where did she pick that up?

"Excuse me, Professor Cormick, would you sign my book?" a female fan interrupted.

"Why yes, of course." He turned to Lila's mother and said, "liability of the trade."

"Let's get out of here." Lila tugged at her mother's arm, leading her to the lobby.

"I want to buy Cormick's books," her mom insisted, getting in the long queue.

"Where did you find that T.S. Eliot quote?" Lila asked.

"The intro to that anthology you liked so much," her mother said. "I read everything you send me. Sometimes two or three times. I didn't love your last poem, about the snake."

Lila hoped she wouldn't initiate the sex talk they never really had. At sixteen, when she'd asked if her mom liked making love with her dad, Hannah had said only: "First it hurt. Then it got better." When Lila confessed she'd lost it to Jeff in college, her mother cried for two weeks, then concluded the conversation with, "Well, the Goodman women were always hot blooded." Lila loved the way that sounded, as if the Hebrew females in her family line were filled with secret ardor and unquenchable fire. But her mother never explained further, so Lila had to figure out the rest herself.

"Listen, my folks just got back from Armenia. I have to meet them uptown," Sari interrupted, hugging them both goodbye before taking off.

"Isn't Sari the coolest?" Lila asked. "She really liked you."

"Very cool. But the one she really liked was your brother."

"What are you talking about?" Lila was surprised.

"After you watched the ball drop in Times Square on New Year's, where did she sleep?"

Lila had left Sari and Mark together at two a.m. when she'd taken the R train downtown to the dorm. She thought he was just displaying good Midwest manners when he'd promised to get Sari home safely. "Why? Did Mark tell you something happened between them?"

"He mentioned how much fun Sari was. I took it as a euphemism."

"Damn." Lila was shocked she'd missed sparks between her brother and best friend. But that was why Sari offered to borrow her dad's Mercedes to drive Mark to the airport. Now she wondered if her mom was right, if the two had slept together on New Year's Eve. No way! But Mark was such a player, and Sari was on the wild side too. If they were sleeping together, it would be hard to figure out who'd screw over who worse.

At the book table, Lila's mother took ten dollars from her purse to buy Cormick's *Celtic Songs of the Heartland*. Lila couldn't find Daniel's book. Too small a press or did it already sell out? She was about to ask when she turned to see Daniel beside her. Flustered, her forehead was sweaty.

"Professor Wildman," Lila said, trying not to sound startled. And horrified her mom was caught holding Cormick's book, the worst scenario she could imagine. "You killed tonight."

She jumped in front of her mother to hide her purchase, self-consciously tucking her hair behind her ears. She didn't introduce them, knowing they'd hate each other, especially now.

Daniel did a side step, thrusting out his arm. "The infamous Hannah Lerner," he said, his eyes catching Cormick's book slipping into her purse.

"The infamous Daniel Wildman," her mom replied, shaking his hand robustly.

"Thank you again for sending that wonderful Thanksgiving dinner." He smiled, looking as uncomfortable as Lila, who felt claustrophobic and ill thinking they were the same age.

"You're very welcome," Hannah smiled bigger. "So glad you enjoyed it."

"Your daughter is very special," he went on.

"I can't tell you how much I appreciate your kindness to her when she was new in the city. She loves it here."

"We love her too," he said. "I mean, the program. She's one of our best students."

Lila's mother caught her eye. Luckily a group of students interrupted.

"Hey, Prof, buy you a beer at Dojo's," said Keith, a Mark Strand groupie from class.

"Your public awaits you," Lila said, shooing Daniel away so nobody could tell she was into him. "I'll see you in class Monday."

"I hope you're having a nice birthday," he threw in before walking off with his posse.

Lila waved goodbye, putting on her coat, distractedly watching Daniel leave without her. She hoped there wouldn't be other girls coming to his dinner at Dojo's.

"That looks magnificent on you," her mother said, straightening the collar of the black knee-length wool jacket, a birthday present she'd bought Lila on sale at Loehmann's that afternoon. In the store mirror it looked so regal. But now Lila wished it were lighter and cashmere like Judith's gray jacket.

They walked out the side door. It was balmy for January, hundreds of students lingering around. Flushed from the awkward encounter with Daniel, Lila steered her mom toward a quiet bench at the side of the building and sat down.

"Are you sleeping with him?" Hannah asked.

Lila's mouth opened. So much for the subterfuge. "No. I'm not."

"Why not?"

"Why do you think we are?" Lila was stunned by her bluntness, hoping nobody heard.

"The way he was trying not to look at you. And the way he was trying not to look at me," she said. "He's obviously crazy about you."

"You think so?" Lila was jolted by how casual her mom sounded. And wildly intrigued. She sensed Daniel's feelings for her had changed over Thanksgiving. But he hadn't even tried to kiss her or ask her out. Her emotions were so all over the place, she didn't trust her own take.

"You're only attracted to him intellectually?" her mom probed.

"No, I'm totally into him. He's the one who doesn't want to get involved." Lila had never been able to keep secrets from her mom for very long. "He said he's never been with a student."

"He certainly wants to be with you."

Lila tingled at the thought. "You think so?"

Her mother nodded. "No doubt in the world."

Lila was thrilled to hear that, especially since her mom was on the psychic side. Uncle Ezra used to call her a Jewish witch. "Did you catch his line about loving me too?"

"And I bet he doesn't know any of his other students' birthdays," Hannah said. "Maybe that's why my Thanksgiving food bothered him. Cooking with you would be more intimate."

"He used to cook holiday meals with his mom as a kid, before she died."

"How old was he when he lost her?"

"Twelve and a half," Lila said.

"Oy, right before his bar mitzvah." Hannah nodded vigorously, as if that explained everything. "People never recover from that kind of a loss," she said.

Was her mom talking about herself? Or Lila not recovering from her father's death?

"That's why I wanted you to get out of Baraboo. I didn't want you to marry the first guy who got you in bed, like I did."

"You were madly in love with Dad."

"I was. But I gave up going to college in a big city. I want you to get your degree and be a success here and get everything you want. Don't screw up your dreams for a man."

"But Daniel's helping me," Lila said. "He introduced me to his whole New York gang."

"So you want to marry him or *be* him?" Hannah asked her daughter.

Wow. Lila was mind blown by the thought. "He hasn't taken advantage of me—in any way. Some profs here—like Cormick—get too close to students. But Daniel doesn't. Ever."

"Morals are good, my *shayna maidel*." She used Lila's Yiddish nickname, pretty girl. "But there's a reason why a smart, handsome Jewish man his age has never married."

"Maybe he hasn't found the right one yet because it's me," Lila told her. "You think that's impossible?"

"It's not impossible. I know how exciting an older man can be." She moved closer and whispered, "When I was a secretary at the Madison newspaper company, I went out with my boss. Frank was smart, successful and twenty years older than I was."

"Really?" Lila hadn't heard this story before. She never pictured her mother with a man who wasn't her husband. The thought was both disturbing and dazzling, as if there were all kinds of sexy mysteries lurking behind her mother's eyes that Lila might now be privy to. "When you were younger than me? What was he like? Was he hot for you? Were you in love with him?"

"Maybe I was, a little." Hannah blushed. "He seemed important and impressive."

Lila couldn't talk to Sari about this—her roommate thought having an unrequited thing for an old guy was gross. She didn't want her classmates to think she was a cliché. How weird that her mom was the only one who got why she was falling for Daniel. "So what happened?"

"Then I met your father at the company Christmas party. He was so jealous, I'd find him waiting in the bushes when Frank brought me home from dinner. I wound up falling for your dad. I decided an older divorced guy with a son was too complicated."

"But Daniel's not divorced or anything!" Lila told her. "He never had a wife or kids. It would be way worse if he had that baggage."

"Honey, a Jewish man who's never been married by forty-two is schlepping a different kind of luggage around," her mother said. "One with a dead body in it."

"He's forty-one," Lila corrected, intrigued by her mother's twist on the metaphor.

"You're too young to be Daniel's porter. You got your own ghosts, Sweetie," Hannah said. "Come on, I made dinner reservations uptown. I have a half-off coupon for Sardi's."

Lila wanted to go to Dojo's but it would be too obvious if she wound up where Daniel was. Yet if he really was that crazy about her...

"Let's get the bus uptown," Lila decided, hesitant to leave downtown, where he was.

"You're never moving back home, are you?" Hannah asked at the bus stop.

"Probably not." Lila put her arm in her mother's.

"I get it. You walk taller and talk better here. You're not afraid. I'm so proud of you."

"Sari teases me when I rush home to call you the second the rates go down at 11:01."

"It's been hard since you left," Hannah admitted.

Lila felt guilty for leaving her mom in Baraboo. "You should move here someday. We'll get apartments in the same building, like Mary Tyler Moore and Rhoda."

"I'd be more like the loud-mouth Ida Morgenstern," Hannah joked, refer-
ring to Rhoda's mom on the TV show. "You sure you won't stay with me at
the hotel tonight?"

For the first six months after her father died, Lila slept next to her mother
in their king-sized bed, afraid her mom might disappear too. Now she felt
too old to crash with her. Besides, there was another bed Lila had in mind.

8

January 1982

DANIEL

Daniel was surprised to see Lila through his peephole. It was almost midnight. She was still dolled up in her velvet dress, under that regal black coat. Was it new? She'd never come by without calling before. Something was changing. At the reading he'd caught her staring up at him adoringly from the front row. But their flirtation would stay innocent, of course, with her mother in town.

He'd just arrived home, glad he hadn't changed out of his best professor clothes: brown corduroys, button-down gray shirt with pleated shoulders and rubber-soled suede shoes that gave him a few more inches. He opened the door slowly. She was leaning against the wall. Her coat was swung open, her frock's velvety fabric clinging to her, showing off her curves. Her heels made her legs longer. She was taller than he was. She'd never shown up at his doorstep this late, arriving like a present. She was everything he wanted: a beautiful, smart woman with a soul. Seeing how good-looking her mother was proved she had good genes and would also age well. Too bad Lila didn't wear colors anymore. Maybe he'd buy her a light blue scarf to offset all that black.

"Can I come in? It's getting cold," she said, sounding raspy, tilting awkwardly on his door frame like she was imitating Barbara Stanwyck in *Double Indemnity*.

Her eyes were bloodshot. He could tell she'd been drinking. He'd had five beers himself, celebrating his minor triumph tonight: he'd read better than Cormick. But his first tryst with Lila should not happen while they were inebriated. Not that it should happen when they were sober either.

"It's late." He let her into his vestibule. "What's up?"

She inched close, staring into his eyes too intensely. "Do you have feelings for me?"

He was taken off guard. "Listen, Lila, you shouldn't come over here drunk. I can smell pot too."

Mixed in was a whiff of her tangy-sweet perfume. Instead of dabbing the scent behind her ears like other women, he imagined Lila impatiently splashing a bottle all over herself in the slapdash way she did everything. He wanted to rip off her coat, put his hands under her velvet. Yet he refused to take advantage of a drunk and stoned woman, let alone a student, the way Cormick would. He folded his arms across his chest, not inviting her in. After all, her mother was here. Daniel was old enough to be the father she lost.

"It's still my birthday," she said, pushing past him, waltzing inside anyway.

He'd slipped her a card after class on Friday. After rejecting several that seemed too romantic or serious, he decided to be light and fun for once in his life. He found one showing four mod Barbie dolls dancing in sequin outfits, a long ash blonde beauty in the center. Inside it said: "When they made you, they broke the mold. Happy birthday to the one and only." He recalled a poem Lila had written about her Barbie dolls—how as a kid, instead of changing their little clothes, she'd just switch their heads. So he bought that one, knowing she'd catch the inside reference.

Yet the card and his salutation at the reading weren't enough, she clearly wanted more from him. A gift? An affair? She wasn't the casual type, her poetry thesis had already revealed that she'd only taken one man to bed before: the football player. Now Daniel followed anxiously as Lila slipped her coat off her lovely shoulders. She tossed it over the antique green chair and plopped down on the sofa. If she weren't his student, there would be nothing wrong with having a girlfriend taller than he was, he decided. He could live with that. He stood by the kitchen, watching her drape herself over his couch, slithering in that soft fabric. He could make love to her right here— the way he'd fantasized—and nobody had to know. Not even her mother. But Lila had a big mouth, confessing all in her poems. He could be her next subject. She'd report everything, read it aloud to their class. She couldn't hold a secret to save her life.

"Sit down for a minute. Please?" Her voice was tipsy. She patted the seat beside her.

He sat down on the last cushion, the one with the button missing. When she moved closer, her dress inched up her thigh. Her shimmery nylons made her legs look sleek and endless. He put a throw pillow over his lap to hide his erection.

"Tonight was so awesome," she said.

"It was a good reading," he conceded.

"It wasn't the reading. It was you. You're in my head and poems and notebook. You're like this brilliant psychic taking over my mind. You get me more than I get myself. "

"So you rushed here to say you like my brain?" he asked, annoyed. Her juvenile, impromptu speech fed his paranoia that she felt only intellectually connected to him. He feared nubile young women no longer found him physically attractive.

"No! I'm totally into you. I can't play the hard-to-get games I'm supposed to."

"Just a freckle-faced Jewish hick from the boonies?" he asked.

"See. You're the only guy who remembers my poems."

"Because I'm your poetry professor." He stood up. Sleeping with her was a bad idea. She could get too emotionally involved. Zalman had warned him away from her, repeatedly.

"A bunch of teachers turn me onto books. But you're the only one I dream of."

She'd dreamt of him? Sexually? He crossed his legs and pictured peeling off her pantyhose, the way her football player removed them like a snake-skin. She knew reading him that poem was seductive. If only they were sober. No, he had to wait until she finished the program.

"You know, I talk to you all the time. Even when you're not around," she went on. "Whatever happens, I tell you, and I can hear your voice talking back."

"You're hearing voices and talking to yourself?" he teased. "They have special strait-jackets reserved for poets at Payne Whitney. I bet we can get you one in black."

"Will you bring flowers when you visit me at the loony bin?" She laughed.

"You have to leave, Lila," he told her, trying to sound resolute.

"If we don't try, I'll spend my whole life mourning what we were afraid of," she said.

"Now you're playing Masha, who wears all black, in mourning for her life."

"I'm not playing anything, Daniel. I know it sounds dumb, but just know-ing you're here always makes me feel less lonely."

It didn't sound so dumb. Lately, when he read a poem he liked, he'd leave it bookmarked to show her. If she was tardy for his class or workshop, he'd watch the door, relieved when she'd barge in, pull out her pink can of Tab and pop it open, interrupting everything. He'd wait for her rapid-fire, off-the-wall, wildly perceptive criticism to instantly animate the room. He'd never met anyone more bouncy and alive.

"You're still confusing inspiration with romantic excitement," he said, his throat parched. "Want some water or something?"

"You know that Auden line about believing your pain? Even if you think I'm just a pathetic girl with unrequited longing, you have to honor what I feel. You can't deny it."

She was trying to argue her way into his bed. She spread her arm over his couch and crept lower on the cushions so he could see her cleavage. It was bizarre that she was acting so brazen the weekend her mother was in town.

That was all he'd need, for Hannah Lerner to show up at his doorstep, following her hot daughter and her fat turkey.

"Lila, listen. I don't want you to get hurt."

"I won't," she said, leaning on her elbow, then slipping and almost falling.

As she gathered herself together and sat up, he went to the kitchen. He untucked his shirt, still hard, trying to hide it. "Do you want water or that vile diet soda you like?" he called. Last week he'd bought a bottle of Tab, her favorite, before his workshop. But she wanted water and he poured them both a glass, then came back and put the glasses on the end table. She was still talking.

"You push me to be emotionally brave in my work and tell me to see a shrink," she said. "But you're the one who's really freaked out about taking a risk with me."

It was a risk he should avoid. He wasn't someone who could get close easily and detach easily. Last week, when Roxy called crying, he'd paid the doctor bill for her daughter's sprained ankle. He couldn't let her down. His previous affairs had ended in heartbreak and disaster. He needed to protect himself—and Lila.

"You just moved here. This is where I live, where I've worked for twelve years, where I know everyone," he said, starting to pace. "I care about my reputation."

"We're both adults here. What's the worst that could happen?" she asked.

She might compare his body to her football player's and feel revolted. He could come too fast and not satisfy her. Maybe she would publish a poem about how lousy he was in bed that Cormick would read and his reputation would be ruined forever.

"I'd get over it. I've been rejected before. I didn't lay down and die," she said.

He worried he'd be the one who wouldn't get over it. "Maybe in other circumstances…"

"What circumstances?" She caught the tiny window he hadn't realize he'd just opened.

"Maybe, if I wasn't your teacher… I can't have an equal relationship with a student because I'd have all the power. When I mentioned it to Dr. Zalman…"

"You told your shrink about me!" She sounded ecstatic to have extracted this fact, as if he'd brought her home to meet his dad, which he kind of did. But Zalman disapproved.

"This issue came up in regard to how amoral Cormick is about his affairs," Daniel said, trying to worm his way out of admitting his growing attraction to Lila. How could he not enjoy her attention? This luscious lively girl had looked up every poem he'd published, quoting him as if everything he said was dazzling and memorable. When he complained that Howard and Cormick did better with editors, Lila said, "But your work is deeper and darker. You're a perfectionist who demands more of yourself than the others do. Your talent will be recognized. It'll just take longer for the world to catch up with you."

"So Lila's flattering her way into your pants?" Zalman had asked. "Boy, are you easy. But a protégée's idealization is not love. Confuse the two at your own peril. And hers."

"You never mentioned me specifically to Dr. Zalman?" Lila was pushing, as usual.

"A few times," he conceded, leaning on his bookshelf. "But I don't want to hurt you."

"That's why I like you so much." She took off her shoe and rubbed her heel. "You're like the coolest, most moral guy I've ever met."

Funny how she never monitored herself. She merely spit out her every thought, unsullied by the normal rules of protocol and discretion. He took a sip of water, spilling it on his shirt like a nerdy teenager. He wished he could be like Cormick, just rip her clothes off and take her because he felt like it. He sat down next to her on the couch. She moved closer, her golden hair brushing against his shoulder.

"I love being with you," she whispered. "Don't you feel anything for me?"

She was sure flinging around the word love a lot. She put her hand on his leg. He removed it. "Lila, of course I care about you. But I can't take advantage of a student."

Damn, Cormick would have her dress on the floor by now, alongside her bra and panties. Hell, he'd be tying her wrists to the bedpost with those glittery hose. "After you get your degree we can…"

"Sleep together the night of graduation!" she jumped in, her hand suddenly back on his leg. "Until then I'll be your student, advisee and assistant and we won't tell anyone."

He didn't like the way she was steering everything, acting out an undercover pact to heighten the dramatic tension. The point of paying a shrink was to get the drama out of his life. He looked down at her hand but didn't remove it.

"I can wait, as long as I know you want me." She nuzzled his neck. "But if you don't…"

"Of course I want you," spilled out.

"That's what my mother said."

"You told your mother about us? Oh God! Your mother is involved already!" He pushed her away, appalled, suddenly feeling imprisoned and claustrophobic. Or was it guilt that he'd found her mother so attractive? He'd expected a loud, wrinkled lummox from the sticks getting off the plane holding a bucket of chicken soup and a loaf of challah. So he'd been startled to see a slender woman with the same ski slope shiksa nose, aqua eyes and pale freckled skin as Lila. It bothered him to think he should be with someone her age, not her daughter's.

"Don't worry," Lila reassured him. "I told her we weren't sleeping together."

"We're not!" he yelled, as if Hannah Lerner had just walked in and caught him mounting her daughter.

"Even if we were, it's not like you're my boss who'd fire me or we're politicians with spouses and kids causing a scandal. We're poets in Greenwich Village. We're both legal and single. It's kosher."

The word kosher made him cringe. Instead of Lila's lover, he was now

Hannah's turkey.

"I told my mom you were special and I couldn't stop thinking about you. That's all."

He wiped sweat from his forehead.

"You think women in the program drool over Cormick, but you were incredible at the reading. All the girls fantasize about you," she said. "You were the rock star tonight."

They did? Really? He knew Cormick and the other long-winded egotists read too long, so he picked short political poems. It was a good strategy. The students did swamp him later, buying his book and asking for his autograph.

"What's the big deal if I told the most important person in my life I have a crunch on you?" Lila asked, using one of her kooky colloquialisms.

"That sounds like you want to chew me, suck out the flavor and spit me out," he said.

"You're getting all that from one "N"? She laughed, rocking her leg nervously.

"It's late. You should go. We'll talk about this after your mother leaves town."

She put her shoe back on again and stood up. "I'd much rather stay, but if you insist on denying your feelings and really want me to leave then…"

He wanted to shut her up. He wanted to throw her to his living room floor and take her right there. But he was in control of what happened—and when. Not her. Or her damn mother. "Get out of here. Please."

She turned her face to the floor. Tiny tears spilled down her cheeks. He gave her a Kleenex, guilty he was ruining her birthday. Wanting to give her something special, he grabbed a slim volume from his shelf called *Despair*. "Here's a chapbook," he said. "My earliest poems."

"Before *Beyond Despair!*" Lila grabbed the book and clutched it close to her.

"Yes, before I was beyond despair," he conceded the in-joke from his past.

"Really, it's the coolest gift I've ever gotten in my whole life," she said.

"I thought you were getting rid of the hyperbole," he teased.

She reclaimed her coat from the chair, which now looked lonely. He helped her on with her wrap and walked her to the door. He meant to hug her quickly, then let go. But they wound up standing too close together in his cramped entranceway, swaying back and forth, slow dancing without music.

"May is less than five months away," he said. "That's not so long."

"I could stay and cook you breakfast," she whispered in his ear, her breath on his neck.

"Raging feminists don't cook," he said, holding her closer, not wanting her to leave.

"Don't tell anyone, but I make mean scrambled eggs and cheese," she said, touching his hair, then desperately running her fingers over his face like a blind girl reading Braille.

"Sweetheart, your mom is in town," he said. "You have to go home."

"When I'm with you, I feel like I am home," she told him.

"Me too," he said.

She came closer, her lips brushing against his as they fell into a long deep wet kiss he let himself get lost in. He wrapped his arms around her, pulling her warm body to his. He finally reached inside her coat to trace the arch of her back, running both of his hands over her velvet dress, her soft, shiny, blond hair tumbling all over his face as he inhaled her reckless perfume.

9

March 1982

LILA

He wasn't into her anymore. On the phone last night, he was weird, pre-occupied. She shouldn't have called at midnight. "Play harder to get," her mother warned in high school, with her first boyfriend. "Let him chase you. Make him miss you." Lila always missed the guy first, found him before he could find her. That was why Daniel didn't want to sleep with her.

"What straight old geezer doesn't screw a hot younger woman who's game?" Sari taunted. "I don't buy all Daniel's morality bullshit. Something's wrong."

Lila regretted wearing torn jeans, a black sweater and cowboy boots to class this morning. He preferred women in dresses, lipstick and done-up hair. Like her mother—and Daniel's red-headed actress, who was decked out in elaborate outfits and makeup in the pictures Lila found sneaking around his bedroom closet. He wanted an older, sophisticated woman, someone hard to get, not a girl in ripped jeans and macho boots who called and found him first.

"You have a minute? I need to talk to you," he said as she put her books into the black Strand bag he'd given her. His eyebrows were scrunched up, it was serious.

"Sure." Her back stiffened, sweat forming on the back of her neck. He was breaking up with her now, at school, where she'd first fallen for him, so she couldn't cry or cause a scene.

"What do you think about calling my new poetry series *Bard of the Ring*?" he asked. "Five Sunday readings at a boxing gym. I'll debut with Howard. A host can referee."

So that was why he'd been so preoccupied -it wasn't the siren actress, it was a reading series. Lila's whole body relaxed. Was that really why he'd been elsewhere, not here with her?

"Sounds cool," she said, following him out of the classroom. She tried to picture what "poetic sparring" in a boxing ring would look like. That was why she loved the Village, where literary happenings were staged in strange places nobody else would ever consider.

"The second week we'll pair Cormick with Merwin," he said in the hallway.

"But why include the guy you most hate on the planet?" she asked quietly.

"Well, he's the biggest name at NCU." Daniel pressed the down elevator button.

"Because subconsciously you want to beat him up?" she asked.

"I like it better when I analyze you and you don't analyze me back," he said, smiling. "Especially when you're right," he added. Then he winked at her. He'd never winked at her before; it made her legs tingle. So he was still into her. That was what winking meant, right?

"I get free therapy from you by osmosis," she said. Should she wink back? No, that would be contrived. Double winking had to be faster, spontaneous. Nervous, she wondered if students walking by could tell they were secretly a couple. She wished he'd push her against the wall for a passionate kiss right there. She pictured wrestling with him on the floor like they did last weekend, when they'd smooched and fondled and caressed each other with clothes on and he'd grabbed her roughly, pinning her to the ground. Finally, he'd stopped treating her like a porcelain doll that would break.

"I bet we could get Philip Levine to do it," he went on, pressing the down button again.

"What about female heavyweights, like Sharon Olds and Adrienne Rich?" she asked.

"Good pun." He patted her shoulder. She wanted his arms around her.

"You could mix in lightweights too," Lila said, wondering whether to pitch herself as a featherweight. But she didn't want to push the metaphor. Why didn't he ask Lila to read? She intentionally brushed against his arm as she pressed "up."

"You always do that." He pointed to both lit buttons.

"If you get inside and press a lower floor, the elevator will sometimes change its mind and take you down to the lobby."

"So it's a control issue?" he asked.

"Unless the elevator wants to go up first."

"Ah yes. Zee elevator's needs are always as important as your own," he joked in his Freud voice.

He was the smartest, funniest, most analytical man she'd ever met. She imagined becoming a professor at NCU too. Then they could teach poetry classes together.

Lila had lingered in the hallway while his other students filed out of class. Now she could be alone with him. She'd memorized his schedule—no other classes on Thursdays, no office hours. She hoped he'd invite her to his place for leftover Chinese lunch again, their code for fooling around.

"We could get champion novelists to do it, like Mailer and Gore Vidal," he threw out.

She nodded though he seemed more interested in this literary man-fest than in her.

"If the 92nd Street Y doesn't want me, I'll do a downtown series and steal their audience."

"Who rejected you from reading uptown?" Had that sparked his new obsession?

"Rage and vengeance can be good motivators," he joked.

He seemed to have a slew of hidden ghosts he always wanted to one-up and avenge.

"Guess where the Gramercy Gym is?" he asked as the elevator came. They stepped inside, joining two bedraggled old professors. "14th and Irving Place, right near you."

She tried to understand the significance of the location as they stepped out of the cage and into the lobby. "So you want me to join a gym?"

"No. I want you to host the reception afterwards," he said, holding open the door for her.

"You do?" she asked, as the spring sunshine hit her face.

"Think Sari would mind?"

"No, she'd love it."

But in Lila's mind Sari disappeared from the picture and Daniel became her roommate instead. She envisioned coming out as a couple at the party. They'd never had a real date in the open before, though some insiders knew. "It's obvious you two are mooning over each other," Judith had said. "When he lectures in class, he stares right at you." Judith was growing on her.

"We can invite the editor of *Poets & Writers* magazine," Daniel said.

She loved how he used the word "we," as if they were an established couple sending out important invitations together.

"Maybe they have a job. You are graduating."

"I know. I can't wait." She followed as he turned left on University Place, then walked her up Fifth Avenue, to her apartment. They passed rows of regal brownstones next to lightening-high skyscrapers. She felt so sophisticated, strolling downtown streets and talking, still awed to be living in a city where you didn't need a car.

"If you stay here, you have to stop waitressing and get a real job," he said.

If? Of course she was going to stay in his city, with him. She was never going back to Wisconsin. Waitressing wouldn't cut it anymore. He wouldn't want to date a waitress. To be his partner, she needed a more prestigious profession. She recalled he was ambivalent about the actress too. He was an intellectual snob. He wanted a serious woman with a serious career. She liked that about him. Lila wanted to be intellectually snobbish herself one day.

"I bet we could get the poetry editor of *New Urban Magazine* to be the referee," Daniel said. "I'll introduce you, then send a recommendation." He took her Strand bag, put it over his shoulder. He was more chivalrous than any of the other guys she knew.

This scheme he was conjuring seemed to be his subtle way of introducing her to all his colleagues. Hopefully, someone would publish her poetry and offer her a full-time teaching or editorial job. She did have all A's and she could type a hundred words a minute, no mistakes.

"And you should meet Tim Holmes, from the *Paris Review*. We'll invite him too."

"I can't wait." Lila felt elated, strolling up the avenue with Daniel next to her. She couldn't wait to sleep with him already, to hold hands and walk arm in arm everywhere, their romance exposed. He promised it would happen after she graduated—just eight more weeks to go. She felt like an old-fashioned bride waiting to lose it on her wedding night, the way her mother waited for her father when she was Lila's age. This boxing event meant Daniel wanted their clandestine days over soon.

She did too, though she'd been totally into their undercover courtship these last few months, trysting inside movie theaters, meeting at hidden ethnic dives where nobody from school would catch them, reading poetry aloud until dawn, lying around together, making out and spooning. They'd even bought matching silver Cross pens –a slim one for her, a thick manly one for him. Though on sale for ten dollars each, they were special, reserved for marking up each other's poems.

"I'll get my mom to send deli," spilled out before she could stop it. Damn! Why had she invited her mom into this talk? She waited for his disdain, another lecture about how she was too dependent on her mother, whom she shouldn't phone every night.

"Yes, let's ask Hannah," he surprised her by answering. She was so relieved.

For a second she feared he suddenly decided to like her new apartment, mother and Jewish food because it fed his boxing bard fantasy. Passing 10th Street, he was walking quickly. It was hard to keep up with his stride in her three-inch boots. She walked better in sneakers. But he'd made fun of working women who walked home wearing gym shoes with skirts, saying they looked like ducks. He didn't like her high heels, he wanted to be taller.

"I thought you said it was stupid to leave the dorm for an illegal sublet?" She'd argued that the 800-square-foot one bedroom at 69 Fifth Avenue in a doorman building for 800 dollars, four hundred bucks each, was classier and cheaper than the dorm and for four times the square feet.

"My parents like the Fifth Avenue and Sari said guys will dig the 69," Lila told him.

"She has a dirty mind," Daniel said, smirking, as they stopped at the light on 12th Street and Fifth Avenue. She figured out why he was walking her all the way home today.

"You want to check out my place to see how many people it'll hold, don't you?"

"You got it, kiddo," he told her, nodding.

"My dad used to call me Kiddo," she said. "It's juvenile." Then she regretted bringing up her father. What if Daniel just wanted an assistant and wasn't so into her sexually after all?

"It's a term of endearment," he said as he put his arm in hers—right there on the street!

"So you find me endearing?"

"I find you enchanting," he said, which embarrassed her.

"I can send out fliers to all the students," she offered.

"We'll make a good team," he told her.

"A great team," Lila said, thinking she could get cute boxing cups and matching napkins at the party store and maybe even make some goody bags with candy or caramel corn. What food did they sell at boxing matches? Lila had never been to one before.

"I'll call Mom. She hated that wine and cheese reception. I bet she'll order us some of that kosher chopped liver. This is so exciting."

She pictured them inviting all the Manhattan poets and editors as she hosted the hippest poetry reception with the best food ever. It would be the first party she'd thrown in her new apartment. She'd serve red AND white wine and appetizers from Dojo. Did they deliver? She'd show him that she could be sophisticated and dress up for him. There was a hot black dress on sale she'd been eyeing at Unique and she could have her nails painted and her hair done at the hip East Village salon Sari turned her onto. She was finished being his student and little protégée. She needed to look the part, making her debut to everybody who knew them at school as Daniel's girl-friend and his lover.

10

April 1982

DANIEL

"Great bout today," Lenu said as Daniel walked into Lila's.

"Yeah, you knocked him out, dude," Tarik added, mock-punching his arm.

Daniel's goal to get the young guys excited about the boxing event clearly worked, anything to make poetry more macho. And the idea was surprisingly popular—more than a hundred people showed up to catch his first bard boxing match. A *Daily News* reporter came with a photographer to cover the story, so he and Howard posed with gloves on. Cormick had even patted him on the back and said, "Genius idea, Danny Boy."

"You killed it," Lila said, rushing him a bottle of Heineken.

"Thanks." He stared at her, not used to her new shorter hairstyle. She didn't look as pretty. He'd spent his entire night of triumph trying to figure out why she'd cut off her tresses—without mentioning it to him. He always told how much he loved her glorious mane. Had she done it to spite him? To make a feminist statement—I am my own woman, not yours?

"Wentworth, have you met my boy Wildman here?" Cormick asked.

Recognizing the name, Daniel's back immediately straightened as he firmly shook Wentworth's hand. "Glad you could make it," he said casually, pretending *The Urban Review's* poetry editor showing up for his event wasn't the highlight of his life thus far.

"He's been in *Poetry* and *APR*," Cormick added.

"Send me some of your work," Charles Wentworth said, giving Daniel his card.

Flattered by Cormick! And now invited to submit poems to the best magazine in the country! As they walked away, Daniel stood there, stunned by how easy it suddenly seemed. He'd waited his whole life to play with the big boys.

Lila, back by his side, said, "Sorry I left before Howard finished. I needed to set up. Couldn't have gone any better."

He nodded. He didn't care if she'd missed Howard's subpar reading at all as long as she saw him give his stellar performance.

"Oh, you need a bottle opener," she said, rushing off again. She seemed nervous.

He couldn't wait until later, when he could tell her what just happened with Cormick and Wentworth. And how the National Book Award winner Gerald Lewis, in the audience, asked Daniel if he'd book him for a future reading. And the owner of the gym said he could expand the series to a year if he wanted. Too bad Faith couldn't come tonight. Daniel also would have wanted his banker father and brother to see him, a winner, with an entourage, in knockout mode. If his mother were alive, she would have been proud.

As he watched Lila rush to her tiny kitchenette, he studied her, wondering why she made her long delicate ash-blond locks so much shorter. Tonight of all nights. He knew he was overreacting and he shouldn't care so much. But he feared it could be a sign she didn't really want to sleep with him. She acted like she did but then, right before the reception at her apartment that he'd invited everyone important to, she'd desexualized herself.

"You really like it?" she asked, handing him the opener, then taking his beer and popping off the cap herself.

"Of course. You look beautiful," he lied, missing her tresses, mourning them. He tried not to over-focus on something superficial before everyone would be shuffling into her place. He flashed to the first time they'd met at the orientation party last September, when Cormick had bellowed Yeats, trying to seduce Lila first. "Never shall a young man/Thrown into despair/By those great honey-coloured/Ramparts at your ear,/Love you for yourself alone/And not your yellow hair…" The poem now seemed ironic, haunting, his night of glory marred. It was impossible for Daniel not to take Lila's bold action as a sign that she didn't want to look sweet and feminine for him. She was in a jagged leather dress. He preferred the softer cut of her velvet frock. Tonight she was copying Sari's masculine look instead. A butch haircut, then what would be next—a big snake tattoo on her chest?

Lila was graduating in three weeks. He wanted to introduce her to all of the editors and publishers coming so she could get herself a job worthy of her brains and talent and stay in New York with him. He'd been so excited to let his friends and colleagues—especially Cormick—see them together. Not a fling, but the real thing.

"It was just a big surprise when I saw you at the gym, that's all." He sipped the beer.

"Javier wanted to try something spiky and fresh," she told him, running her hands through her new cut.

She was still gorgeous, but she was emulating the female rockers on that new MTV station she'd been talking about. He hated that dumb cliché Pat Benatar song Lila kept singing to him: *Love Is a Battlefield*. No, love was escaping the battlefield. It was the end game, the prize.

"I wanted to look great for you. I knew tonight was special," she said.

"It is," he conceded, now feeling guilty that he was being such a conservative prig. "You have to meet Charles Wentworth," he whispered. "Poetry editor of *Urban Review*."

"Wow, he's in my apartment. Fucking awesome," she said.

He wasn't used to her swearing either. He watched as she walked over to her classmates by the TV. Who wanted to watch a screeching video at a literary party? He went to turn it off.

"Nice job tonight, tough guy," Sari teased him.

"I appreciate you letting me use your place. Really," Daniel told her.

"Yeah, classy digs," Lenu said.

"Love the haircut," Tarik told Lila. "Very chic."

"Thanks," Lila said, blushing a little.

Daniel wondered why Tarik was standing so close to Lila.She'd confided that he'd taken her to dinner once, last Valentine's Day, but it didn't end well and they'd never gone out again. Suddenly Daniel worried that she was still interested in him. He was tall, casual in black jeans and a button down shirt. Maybe Daniel—in his brown pants and sports coat—was overdressed. Tarik was a good-looking guy from a wealthy family, twenty years his junior. Lila might want someone younger, closer to her age.

"Who's that?" Daniel pointed to the band on TV playing some "tattooed loveboys" crap.

"It's Chrissie Hynde, from the Pretenders," Sari said.

"Sorry. Want us to turn it down?" Lila asked.

"No, no. It's cool. She rocks. Love the Pretenders," Daniel lied, pretending himself, to be younger and hipper. He'd been playing Lila albums by Lou Reed, Bob Dylan, Leonard Cohen and Patti Smith—troubadour poets with scathing lyrics that really meant something.

When the bell rang, he rushed to greet more guests at the door, taking coats, man of the house, as if he lived here. He hung the wraps in the walk-in closet, which was bigger than his. He scanned the white walls and wooden floors with long windows. His place had more charm and history. But hers was larger, newly painted. He pictured living here with Lila, cooking dinners, throwing poetry receptions together.

She'd put out the beer and wine he'd ordered on the makeshift bar table. She'd placed a nice cloth over another tin table, filled with deli trays, the chopped liver platter and crudités her mother had sent. He'd regretted his resentment of Hannah—it was good that Lila had such a warm, generous role model in her corner. If he'd had his mother around longer, he would be more confident, Zalman told him. Not as afraid to get close to a woman who'd love him back.

Daniel was touched that Lila had gone to so much trouble to please him tonight. Zalman was wrong. Though she was young and obsessed with her art, Lila could be very nurturing. Maybe Daniel should stop focusing on what was missing.

"The space works great for events," Lila said. "Some of the guests think I have my own pad in a doorman building. Nobody has to know Sari has the bedroom and I'll be sleeping on the futon in the living room, right?"

He hoped she still wanted to sleep beside him in his double bed soon, fearing she'd changed her mind and wanted someone taller and younger and hipper than he was.

"Everyone's saying how awesome you were at the reading." Lila smiled. "I'm sure you read way better than Howard and you were the best one there."

"But Brodsky and Sharon Olds didn't show up," he blurted out.

"At parties you think only of who's not there," Lila told him.

"Good line, I might have to steal it." He laughed. He did read better than Howard, no doubt about that. But Daniel couldn't help but note that Betsy, Howard's girlfriend, had long chestnut hair down to her waist. It was as if he'd perched Betsy right there, in the front row, with her long, flowing mane, to mock him.

"Next time, don't cut your hair without warning me," he told Lila, slipping his arm firm around her waist in front of everybody. Daniel saw Cormick notice and do a double take.

"Now that I'm yours, you get to control how my hair looks?" she asked, snuggling close.

"Yes, I get to decide," he said. "Now that you're mine."

11

June 1982

LILA

On the couch in his living room that Thursday at midnight, sitting close by candlelight, listening to Louis Armstrong's *What a Wonderful World*, it seemed just as romantic as Lila had imagined. The V-neck strappy black cotton dress her mother sent fit her perfectly, she liked how the waist was pulled in and the skirt flared. She lifted his fancy flute of bubbly to toast, gently touching Daniel's glass, flattered he used his best stemware to celebrate her graduating—and their first real night together.

"I fantasized about you all day," he whispered, blowing in her ear. It made her tingle.

"You did? What was your fantasy?"

"Taking off your graduation gown." He twirled a strand of her hair.

"You want me to go get the gown? It's in my dorm room."

"No, no." He laughed. "You're perfect just like this. 'Poised with porcelain skin, buoyant/beauty Venus lost in Botticelli's eyes.'"

"More like a cartoon ghost. My nickname in high school was Casper." She giggled, but the way he recited the poem while looking at her made her feel beautiful. Or made her believe he thought so. She took off her high heels, which were cramping her feet. She was relieved to feel the breeze seeping through his open window. But the jack-hammering outside rattled her. Was there an emergency, a burst pipe that made them rush to fix the street so late?

"These glasses were a graduation present from my grandmother Yetta, the last gift she ever gave me," he said, pouring another flute of champagne.

Lila had already downed three glasses of white wine and smoked half a joint at her dorm party, sure it would make her feel looser, breezier, freed up like she wanted to be for Daniel. But she'd eaten too many handfuls of peanuts. And it was too muggy in here, with no air-conditioning. She was getting claustrophobic, the construction noise echoing, boxing her in.

For months she'd turned off the lights at her place every night, making herself come, picturing Daniel ravaging her on his living room floor. Illicitly sneaking around in limbo had enhanced the lust and intrigue. All the anticipation turned her on so much while she was alone on her futon. But tonight at his place, with nothing in their way, she starting feeling a little fat and fidgety. It seemed surreal to finally be free of the restrictions of their roles, as if she were a master spy during a war suddenly declared over.

Daniel went to the bathroom. She drank more champagne. It made her lighter. But when she put the glass down, she missed and hit the edge of the table, nicking the stem. Damn it! Her clumsy fingers broke his irreplaceable family heirloom. It was just a tiny chip at the bottom but what if he noticed? Should she tell him? No, it would wreck the whole night if he knew she'd ruined his fragile antique. She turned the marred side away so he wouldn't see. Her bare foot was falling sleep; she jiggled to get it awake.

"Are you nervous?" he asked when he came back, putting his hand on her leg.

"Sometimes I get *shpilkes*, as my mom calls it."

"Let's not mention your mother tonight," he said.

But he'd already brought up his Grandma Yetta and her glasses. Lila's heart was racing, her palms sticky with sweat. "Mind if I get high?" From her purse she pulled out the half joint of Sari's light green Hawaiian leftover from the party. "To chill me out."

"Can't I chill you out?" Daniel massaged her neck with his strong hands.

"You wrote about smoking *ganja* at Hedonism Hotel in Negril," she reminded him.

"That was twenty-one years ago," he said.

It struck her as odd that he had a memory as old as she was. Lila wondered what Daniel was like at her age, with long hippie hair, getting stoned with Rastafarian musicians on the beach. She wished she could slip into that scene from his poem to party with him now. She imagined him as a student at Iowa, suddenly worried she'd missed his youngest, coolest years.

"I'm so relieved we can stop sneaking around," he said.

"Me too." She licked the edge of the joint, the way Sari did. "Just a few hits."

When he went to the kitchen, she moved down on the couch, farther from the glass so he'd be less likely to notice. He came back with an ashtray and pack of matches from the Odeon, a hip bistro he'd promised to show her now that they were going public. She sparked the flame and sucked in, hitting it deeply. "Sure you don't want to?"

"No, I'm fine, sweetie," he said.

Daniel calling her "sweetie" seemed a little patronizing. Then again, Jeff still used her college nicknames: "Casper," "Blondie" and "Lerner." She'd told Daniel that Jeff had been her one serious boyfriend from the past, but Daniel didn't seem to know that meant he was the *only* guy she'd ever taken to bed. Lila had wanted to clarify, but didn't want to turn Daniel off by her lack of experience. He'd already refused to sleep with a student; she didn't need to hammer home how innocent she was. She smoked the joint halfway down, then stubbed it out. When he went to flip the record, she slipped the remainder of the spliff in her purse. Who listened to albums anymore? It was so old-fashioned. All her music was on cassette tapes.

"I'm so glad your hair's getting long again. You look so sexy tonight," he said, inching her dress up her thigh. He ran his hands over the shiny Givenchy hose her mother had sent. Lila was glad his nails were short; the stockings cost twelve dollars a pair.

"I wore this for you," she admitted, a tiny bit buzzed, wishing she felt looser and higher and uninhibited already. She recalled the George Carlin tape her brother sent where the comedian stood on stage, fiddling around, saying nothing. Then he finally said, "Just waiting for the drugs to take effect."

"Really, you're such a gorgeous woman," Daniel cooed.

Nobody had ever called her gorgeous before. She kissed his neck, which smelled musky, unbuttoning his shirt to find a rug of dark chest hair. He was really hairy, like a big hot gorilla. Why hadn't she known that before? She rubbed her hands over his pants, feeling his erection under the soft brown corduroy. He pushed her to the floor. She wanted to be overpowered by his body on top of hers, his strong arms pinning her there. His scruffy chin hairs scratched her face.

"When did you last shave?" she asked.

"Is my shadow hurting you?" He sounded worried.

"I like your shadow hurting me." She ran her fingers over his rugged shoulders. She squirmed, entangling their legs, getting lost in the rhythm of rubbing against him, as if they were slow dancing lying down. Starting to get light-headed, she tried to forget about his excessive hair and breaking his glass and focus on his warm hands underneath her dress.

But then he stopped and stood up. "Come on." He reached for her.

Oh no! She wanted to stay there and do it on the floor. In her fantasies they were always making love in his living room, where he led the workshop. But it was too weird to explain, so she let him lead her to the bedroom. She reluctantly lay down beside him on the bed and they made out. The room began swaying but his lips were her anchor. He kept kissing her, his hands brushing over her breasts, her hose, her hair.

"Let's take off your clothes," he whispered.

She shut her eyes, but he didn't take off anything. Did he expect her to disrobe herself? She was too embarrassed to say, "You do it," or admit she wanted to be undressed. Rays from the streetlight coming in through his window shifted colors across his bed like a kaleidoscope. The joint all of a sudden seemed stronger than she'd expected. She recalled Sari calling it "creeper weed." Lila just figured out that meant the high crept up on you slowly. She hoped this wasn't the dangerous stuff you were supposed to smoke lightly and savor. Too late. She felt like she was being hit by a train of highness.

He just laid there, holding her, slowly kissing her neck and shoulders. After nothing happened for what seemed like hours, Lila finally pulled her dress over her shoulders. She hoped Daniel would notice her new black lacy bra. It cost twenty-two dollars at La Petite Coquette, a graduation present she bought herself, really a present for him. It was the most expensive brassiere she'd ever owned. Didn't he like it? Feeling self-conscious in just her bra and hose, she unzipped his pants. He took them off to reveal blue and white boxer shorts. Jeff had always worn Fruit of the Loom briefs. She'd never seen boxers up close before. Lots of bunched up material. They fascinated her. Did all old guys wear them?

He kept kissing and caressing her—endlessly. It was too much already. But he didn't take off her hose or bra, as if she were supposed to remove her lingerie herself. She wanted to shut off the lights, but to do that she'd have to get up and parade around half-dressed. Why wasn't he ripping off the rest of her clothes and jumping her, the way Jeff used to? Silver triangles started flashing around his head. She wished they'd stop.

"Are you okay?" Daniel asked.

"Just a little dizzy."

"You need some water?"

He brought her water in the fancy flute. She checked the stem. Luckily it was his, not the one she'd chipped. He sat up in bed, leaned against the headboard. She put the glass down carefully on the table, not wanting to destroy another one, then rested her head on his shoulder.

"You're still into me?" she whispered.

"Of course. You're such a luscious woman." He wrapped his warm arm around her. "You smell juicy and delicious."

Almost naked over the covers, she analyzed the words "luscious," "juicy" and "delicious." They made her sound like a ripe plum. Couldn't a brilliant poet like him do better than that? She recalled *Lovesong*, the Ted Hughes poem Daniel had read her. "Their heads fell apart into sleep like the two halves/Of a lopped melon, but love is hard to stop." A melon was more specific. You could just see their heads looking like half cantaloupes. Daniel wrote in her margins: "be more idiosyncratic," "get rid of generalities," "flesh out." She couldn't stop thinking of his bold handwriting on her pages now, of all times.

"I've never waited for anyone so long before," Daniel was saying.

"Me too," she answered.

Wait, was that true? Depended on how you counted—from when she met Daniel, or when they'd first kissed. In high school she'd refused to go all the way with Jeff for eight months. She was the only girl who wouldn't give it up for him fast, he'd later told her, which gained his respect. She never revealed it had less to do with her morals than not wanting him to see her thunder thighs.

"I haven't been with anyone since Jeff," Lila confided. Once, when she'd asked, Daniel admitted he'd already taken more than twenty women to bed. She liked being the only student he'd ever touched. It made her feel special. Was she the youngest and least experienced? She stared up at the beige light fixture on the ceiling, silver rays now fluttering around like fireflies.

"Jeff was the guy in your snake poem?" Daniel asked, stroking the long strands of her hair. "You're still in touch with him?"

"What? Oh yeah, he hangs out with my brother in Wisconsin. We all stayed friends," she said. "I was in love with Jeff for, like, six and a half years. He's the only guy I was ever really with before. I mean, sexually," she finally blurted out before she could stop herself.

"Really? I didn't know that." His hand stopped playing with her hair midstroke.

"We were together all through high school and college. We were gonna get married," she said. "When we met he was the star defensive tackle. He'd see me in the hall and jump to the floor for 100 push ups to show off. I was this nerdball editor of the school newspaper, shocked he was even into me." She chuckled at the memory.

"You don't have to make him sound so virile," Daniel joked. Or was it criticism?

"He's a goofy jock. He's twenty years younger than you. He could be your son."

Daniel put the pillow in front of his stomach.

Oh God, had she insulted him by babbling on about Jeff? "I'm sorry. You're so much smarter and more sophisticated and better read than he is," Lila tried to recover. "I mean, he never even read any poetry at all. Except for mine."

"You prefer my brain but his body?" Daniel asked.

"No. I'm totally into you. No competition," she assured him. "Don't be crazy."

As he put down the pillow and pulled the covers over himself, she noticed—through his boxers—he'd gone soft. Damn it, she shouldn't have brought up her ex-boyfriend. It was her fault that Daniel's aggressive moves -which were getting her so hot on the living room floor—were now replaced with this mistimed interrogation. Did she still care about Jeff? Little light animals seemed to be scampering across his ceiling. Lila felt like she was taking a lie detector test where wires were hooked up to Daniel's penis and any deception would cause him to lose his stiffness. She told herself to stop talking and thinking too much; it must have been pot-induced paranoia sweeping over her.

"Well, you do talk about him a lot," Daniel said.

"Everyone gets hung up on their first. Not that I'm hung up." Was she supposed to say that Daniel was the only man she'd ever loved? She couldn't lie to him. Their connection was based on unvarnished truth. Leaning on her left hand, it became numb. She shifted around.

"I'm sorry," he said. "Sometimes I get insecure with women I really care about. Comes from losing my mother so young."

Jeez, he was thinking about his late mother *now*. She felt guilty for not being empathetic. "That must have been so hard for you," she said, then kicked herself for saying "hard." She should have said "difficult." Why couldn't she shut the fuck up? She sat up, pulled the covers over herself.

"It's my fault," she said, blinking away the glittery spots. "The weed turned out to be stronger than I expected."

"Don't worry," he said. "We can wait. It's no big deal."

But she didn't want to wait, she wanted to get it over with already. She should have torn off her bra and nylons when he'd asked her to. He'd wanted her to strip, that's what turned him on. The problem was, she wasn't as wild or thin or experienced as his flamey redheaded actress—who probably did a whole strip tease routine under bright lights.

Daniel sat at the edge of the bed, rubbing her back. "Want to take a walk? Get some air?"

He was giving up already? She felt dejected and embarrassed that he no longer wanted her. She'd aced graduate school but managed to flunk her own seduction.

"Listen, I have that interview at *New Urban Magazine* you set up for me at ten tomorrow morning. So maybe I should get home?"

"You sure? We could just sleep here tonight," he said.

"No. I should go." But she wanted to try again. "Unless you want to finish the champagne…"

"Maybe you shouldn't be so high our first time," he said. "I want you to really be here with me."

Damn, he was turning into a fucking narc. Just what she needed, a critique on her bedroom etiquette. How insulting. Holding back tears, Lila got up and quickly threw her dress on. The strap of her new bra was digging into her skin, so she unclasped it under her dress and slipped it into her purse.

"So come over after your interview," he said.

She prayed he would save the night by saying, "Stop. You're not allowed to go," throwing her to the floor and doing it right there.

"Let me walk you home," he said. But he didn't stand up.

"No, that's okay. I'll hop a cab. See you tomorrow." She waved goodbye, getting out of his bedroom before he could see her cry. She put her shoes on, grabbing her coat.

It was a loud, crazy night in the Village, the kind she usually loved, tons of people in bizarre outfits. Plodding past Village Cigars on Christopher Street, Lila took out the joint and lit it, wanting to erase her whole disaster with Daniel.

"How ya doin' tonight, girlfriend?" asked a tall black transvestite in criss-cross hose and leather, standing at the corner next to her.

"Not so good."

"Oh, that smells sweet. Can I have a hit?"

She handed over the joint, noticing she had the same lacy bra as Lila's, in red, which was prettier.

"Thanks, baby doll. Don't worry. It'll all work out the way it's supposed to," she said, handing Lila a flier for her midnight show at the Duplex cabaret.

Lila was far away and outside of herself as she stood at the curb, getting higher, soothed by the words of the cross-dresser instead of the lover she now desperately missed.

12
June 1982
DANIEL

The Holy Land offered the perfect escape hatch. Daniel couldn't wait to take Lila in his arms, carry her to his bedroom and make love to her for hours, the way he should have last night. Then they'd plan their getaway to Israel, flying there together for his prestigious fellowship. But when he opened the door on Friday at noon she looked different, in an oversized navy blazer, with broad shoulder pads and thick buttons. He'd never seen her in a suit. Or with so much makeup, her pretty blond hair clipped away from her face.

"Got your message," she told him, stepping into his foyer. She leaned in to kiss him quickly but barely brushed his lips. "So you already know?"

"I just heard." He led her inside, relieved she seemed happy, pretending nothing bad had happened, as if she hadn't gotten too stoned and backed out of sleeping with him at the last humiliating second twelve hours earlier. "Who told you? Howard?"

"Howard knows about my job?" she asked.

"What job?" Daniel detected the edge of the lace camisole she was wearing underneath the jacket he wanted to unbutton.

"I just heard you say we'll celebrate. You don't know? *New Urban Magazine* hired me!" she squealed. "Can you believe it?"

"They did?"

"I'll be working for the most brilliant magazine in the country. It's the best thing that ever happened to me."

He thought he was the best thing that ever happened to her?

She plopped down on the couch. "I'm in shock. It totally blows my mind. It's like this dream I didn't know I had coming true. All because of you."

Daniel sat down next to her. "Mazel tov." He kissed her forehead, realizing how off the gesture was, as if congratulating his daughter on a good report card. Damn. Why had he used Yiddish, as if she'd just been bat mitzvahed? He was still self-conscious from the night before, too inhibited to touch her lips, or look into her eyes for fear he'd see his failure.

"I didn't know about the magazine," he said. "I meant to celebrate my fellowship."

"What fellowship?"

He was glad she was learning how to give a good interview, but she obviously had not listened to his whole message divulging his seriously stellar news. Just as well, he could tell her in person right now himself. He took both of her hands. They were a little clammy. He wished she would take off the masculine blazer, wipe off the paint covering her lovely face and undo her barrette so he could run his fingers through her hair which would hopefully soon grow back as long as it used to be. "Lila, remember my meeting with the Dorman Committee?"

"Vaguely."

"Well, I just found out they chose me!"

"They did? How cool! We both got awesome news today."

She clearly wasn't grasping what this meant.

"Honey, they offered me a fellowship to teach poetry at Hebrew University in Jerusalem. They only choose one author every two years."

Her mouth opened and she took her hands back. "You're leaving me?" she asked. "You already decided you're going away? When?"

"It just happened. I walked in the door a half hour ago. You're the first person I told."

"You said Howard knew."

"I had to ask him to take over my fall classes." Daniel had also left a message with Cormick, to gloat, to say *Fuck you, you old creep. I'll no longer be your overworked, underpaid doormat.*

"You gave up your classes? But you only mentioned Israel a few times in passing, like there was no chance it would happen." She leaned on the couch arm, tapping her foot on his wooden floor.

"I didn't think I had a chance. This two-year fellowship was a big longshot."

"Two years!" She looked horrified. "Can't you just say no?"

She clearly thought he was abandoning her. But she had no idea of the romantic plan that his brain had been hatching all morning. "I'm not leaving you, Lila. I want you to come with me!"

"You do? Really? Where again?"

"Yes, I do. I want to take you to Jerusalem." He reached over to hold her, but she jumped up.

"When is this happening?" she questioned, squinting as if the sun were hurting her eyes though his blinds were drawn.

"I officially start in September. But we could get out of here sooner, next month." He reached out his hand to coax her back, but she wouldn't come. "You know a little Hebrew. We'll can get more fluent doing an Ulpan together. You could be an international poet, in two languages. You can teach at Hebrew University too." It was the most spontaneous decision he'd ever made. He was sick of over-thinking everything. His adrenaline soared at the thought of just taking off with her.

"But *New Urban Magazine* just offered me the editorial assistant gig starting Monday. To work with the best writers and editors in the world. They come in and out every day. John Ashbery. Ian Frazier. John Updike. Philip Roth."

Every name she rattled off—each man more famous than he was—felt like a stab in his gut.

"Robert Penn Warren was the last Dorman winner. He went on to win the Pulitzer," Daniel countered.

When he'd left the phone message for Lila, he was exhilarated, picturing her rushing back into his arms where they'd rip off each other's clothes and spend all afternoon in bed. But her cold and confused reaction was throwing him. He couldn't touch her now if he tried.

"You really didn't know I got the job?" she asked, as if she didn't believe him.

He shook his head.

"Why do you want to leave New York?"

She had no idea how demoralizing his last few terms at New City had been. While Lila and his students looked up to him, among the faculty he'd become a joke. His last book came out a decade ago and it was only a slender paperback. His biggest triumph was a reading series. Cormick—who popped out fat hardcover poetry collections yearly—had never respected Daniel. Even Howard was surpassing him lately with impressive bylines. The deans refused to consider Daniel for the tenured faculty job they were offering Faith— along with Daniel's corner office. She didn't have the heart to tell him herself that he was losing his shot at a solid position and his workspace. It was wrecking their friendship.

But now all that was history.

"It's such an exciting offer for me," he told Lila, stunned she wasn't getting it.

What a thrilling two years they could have in the Middle East –lying on the beach, her hot body and brain beside him as they'd edit their poems together. They could explore the desert hand in hand. The Dorman committee ran an institute for global peace, with political summits in Jordan, Cairo and Istanbul. He could have an important international life. When he'd renewed his passport on his way home from the meeting, Daniel saw that he hadn't been out of the country in seven years. He had already started packing. He just assumed she would jump at the chance to accompany him. He hadn't really considered leaving without Lila—over a job that barely existed.

"You're sure it's not temporary?" he asked. "Filling in for summer vacation?"

"No. I met with four editors who said full time, ten thirty to six. Perfect hours."

Of course, Lila was smart and talented. But she was so naïve. Her main editorial experience was being his assistant, which he now regretted telling her to play up on the résumé he wished he hadn't edited so well.

"It'll just be typing and filing to start," she said.

"I'm sure you'd do great there. You're smart as a whip."

"That's cliché."

"Touché," he said. She hadn't even started the job and she was already correcting him. He was losing her before he even had her.

"I told Charles Wentworth I studied with you. He admires your work."

"Then why does he keep rejecting it?" he asked.

"He wants to see more. I told him what a genius you are."

The thought of her talking him up there was flattering, but embarrassing. Did they know she was his girlfriend? Did she know?

"The managing editor came in too. Turns out he's the one I'll be working for directly, he seemed proper, standoffish, really. On the skinny side, tall, kind of formal, almost British. Do you know him?" She said all this quickly, as if it was all one sentence.

As she shifted her arms, the top button of her blazer came open. He saw she wasn't wearing a bra underneath the lilac camisole, her nipple peeking through the sheer fabric. She seemed more enthralled with *Urban Review's* male brass than with Daniel. He worried her looks had really charmed the editors. But he had to keep that to himself and stay rational, to remedy this mix-up.

"Listen, you just graduated. You could take some time to figure out your next move."

"But this is my move. I start Monday morning," she said. "I need to go home and call my mother. I wanted to tell you first."

Half-turning towards his bookshelf, she nervously ran her hands over a dusty row. She picked up the paperback *Diving Into the Wreck* lying atop Adrienne Rich's hardcovers and turned it straight, standing it up in the stack.

He could feel her slipping out of his apartment.

"Don't go yet," Daniel said.

This was all his fault, offering such an over-the-top reference, saying Lila was "the most brilliant, impressive student I've had in ten years." He'd sent it long before he knew he had a shot at winning two years abroad, and would want to take Lila with him. He thought of a different tactic.

"I can't wait to show you Israel. My mother took the Passover line 'next year in Jerusalem' to heart. But she never made it," he said. "She'd be so proud of me."

"I'm really proud of you. I couldn't be prouder. It's incredible news," Lila said. Then she added, "But I already went on a Birthright trip—with Jeff."

Him again! "That's right. Subject of your poem. 'On the ancient sands of Zion, we were supposed to be free.'" It was about a fight she and her football idiot had on the beach after he'd fucked someone else. Daniel would never cheat on her. "Look how inspiring you found it."

"I find New York inspiring," she said, brushing her fingers over the tier of paperback fiction. She was refusing to make eye contact.

For two years she'd been following him like a lost little puppy to every class, workshop, office hour and poetry reading, begging for his attention and praise. He thought they both had the same goal—to write and to be together, in the open. How could their dreams be clashing now? *Shvitzing*, he opened the window. Con Ed was still jack hammering outside. There must have been a leaky or burst pipe below the pavement. There had to be a way to fix this too. "How about you work at the magazine all summer, get great experience. Then, in September, you could join me for a few months. Come sit back down with me for a minute."

She reluctantly returned, sitting on the next cushion over. "But once I get in the door, you never know what'll happen. I mean, what if I wind up with my first byline in *The Review*?" she asked. " Or I could become a staff writer. Doesn't that sometimes happen –if you work hard and they really like you?"

Most peons wound up eternally stuck in their low level positions, from what he'd heard. Few ever moved up. They would probably pay her two hundred bucks a week to be a secretary—not a poet. "I'm sure they'd let an employee take a leave of absence," he tried.

"But how can I think of getting out of there when I'm dying to get in?" she asked. "Hey, can you postpone your fellowship till next summer?"

He'd already resigned his teaching job and postponing could risk losing the highest honor he'd ever been paid. He couldn't fathom why she would rather be a typist than go away with him. When he was her age, he'd rushed headlong into wild adventures in Negril, Belize, South Africa. "My fellowship is all expenses paid, plus a stipend. You won't have to waitress or type or answer phones in an office. I'll take care of rent and bills and you can write all day. Just try it for a few weeks in the fall."

"Okay, maybe in November. Or December." She stood up again, edging towards his door. "But I need to call my mom to tell her." He couldn't let her go.

"Can't you tell her later?" he pleaded.

"I rushed over right from the interview. You're the only one who knows."

"Wait." If she told her mother, it would be a done deal. "I'm offering you every artist's fantasy. Don't you want to go away with me? I thought you said it would be fun to take a trip together over the summer."

"It would be awesome to go the beach on July 4th weekend. Or Labor Day. But I can't just take off with you for two years. We've never gone away together before. I haven't even been here for two years yet."

"But travelling to Israel together would be awesome." He stole her juvenile word.

"What would I even say if someone asked what I was doing there?" she asked.

"You'd say 'I'm teaching and writing here with my boyfriend, who's a Dorman Fellow.'"

"Yeah, like I'm really gonna show off, 'My boyfriend's this big shot poet. So I'm here mooching off of his money and prize.'"

"No, of course you wouldn't do that," he said.

"I just got my *own* job."

You mean, *I* just got *you* a job that now I don't want you to take, he didn't say, his temple throbbing.

"I'm not the type who wants to just be a guy's armpiece," she proclaimed.

"No, of course you don't. You wouldn't be."

Oh, that was the problem! He should have known. She wasn't like Roxy, a divorced actress who'd had an array of past lovers and a kid with a gay co-worker. Lila was raised in a religious family in Wisconsin. She had slept with only one guy in her whole life, in a long-term serious relationship she hoped would lead to marriage. That was why she was so nervous the night before and kept bringing up Jeff. She was trying to let Daniel know she couldn't be casual about sex. She needed the commitment first. He could do that!

"Lila, how about this?" He rushed over to her. "We can make it official before we go."

"Make what official?" she asked.

"We can get hitched." He leaned his arm against the bookshelf above her. "Down at City Hall." He knew it was crazy—they were just becoming an official couple. But he was tired of being broke and breaking romances, with all the headaches and rejection. If that was what it took, he would get out of his head and act like a man this time. The man Gabrielle and Roxy and Faith had once wanted. The man he'd never been. He had his mother's wedding band, platinum with a tiny diamond chip. But Lila had big fingers and Daniel's mother had been a petite bird with tiny bones. He'd have to get the ring resized. He could do that—they had jewelers in Israel.

She back-stepped near his kitchen alcove, her eyes staring wide. But she looked more shell-shocked than overjoyed, like she couldn't believe this was happening.

He'd said it too casually, that was the problem. Should he get on his knee? He needed to convince her, to keep her. "Yes. Married. I'll be forty-two in September. I see what I've been doing wrong. I've been too scared to act. Too selfish and self-involved."

"Wow. Daniel, that's so heavy. I'm touched. I mean, I really love you. More than anyone. Ever. But it's like, way too soon." She took another step back, crossing her arms across her chest. "I mean, we haven't even slept together."

So that's what this was about: He had failed to make Lila his last night! Although she was stoned and sending mixed signals, he should have taken her anyway. Was that what she wanted? Is that what she wanted now? He no longer knew. He was misreading her, botching everything. He wished he could slow down, take back his proposal, postpone the trip. He should apologize. No, he should shut up and stop talking and being so rash, which was scaring her off.

"I know, but we don't have to figure it all out now," he tried to backpedal.

"I do. I have to start work on Monday," she insisted, buttoning her blazer.

Everything he said was wrong today.

But maybe it wasn't him. Zalman had been railing against their romance repeatedly, insisting she was too young, unformed, ill-equipped for intimacy. She was so hungry for acclaim and validation that she saw the magazine as God, making the worst decision imaginable, picking the low-level job he'd found her over long-lasting love. Had Lila been using him for his connections all along? He should argue or convince her or compete, but he was so ashamed he just wanted to sink into his brown carpet and hide.

"Listen, I have to call my mom," she reiterated, blowing him a kiss, then turning her back on him. He couldn't follow or stop her.

He couldn't handle it anymore, her mother Hannah always looming, Lila's preoccupation with the Wisconsin football jerk, the local-yokel routine she kept using to worm her way into the New York literary circles he couldn't wait to shake off. He went to shut the door, locked and double bolted it. He was glad she was gone. He just needed to escape his lousy job, this shit-hole in this cruel city and all his years of failure to start over by himself, somewhere else, in Israel. Where he could win.

PART THREE: 2010

13

April 2010

LILA

Dropping Daniel's hardcovers on a chair, Lila flew out of Barnes & Noble, humiliated that Lip Ring saw what happened. Rounding the registers, she pulled out her cell, pressed #1 on speed dial. "I shouldn't have gone," Lila confessed.

"Oh God. Where are you now?" Sari asked.

"Just leaving." Lila rushed past the maze of toys, video games, and stationery taking up space where books should be. Trying to disappear fast, she felt trapped in the dumb high heels she shouldn't have worn, now hampering her escape. How could he not remember *her*? He knew everybody else. Standing on the slow escalator, she teetered down the moving steps, perspiring, disoriented. Pulling a Kleenex from her purse, she dabbed her forehead with her left hand. Damn, she hoped it wasn't another hot flash.

"How bad was it?" Sari sounded worried.

"I thought I could handle seeing him again." She leaned the phone against her ear so she could hold onto the rail for a minute, trying to breathe.

"Nothing happened, did it?" Sari asked. "I mean, you didn't tell Daniel…"

"Well no…"

"Mark is going to kill you."

"Don't tell Mark!" Lila yelled. As she reached the bottom of the stairs, she pushed the heavy glass door. She didn't need her brother entangled in her affairs again.

"Lila—I thought it was you." She heard his voice from behind, an arm on her elbow.

She swung around fast, sure it was Daniel. But it was a much taller, middle-aged guy with cocoa-colored skin, holding a shopping bag full of books. He was nicely dressed in a navy sports coat and tie. "It's Tarik," he said, opening the door for her, following her outside. "From our program. You don't remember?"

Was his faint accent Middle Eastern? She'd ask Sari who he was if he wasn't standing in front of her. "I'll get back to you," she told Sari, ending their call.

"Wildman's private workshop." He looked at her, expectantly. "Tarik Adivar."

"Ah Tarik, yes." The Turkish fiction writer. She recalled a story about his father's multiple wives that had intrigued her thirty years before. He was thicker now, less hair, but looking at him closer she vaguely recognized his lovely oval green eyes and long lashes.

"You didn't hear me yelling your name?" he asked.

She winced, slipping her phone back into her purse, wondering how much he saw at the bookstore. But if Tarik knew who she was, why didn't Daniel? Everyone said she still looked the same, much younger than her age. She was mortified, she just wanted to get home and hide. Lila checked her watch, eight o'clock, summer light outside. "No, sorry. Late to meet a friend," she mumbled.

"You always said Wildman was the true genius, not Cormick. Great reading, huh?"

She nodded, relieved that he obviously hadn't witnessed the way Daniel had dismissed her. "Yes, great. Well, nice seeing you." She started walking down Warren Street. Tarik strode alongside.

"I was hoping you'd be here tonight," he said. "You look the same." His eyes took in her dress and heels.

Had they once gone on a date? She faintly recalled an awkward dinner with him.

"I'm glad I stayed in the city late to catch the reading. We're in Westport. I told my wife that my old professor had reached international stature. I haven't gone to a reading since grad school." He chattered on with no idea she could barely focus. He pulled out his Blackberry, showing her a picture of his spouse, a WASPy brunette in a plaid jumpsuit. "Here," he pointed to his three kids.

"Adorable. So you're in Connecticut?" She was surprised he lived so close by. In her mind she'd somehow exiled him back to Turkey after grad school. Just as she'd relegated Daniel unreachable in Israel, ignoring years of bylines that called him "A poet living in Vermont."

"Yes, but I work in the city. My uncle's investment firm. Selling out, as you artists say. 'You can't eat your dreams,' my father used to warn me. I saw your book reviewed in the magazine and heard you were on Charlie Rose. I'd love to have watched. Did you post a link to your Facebook page?"

"I've been meaning to." Were they Facebook friends? Her publicist said to accept all requests to build her following, but she didn't recall seeing Tarik there. This morning at the office when she typed in her professor's name, nine Daniel Wildmans popped up, four on LinkedIn, none him. She felt so Linked Out. She was psyched to see @DanielWildman on Twitter, but it turned out to be a hunky Latino skateboarder from Encino she'd accidentally followed. "I have to link it to my website too."

"We're all going for drinks at The Theater Bar," Tarik added. "You should join us."

"Who's all?" she asked, paranoid, turning back to see if Daniel's reading had let out yet.

"Wildman, Powell, Fell…"

"Howard was there tonight?" Thankfully she'd missed him in the crowd. She'd zeroed in on Daniel at the podium. At first, he looked older, heavier, grayer. But then he'd opened his mouth to read the majestic title poem about his father's failure. Time fell away and the entire room became silent, mesmerized by his power. Or at least she was.

"Yes, Howard seemed very talkative," Tarik said. "More friendly than he used to be."

She hadn't been in the same room with Howard and Daniel since 1983. She pictured them leaving the bookstore now, catching her with Tarik, assuming something was going on between them. But if Daniel didn't remember her, he wouldn't care. And why should she worry what he thought anymore? She was fifty and married! She strode faster, blinking back tears, turning down West Street. Passing The Palm, her local bistro, she decided to duck inside and lose Tarik. "Well, here's where I'm going."

He opened the door for her again. "Wildman and Fell looked so much older. Right?" He kept talking and walking her inside, oblivious. "Hard to believe that Fell almost died."

"What do you mean?"

"Didn't you hear? He's had heart trouble."

"What?" Lila was taken aback –and hooked. "How serious?" She'd hadn't heard anything about him in a while. They were in different circles now.

"Some kind of arrhythmia."

"How are you this evening?" Martino greeted her, eyeing Tarik. "Will your husband be joining us too?"

"No. He's out of town," Lila said, self-conscious, as if the maître d' would think she was really *with* Tarik, concerned about Howard. Though an irregular heartbeat seemed an apt condition for a poet.

In class, Daniel had called her use of the word "heartbeat" in a poem cliché. She'd shot back the line by Ted Hughes: "The heart beats thick,/Big trout muscle out of the dead cold." But then Daniel published "as if the heart is a prism." The hypocrite.

"Is your friend here?" Tarik asked, interrupting the argument with Daniel she'd resurrected in her head.

"Who? Oh." Lila looked around. Then she shrugged, pretending defeat.

"Let me buy you a drink," he offered.

Lila nodded, needing to sit down. She thought she'd be having a glass of wine with Daniel now. She'd rehearsed handing him the envelope. He'd open it, read what she'd writen and finally understand how fragile she'd been back then. Surely, in retrospect, he'd regret taking advantage of an innocent nineteen-year-old. *I'm so sorry,* she'd imagined him saying, gently taking her hand. *Lila, I'm stunned. I had no idea.*

"Your usual table by the window?" Martino asked.

"The bar's fine." She didn't want anybody from the reading to see her, especially Daniel.

"You look lovely tonight," Martino told her.

"Why, thank you." She pictured Daniel's smart-looking wife laughing at her: a pathetic, overdressed, made-up stranger stumbling out of the bookstore. Sitting on the corner stool, Lila suddenly worried that when Martino had complimented her all those times was just being nice. It was something he said to all women her age, for bigger tips.

"Pinot Gris?" he asked.

Disjointed memories assaulted Lila's brain: holding hands with Daniel on the Spring Street subway platform. Making out with him on the floor at Howard's party. The IV drip hurting her hand at the hospital three decades before. She could still feel the needle pricking a thick vein under her skin.

"A Manhattan," Lila said. "Dry."

"Make it two," Tarik echoed, tucking his bag under the stool beside her and sitting down. "So you must like working at the magazine?"

"Have you been in touch with Daniel this whole time?"

"Not in years. I just emailed Wildman kudos when I heard he won and he invited me to his reading," Tarik explained. "Tell me about publishing a book. I bet that was so exciting."

"Yes. Most exhilarating was first seeing it in bookstores. My husband was annoyed when I told a reporter it was the best moment of my life," Lila admitted.

"You had a Barnes & Noble reading at the same store?" Tarik asked.

"Standing room only," she let slip, then added, "but not as big a crowd as Daniel's."

How many former students had he invited to his event? Not her. She was off his list. Why would she expect to get an invitation when they'd had no contact at all since he'd left town? It felt like another slight: being ignored, cast aside, forgotten. But she heard the voice of her shrink, Dr. Ness: *Feelings misinform.*

"Remember how competitive Wildman, Fell and Cormick all used to be?" Tarik asked.

She hadn't thought about the trio in years. "Is Howard still publishing a lot too?" she asked, suddenly more interested, feeling like a spy desperately gathering a dossier on her former professors.

"He said he won an award for a poem in *Crazy Horse* last year."

She rarely read journals anymore and missed the obscure names: *Sewanee Review, The Bitter Oleander, Aberration Labyrinth, The Skanky Possum.*

When the drinks came, Tarik clinked his glass against hers. Lila ate the cherry on the side, then downed the whiskey. It was sweet and smoky, on the strong side. She felt flushed. Running out of work to get her hair and nails done, she hadn't eaten all day. "Do you think Howard and Daniel are still good friends?"

"Of course. They've been close since they were in grad school together," Tarik said. "Though I never felt Fell's work was as moving or as universal as Wildman's."

"Howard was a good line editor," she said.

"You were the best critic there. I loved your concise notes in class," Tarik said. "You were a good hostess too. I remember you had that elegant Fifth Avenue apartment where you and Sari gave a reception after Wildman's reading at the wrestling arena. You had all that chopped liver and lox. I can't believe I recall that. I'd never had Jewish food before."

Just what she wanted as a legacy: to be known as an ethnic overfeeder, like her mother. She signaled the waiter for another.

"You're still friends with Sari?" he asked.

She nodded, wondering if she should phone Sari back to ensure she wouldn't tell Mark anything. Lila was lucky her husband wasn't coming home until tomorrow. She should call Dr. Ness for an emergency phone session. Dr. Ness would say: "Stop drinking now. Beware of anything that helps you escape, because you always have to return to yourself." Lila ate another palmful of peanuts. "I can't believe Howard has heart problems."

"At the reading, he told Judith he's had four attacks," Tarik responded.

"You know, I remember seeing his poem in *APR* titled *The Heart's Blockage*. I didn't realize it was literal."

"AARP does poems?" Tarik asked.

"No *American Poetry Review*," Lila corrected, laughing. Though the truth was, she no longer read *APR*, the Philly-based paper that Howard and Daniel had turned her on to. "Wait! Judith was at the bookstore too? I missed her." Lila had obviously been so obsessed with Daniel, she'd been blind to everyone else. "With her husband?" So many ancient soap operas were swirling around one New York reading.

"She came alone," he said. "Did you read her Marianne Moore biography?"

"Yes. It wasn't bad." Lila wondered if any students in their program wound up really writing their own material, or if the only ones still getting published were dissecting other's work, as she was. The drink she'd ordered arrived. She dove in, skipping the cherry this time.

"I bought two copies of your book." Tarik ate her cherry. "Beautiful author photo."

Was he flirting with her? "Did you read it?"

"Yes. I enjoyed it," he said.

Not a ringing endorsement. And why flatter her photograph? Was he implying she didn't look better in person?

"I always admired your poems in school," he went on. "I liked your voice better than Wildman's. I always found his work a little overwrought, like he was using fancy oration to make up for his lack of height. Lenu and I nicknamed him Napoleon."

"He was pretty nice to you." Lila defended Daniel—inanely—since he didn't even know who she was anymore. The jealous tinge in Tarik's voice triggered her memory of their dinner date. At the Cookery, which had been closed for decades. It was in the winter—Valentine's Day—the timing mostly to make her professor jealous. Had he sent her flowers?

"I remember you and Wildman used to be an item," Tarik said. He finished his drink, waving for another.

"No, we weren't," Lila said sharply. "He swore he'd never date a student. Cormick was the one who screwed all the women in the program," Lila insisted, tipsy, anxiously fishing cashews and almonds out of the snack bowl.

"Well, everyone saw you together," Tarik told her, not letting it go.

She shook her head, feeling found out, a teenager caught in the backseat at a drive-in movie, not a middle-aged author lifetimes later.

"*After* I graduated," she clarified. It was over with Daniel almost thirty years ago, she reminded herself. "He was more of a paternal figure," she added. Another dad who'd deserted her.

"I still remember lines from a poem you brought to class. 'I've never been good at secrets, unbutton myself heedlessly.'" Tarik recited with his eyes closed. "You know, I used to really have a thing for you," he admitted.

She felt herself blink quickly, flattered but embarrassed.

"Listen, Lila. I know this might seem ridiculous... But it's always bothered me that I acted so badly that night we had dinner."

"It was a long time ago." Had he acted badly or had she?

"I know I came off sexist and pig-headed. I didn't mean to offend you," he said. "I'm not like that. My wife is a corporate lawyer. Both of my daughters are excellent students, even better than my son..."

She popped the last few nuts in her mouth, finishing the bowl, but still famished and angry at herself for going to the reading. She was a mature, happily married career woman, for God's sake. She needed to leave the Daniel disaster in the past and forget the love that could never be fixed—or finished.

"I hope you will accept my heartfelt remorse now." Tarik put his hand on hers. The gesture—and his formality—jarred her. She was touched that he sounded so serious, as if this had really weighed on him.

Why did the wrong men always apologize?

"Of course," Lila said. Hearing her iPhone buzz, she checked to see who was calling, for a second imagining it was Daniel, as if he even had her number. It was her husband, from L.A. She didn't pick up. Yikes. Where would she tell him she was? In the eighties, drunk and lost in a time warp. She had to bust out of here.

"Oh, looks like my friend can't make it." She half-smiled, taking her hand back to signal the waiter for the check.

"Please, allow me," Tarik said when it came, pulling out his credit card. "You made my night. What a thrill to get to catch up with a famous author from my past."

How odd, after all this time, that this middle-aged guy was acting like he knew her so well when Lila hadn't even recognized him. It was as if he'd built up this whole imaginary connection to her over the years, assigning some kind of deep meaning to her old poems.

Then, Lila realized with dismay, that was what she'd done with Daniel.

14

April 2010

DANIEL

Why did I pretend not to know her? Daniel wondered, forcing a smile as he signed another book. He tried to erase thoughts of Lila but her spicy perfume lingered, along with the flash of her long hair hitting her black dress as she ran off. Acting like he didn't recognize her was stupid and immature. When he looked up from the page and scanned the room, she'd disappeared. He was relieved, glad his wife had taken the kids for coffee at the café, so she'd missed the incident. She didn't need to see a tall blonde from his bachelor days. Especially this week, after the prize had renewed the spark in their marriage. The Moët they'd shared numbed the sciatica in his lower back and the hotel suite his publisher sprung for hadn't hurt either. Good idea to let the kids crash with their Brooklyn cousins. Returning to New York as an award winner had changed everything; the city he'd dreaded now seemed so welcoming and majestic.

Yet the pain on Lila's face before she'd left made him want to run after her, take back the charade. *Why did she come?* She wasn't here to congratulate him; she was fiddling with her purse. She'd brought something to give him. He could barely handle the surprise of seeing her, let alone having a tête-à-tête in public. Now he wondered what she meant to show him. An embarrassing photo from Howard's party? A pathetic half-poem he'd scrawled her late one night in the Village? Maybe she came to apologize. After all, she'd taken advantage of his feelings back then, humiliating him worse than any woman ever had. But it was way too late to revise the past.

Wasn't it?

"I'll be right back," he told his publicist, rushing past the line of stragglers still waiting for his signature. He looked at all the kiddie toys, technology and flowered stationery they'd overstuffed the floor with. Where were the books? When he'd asked Pete to set up a reading at Coliseum, Books and Company or Gotham Book Mart, Daniel was shattered to hear they were all closed—replaced by impersonal chain stores.

Still, Daniel was pleased they'd ordered two hundred copies of *Losers Like Me*, which Pete had informed him of proudly. Until he'd added, "More than James Franco." His 24-year-old editor was comparing Daniel to a Hollywood narcissist who thought he was an author because he was playing Allen Ginsberg in an upcoming movie. Franco probably didn't even write his own books. Or "ooks," as Daniel used to call them. But hey, he'd beaten the young celebrity. Nobody would have predicted that at sixty-nine years old, decades after he'd fled town in disgrace, Daniel would wind up the toast of the New York literary world.

As he made his way to the front entrance, he saw Mary Jonas's daughter at the register, with that silly pierced ring in her lip. Next to her was the assistant who worked with Daniel's publisher. No Lila. As he glanced over at the escalators that led down to the sidewalk, the stairs empty, Daniel was hit by a barrage of visceral memories: Feeding Lila a slice of her mother's kosher turkey. The rabbit fur on the bed underneath her before she fled Howard's party in tears. The noxious smell of urine in the hospital's waiting room the next day. To think Howard had almost lost his life over a love triangle.

Daniel stopped walking. What was he doing, chasing her? He turned back to finish signing books. Tonight was what he'd waited decades for. His Manhattan colleagues and family were here, cheering him on. He was touched that so many people he used to know came. He'd promised Tarik he'd have a quick drink with some former students before leaving the city. A rich banker now, Tarik was sweet to buy eight books, as if shopping for ties at Barney's. Daniel recalled Tarik had a crush on Lila in grad school. Who could blame him? She was *still* a looker; even more lovely and poised now. He was pleased she'd seen him read so well tonight. He wished Cormick and Zalman could have been here. And his father and brother too.

"At parties you think only of who's not there," Lila once told him after his class.

He made his way back through the maze of shelves and sat down to greet the last gaggle of autograph-seekers. He prized the signed copies of books by poets he admired, inscribed to him. He tried to be equally eloquent.

"You made it." Howard smirked, dropping Daniel's poetry book down on the table.

"Yes, *boychick*, I did." Buoyed to see him, Daniel lept up to embrace his buddy. Howard offered a half-hug but Daniel pulled him closer, patting his back.

They'd been in touch by email, but he couldn't believe it had been almost thirty years. How old and thin his chum looked, shrunken, granny glasses on a string around his neck, like a *bubbe* in Florida playing gin rummy. Had Howard seen Lila? Daniel wanted to ask but stopped himself. It was the first time they'd all been in the same place since Howard's book party. Ironically the only one here who would understand the salacious gossip was the man who'd caused it.

"I finally came back to town, just to spite you," Daniel joked.

"Standing room only. Unobtrusive as always," Howard cracked.

"Yes, a few friends showed up." Daniel said. "You look good."

"You're full of shit."

"You look like hell," Daniel offered. "So do I. We're *alter cockers* now."

"I spit into the face of time and all that," Howard said.

"Lamentation of the Old Poet." Daniel paraphrased Yeats' title.

"John Hancock?" Howard stressed the last syllable, grinning.

"Yes, of course. Thanks for buying it."

"You didn't send me a review copy. I edited most of these."

"I told my publicist to," he mumbled.

"Publicist?" Howard laughed.

After marking down the date and New York City, Daniel wrote "To My Dearest, Oldest friend." He feared it sounded a bit too elegiac. So he continued, "With immense love and gratitude."

Howard eyed the messy black script on the page and said "String of clichés."

"Fuck you." Daniel smiled. "At least you made it here, a whole ten blocks. Did you have to take a cab?" He was annoyed he'd had to email and phone Howard twice to get him to commit to showing up, as if Daniel's first visit to New York since the early eighties wasn't reason enough.

"Saw your limo out front," Howard mumbled. "Funny ride for a Vermont poet."

"It's a town car. Publisher sent it," Daniel said.

Just a few hours earlier, riding downtown in the black sedan with his wife and kids, Daniel had panicked that nobody would show up. Or that someone from Howard's soiree would open their mouth about that one ancient indiscretion. He was acting like a paranoid adolescent. Jeez, half of the people who'd attended Howard's party were dead. Thankfully his wife didn't know the truth. He'd made sure she'd never find out what happened with Lila. But tonight was about celebrating, not digging up old ghosts.

"So we're all going out later? Since you're rich and famous now, you're treating?" Howard asked with the salty glint in his eye that Daniel didn't realize he'd missed.

"For you, my pal, I am." It was good to see him after so long.

"Did you invite Lila for drinks too?" Howard asked.

Damn him. Daniel stiffened, worried he'd caught what happened. "No. Why?"

"She flew out of here fast." Howard was reveling in this. "What did you say to her?"

"I told her you were here," Daniel joked, trying not to remember.

"Come on up," the clerk called out, summoning another customer. Howard ambled to the front row of chairs and sat down by himself. It was as if freaking Daniel out, then watching him sweat was the show he'd really come for.

"Daniel Wildman, it was such a thrill to hear you read today," said a vivacious redhead who plopped down four books and stared.

"Roxanne McDowell! What a great surprise." Daniel grinned.

"Roxy to you," she said, smiling.

His actress ex was still stunning too. What was in the New York water? Had they had work done? Glancing over to where his wife had been sitting, he was even more relieved she was at the café. He found her natural appearance beautiful. Their political crowd in Vermont made fun of big city folk since nobody in their circle wasted time or money on Pilates trainers and hair dye. So he felt sheepish noting how dazzling both of his old girlfriends were, with their glossy lips and long legs enhanced by nylons and heels. But the eyes must also feast.

Daniel stood up and gave Roxy a quick hug. "You look the same." He recalled reading that she'd wed a big Broadway producer.

"Bet you say that to all the girls." She giggled.

He signed the first book "With love and lots of lovely memories." Nice alliteration, he thought. But one nostalgic "love" was enough. What would he sign on the others?

"I was so thrilled to hear you won the Pulitzer."

"How's your little daughter? Katy, was it?" he asked, proud he'd remembered. His hair and back might be gone, but his powers of recall were vivid as ever. Too sharp sometimes.

"She's married and pregnant in Austin. Can you believe it? I'm going to be a grandma," Roxy said.

He nodded, signing her other two books "Fondly," and "With cherished memories."

"Thanks. This means so much to me," she gushed. "Listen, Daniel," Roxy put her hand on his shoulder, not letting him go. "I tried to find you on Facebook, but you're the only one not on there. I always felt badly about the way we ended. I never meant to hurt you…"

"Oh, that's water under a very creaky bridge." He shrugged it off. He glanced over to see Howard watching. He waved gleefully.

Why was it always the wrong people who were sorry?

"I was actually relieved when I heard you were dating someone else," Roxy continued. "The blond student."

It annoyed him that everyone was bringing up Lila now. Roxy hadn't been at Howard's party, had she? Daniel pretended he had no idea who she was talking about.

"You know, the woman of ambition you published the poem about," Roxy persisted. "I thought you two would have wound up together."

"No, we didn't."

Did everyone know about him and Lila? Damn, it was his own fault for spilling so much of his feelings in those purple lines he had to publish in the best magazine in the country. Howard, staring at them, giving him a thumb's up sign like a stupid frat boy.

"Yes, I saw you married a pretty brunette. In that family picture in the paper yesterday," Roxy went on. "What impressive children you have…"

"Thanks." How asinine Daniel had been, to dodge an entire city because of one drunken slip, when he had so many comrades and stories here.

For a second he felt like inviting Roxy for drinks too. But his marital bed was finally hot again he shouldn't ruin it by being insensitive. He'd finally learned to keep his big mouth shut. "It's never too late to have a happy childhood," he'd once told Zalman.

"For you, it's too late," Zalman had said.

Well, at least he'd dodged the Lila grenade. But what the hell was in her purse?

PART FOUR: 1982

15
July 1982

LILA

"The guy's not worth offing yourself over," Mark told her.

"What? I'm not suicidal," Lila reassured. "Why would you think that?"

"You sent Mom some poetry book she thought was a sign," Mark said, crushing Sari's cigarette in the ashtray.

They were in Chinatown where Lila was sitting next to Jeff at a red leather booth in Wo Hop as they waited for their food. Lila assumed Sari would light another smoke or tell her brother to piss off, but she didn't.

"Sign of what?" Sari asked.

"Everybody in the book killed themselves," Mark said.

"They did not!" Lila visualized the table of contents—Plath. Sexton. Berryman. Celan. Crane. Wow, they all had. There were even poems that Daniel had showed her by Hemingway—who'd shot himself in the head. But they were disappointing, light verse filled with the words "fart," "shit," "bitch" and "whore." Even Daniel, who exalted "Papa"—admitted they were horrible. "Forms aren't transferable," he'd said. "Most novelists can't do justice to poetry. They have too many words."

"Mom thought it was some kind of hidden message," Mark was saying.

"What? I wasn't sending anyone any kind of message. Why didn't you just tell them I was fine?" Lila asked her roommate.

"Are you?" Sari mouthed wordlessly, reaching her hand across the table to touch Lila's.

Lila didn't know the answer. She'd barely been able to eat or sleep or concentrate in the six weeks since Daniel left. It was day forty-three. Every time the phone rang in her apartment, she still jumped to answer. Each afternoon she ran to check the mail, dismayed when there were no letters to her in his messy scrawl. She checked the messages on her machine ten times a day, it was never him. She read his poems over and over, sure there was a code hiding there that would tell her why he left her so abruptly and when he would come back for her.

"It was all I could do to keep Mom from getting on a plane," Mark said. "She gave us strict instructions to bring you back with us Sunday."

"I can't take a vacation now," Lila said. She was working full-time, staying at the office until nine at night, volunteering to type or edit the work of any writers or editors who asked. She was sure Daniel would be proud of her, making such a good impression. She took notes in her journal when Adrienne Rich and George Plimpton came back to the office, in case Daniel would want to know every single detail when he returned to New York, and to his senses. She talked to him often in her head, every day, like he was still here, they way she'd talked to her dad for years after he'd left.

"Mom didn't mean vacation," Mark went on. "She meant for us to move you back."

Staring into her brother's eyes, Lila realized that Mark and Jeff had been sent here to capture her, like bounty hunters chasing after a fugitive mental patient. So that was the real reason her brother had driven his ugly blue Honda pickup fifteen hours to Manhattan with Jeff this weekend: for an intervention.

"Don't be crazy. I just got a great job!" she spat. "I'm not going anywhere."

Then she saw how concerned Mark and Jeff had been. She'd actually been worried herself. She'd never not been able to eat or get out of bed before. The only time she felt alive was at the magazine, which reminded her of Daniel.

There she'd escape into the rhythms of typing or pasting cartoons into bulging black scrapbooks with old-fashioned glue for hours on end.

After work, she'd take the Fifth Avenue bus downtown—and then walk around the Village, looking for Daniel in Washington Square Park, the Village diner, St. Marks Bookshop, even the gym where he'd done his reading series—everywhere they used to hang out. In the middle of the night, Lila kept waking up from bad dreams, in a tangle of tears and sweat. In last night's nightmare, she was at the Baraboo cemetery visiting her father's grave but there was a mistake and Daniel was buried in the plot instead.

"She hasn't been sleeping well or eating anything," Sari reported as if Lila wasn't there at all.

"Hey, can we get some wonton soup too?" Mark called out when the waiter walked by.

"No more order! Too much food! Two almond shrimp, chicken mu shu, orange beef, rice, six egg roll enough," yelled the old Chinese guy. He shook his head in disgust at the four young gluttonous Americans, then stomped back toward the kitchen.

"We waited an hour to get into this dive and he won't let us order soup?" Jeff laughed.

"They're not used to big Wisconsin boys," said Sari, staring at Mark in a moony way that made Lila feel even more alone.

It had seemed bizarre that Lila's brother and ex-boyfriend drove all the way to New York. She couldn't handle company but they didn't give her a choice, barging in, flicking on the lights, insisting she get out of bed and get dressed, dragging her on this strange double dinner date to her favorite restaurant. But Lila forgot how loud, hot and crowded it was here. It hurt her ears.

"Think he'll give us more napkins?" Jeff asked. "Or are they rationed too?"

Lila felt stuck in a tunnel where she was peering out at everyone from a distance but she couldn't talk or touch. She eyed her ex-boyfriend, with his chiseled chin, long Roman nose and blond crew cut finally growing out. He seemed very young and light, like a golden retriever puppy, so effortlessly himself. Daniel—darker, shorter, faster speaking—had been paranoid that there were still lingering sparks between Lila and her first love, but he was wrong. There wasn't anything leftover from the past but friendship. When she'd seen the dozen roses on her desk her first day of work, with the note "congratulations on your new job," Lila's heart leapt, praying they were from Daniel. But they were only from her Wisconsin ex. Now that he was here, she wondered if Daniel could somehow tell—through the air waves. She hoped it would upset him enough to make him return to New York.

"Man, this city kills me. Everyone's a character," Mark said. "Like all the nuts on *Taxi*."

Lila kept replaying the twisted talk about Daniel's fellowship that Friday afternoon in June. She didn't even know it was a fight. After she'd left to call her mother, she met Sari for lunch, to tell her the good news. When she'd called Daniel that night, he didn't answer. She still couldn't believe that he didn't return her phone message on Friday. Or Saturday. Or Sunday. On Monday, after three days of being ignored, she'd shown up at Daniel's apartment building to find him gone. Stanley, his old neighbor upstairs, said he'd left for JFK airport with a big suitcase the day before. He'd gone to Israel without saying goodbye to her. Marching home, she argued with him, swearing out loud how mean and immature and cold it was to just take off, becoming one of those New York characters who talked to themselves.

But that night she started flashing to the hot spring morning when her tall, handsome father woke her up and kissed her cheek, before he left for work. "Bye bye, my Lila head. See you later," he said as he always did. But he never came back. What if Daniel never came back either?

His neighbor Stanley gave her Daniel's forwarding address in Israel, but still Lila had spent eighteen minutes frantically arguing with a secretary who barely spoke English at Hebrew University. They had no record of a Daniel Wildman being there. Where was he? The fifty-four dollar charge that showed up on Lila's phone bill added to the injury. Lila sent him a first class letter, then a telegram he never replied to. Paranoid, she wondered if Daniel was really still in Greenwich Village. Maybe he'd moved in with his redheaded actress and Stanley was in on the elaborate ruse? But then Lila saw the actress's picture in an ad for a new play at The Public this month. And NCU's campus bulletin confirmed Daniel was teaching at Hebrew University, starting at the end of September, right after the Jewish holidays. Lila was afraid that Daniel had erased her, like the way he'd cross out a bad stanza that was ruining a poem.

"Why don't you turn off the TV and read a book? You know, those things with bound pages," Sari was teasing Mark.

What TV? Lila missed what they were saying.

"Look where reading all those poetry books got her—manically depressed cause her old prof took off after she dumped him," Mark said.

Her brother's words—reducing her to a romantic spat—stung. Lila stared at Sari, hurt that her best friend had betrayed her confidence.

"What are you talking about?" Lila yelled. "I never dumped him."

"Well, what do you think turning down a marriage proposal is?" Sari asked.

Was that what Daniel thought? No wonder he was angry; he probably felt like she'd been lying to him or playing games for two years. That was why Lila needed to speak to him so badly. To tell him she'd never wanted their relationship to end. She'd just been so stunned by his offer—and the horrible timing—that she hadn't quite taken it all in. It happened too fast. But she wasn't sure what she could have done differently. She'd never give up the job—for anything. She didn't want to go away for two years or to get married too young, like her mother did.

"Hey, I was pretty upset when *you* moved to New York," Jeff admitted.

"Really? You never told me that," Lila said, recalling how he'd told everyone their split was mutual, that they'd decided long distance was too hard so they'd go back to being friends.

"Well, now I'm just worried how you're feeling," Jeff told her, patting her back.

She felt far away from the table and from herself, as if her falling out with Daniel happened to someone else. It was a story that she'd be able to make sense of sometime in the future. When she came back to life.

"That's because she was the only Jewish girl you'd ever gone out with," Mark threw out.

"The only woman of our faith my brother ever slept with was a stripper," Lila said. "He found the sole Jewish stripper in Wisconsin." She used her old taunt, but her heart wasn't in it.

"Hey, I'm not spilling all of your sick secrets," Mark said in weak protest.

"I like that he's a hot-blooded American male," Sari jumped in. "I am sick of all these urban pseudo-intellectuals who can't buy a woman dinner and screw her without revealing their sob story pasts in heroic couplets."

Daniel preferred free verse. Dating Mark, the biggest beer pong player in Baraboo, didn't exactly give Sari relationship cred, but Lila was too tired to tussle back.

"Have a drink at least," Jeff said, pouring tea into a cracked cup for Lila.

She hated tea and shook her head.

"I know what you want." In a loud Baraboo twang he called out, "Hey, can we get us some diet sody pop for the lady poet, eh?"

"You want a beer, Marky?" Sari asked.

Marky? Only Lila's mother had called him that. When he was five.

"Excuse me, we need two beers, two Diet Cokes, water, and an ashtray," Sari bellowed to a different waiter, this one jumping at her command, bringing it all quickly, along with crunchy noodles.

Jeff grabbed a bunch and put them on Lila's plate. She put them back on his. She wasn't thirsty or hungry. The only bright side of abandonment was losing thirteen pounds. She kind of liked the feel of her hip bones protruding, the enclave of her stomach flat for the first time, like she was physically disappearing.

Mark opened the soda, drank it all in one gulp and burped.

Sari laughed.

"Mom would be so proud," Lila muttered as the waiter plopped all the food down on their table. Mark and Jeff devoured the soup and greasy egg rolls. Sari spooned rice, beef and chicken on Mark's plate. It confused Lila to see her rough-and-tumble pal turn so oddly solicitous around her brother.

"Okay, this grub was definitely worth waiting for." Mark talked with his mouth full.

"It's, like, the best Chinese food I've ever had," Jeff echoed.

"Don't use the word *like* so much," Lila corrected. "You sound uneducated."

"Gee, sorry, Miss Masters in Poetry," Mark said. "Who's making a whole two hundred bucks a week typing."

"At a big Manhattan magazine," Jeff slipped in, scooping sautéed shrimp and almonds on her plate. "Have some." He forced a forkful in her mouth. It wasn't bad. "Can we get another shrimp dish or will the waiter throw us out on the street?" Jeff asked, winking at Lila.

Though he stood six foot tall, with two hundred pounds of muscle, Jeff had been the runt of their college football team. Lila noticed how much beefier Jeff was than Daniel. She'd never thought of Daniel as delicate before. Even Jeff's neck and fingers seemed thicker.

The waiter marched over with the bill. "Pay now." He pointed to the cashier. "You go."

"Man, you weren't kidding about the worst waiters on the planet." Jeff took the check.

"Fine chow is the one thing your city's got us beat on," Jeff said as they cleaned their hands with the Handi Wipes the waiter threw on the table. "In the paper it said there's a midnight show of *Sleeper* at the Film Forum."

She was the one who'd turned them both on to Woody Allen movies in high school. But it would be sacrilegious to go together now since Lila had seen the last two Woody flicks with Daniel. It would be like cheating on him. "You guys already saw *Sleeper*," she said. "You kept quoting his Orgasmatron jokes."

"Hey don't knock masturbation. It's sex with someone I love," Mark recited.

"That one was from *Annie Hall*," Sari corrected.

"Definitely *Annie Hall*, dude," Jeff butted in.

"*Post* says there's a late show of *Rocky III* at Times Square," Mark said.

"I could be talked into *Rocky III*," Sari jumped in.

"Nobody with a brain goes to late movies in Times Square," Lila said. "Too dangerous."

"Oh you gotta see it with us," Jeff insisted. He went over to the cashiers to pay the bill as she inched towards the crowded stairway, dozens of people waiting.

She wished Jeff would stop using the word "got." Was she becoming Daniel? She felt older, sardonic, critical of all grammar mistakes. She remembered a poem he'd read her about how you become what was missing.

Crammed into the tiny corner booth on Mott Street, Lila stared at Jeff, touched that he'd driven all the way here to check on her. Sari said that wrapping herself around Daniel for two years had brainwashed Lila, covering her eyes with the same cynical, dark-tinted glasses that colored his world. She'd been flattered to be his muse, reading and critiquing his early drafts. She'd spent the last two years building him up and editing his work, protecting him. She didn't feel like she was anyone without him. She hated becoming her mother, overly dependent on a man for her outlook and money and self-worth. That was the reason she'd move to New York and didn't go to Israel with Daniel to begin with.

"Let's get out of here," Jeff said, tugging her sleeve.

On their way up the stairs, he put two fortune cookies in his pocket. Lila slipped her hand in to grab a cookie to see what her fortune said. Maybe it would tell her when Daniel would come back or what she should do next. She found Jeff's hand in there. He smiled, interlocking his fingers in hers, misinterpreting her mistake. But he was so nice. She smiled back, rubbing his skin with her thumb for a minute. Then, as Sari and Mark bolted up the stairs, Lila broke away, grabbed the cookie and opened it. Pulling out the slip with her fortune, she read "Someone new will steal your heart." Could someone old be new again?

As they made their way outside onto Mott Street, Lila noticed that Jeff was wearing the soft denim shirt she'd bought him for his birthday three years before. It made his shoulders look rugged. The gesture touched her. The shirt was a nice metaphor, she thought, crafting a poem in her head, about how he'd "put on the light blue shirt I bought you before I left you, wearing our past as if it could protect you." But then she heard Daniel cutting out her rhymes. He hated rhymes. He would edit it so it read: "the light blue shirt I bought before I left, as if our past could protect you." She wondered what listening to Daniel's voice in her head was protecting her from.

16
July 1982
DANIEL

Daniel had not written a word in forty-three days. He had spent the last six weeks as a dumb tourist, attempting to hike up Masada, inspecting ancient ruins in Safed, the highest city in Israel, getting a backache and sunburn despite wearing his New York Mets baseball cap and overpriced sunscreen. Floating in the Dead Sea, he felt dead himself, cold and lifeless. He hated to admit how much he had relied on Lila's manic energy and constant encouragement. He feared their breakup had ruined him, destroyed his chance for passion in love and work.

But now, back in Jerusalem near his campus apartment, he sat down at his favorite outdoor café. He opened his notebook and took out the silver Cross pen Lila had given him and five heartfelt stanzas poured out. It was a sweet direct address he titled *To My Ambitious Young Woman*, written to her in present tense, as if she were here:"It's true, I can see the joy of your passion,/blossoming with such brilliance/I become more student than teacher," he read. He pictured Lila all dressed up at the magazine, sure she had already met an older male writer more successful and virile than he was. He changed "*My*" to "*An*" *Ambitious Young Woman*; she wasn't his anymore. It was humiliating to think that she had never really been his, not even once.

The short brunette waitress, reading in her usual corner, looked up at him oddly. He must have recited the lines out loud without realizing it.

Daniel read his page over again silently, seeing that it was the apology he owed Lila that he had not been able to send. His anger was gone, his emotional tone was honest, but his rhythm was off. He didn't know how to fix it. He ached to call Lila, to get her eyes on it, so she could help him figure out what was wrong with his goodbye poem to her. As if he could leave her in his notebook, finish her off with the right stanza to get back his power. He envisioned turning her into a poem the way God had turned Lot's wife into a pillar of salt.

"Just what my country needs—another suffering Jew," the pixie-haired waitress commented as she refilled his coffee. She smiled as he noticed the paperback now stuffed in her apron. Probably a Hebrew potboiler.

"It's that obvious I'm suffering?" he asked, going back to work. His next stanza was authentic but also inadequate. There were extraneous syllables, yet something essential was off. He was distracted by the shadow on the edge of his paper.

"In the most beautiful land in the world, you're always stuck inside your own head," she said, this time bringing him a bread basket and a glass of water.

Was that a question or a commentary? She spoke English well, with only the hint of an Israeli accent; she had obviously spent time in the States.

"Ready to order food? Shakshuka? Tabouli? Eggs? American-style, all scrambled up? You're from New York? I can get you a bagel and shmear."

How did she know where he was from? Oh, the Mets hat. "No, thank you."

It was probably rude that he'd once again parked himself at her table for several hours. Today all he'd done was stare at his soliloquy to his ex-girlfriend, ignoring the other chattering, chain-smoking customers, not ordering anything but coffee. From where he was sitting on the patio, he had a glorious panoramic view, from the desert to the sweeping slopes of Mount Zion. But even surrounded by the spicy smells of exotic food everyone around him was eating fervently, he wasn't the least bit hungry. He had lost his appetite when he'd lost Lila.

Daniel knew she'd truly cared for him, in her youthful, hyper, ravenous way. But she wanted the wrong things: to wear hip black clothes to Manhattan book parties and hobnob with the literati at her highbrow magazine rather than seriously buckle down and focus on the work, which was all that mattered. Or was it just Daniel that she couldn't focus on? He still couldn't believe she would rather be a typist at a New York office than a poet exploring this ancient land by his side.

"Do you need anything else?" the waitress asked.

"No, I'm good." He'd leave her a big tip this time. He planned to come back. Taking in the jagged ridge of mountains, he breathed in the fresh air, known for tasting "as pure as wine." He felt calmer here, near the old city. How unhappy, nervous and claustrophobic he felt in *his* old city. In an interview, Philip Roth had extolled the virtues of his solitary home in Connecticut. After his divorce, Roth had sworn off women, saying literature was his only mistress. Maybe for true artists, it was too hard to combine work and love. Nonsense, Dr. Zalman had told Daniel, warning that in real life Roth was a misogynist who'd left his marriage, was too selfish for children and was a lousy role model to pick. Perhaps so, but Daniel wished for a sliver of his acclaim.

He missed Zalman, who wouldn't commit to weekly long-distance phone sessions, claiming he was taking the whole summer off. Daniel worried he was ill. In a decade of treatment, Daniel never knew him to go on vacation for more than a week, even in August.

"Picking someone unavailable is How to Stay Single 101," his psychoanalyst had concluded at their final emergency double session that Friday afternoon, right after Lila had left him. Zalman insisted she was too young and that the unconditional love Daniel strived for did not exist; it was a mother fantasy Daniel needed to get over. He reiterated that an adoring protégée right out of school was not marriage material, suggesting Daniel find a mate in another field —architecture, law, design, nursing—anything. "A relationship needs one flower and one gardener," Zalman opined. "You and Lila are both hothouse orchids. Delicate, sensitive, swayed by the wrong wind. Too easily misguided."

"How so?" Daniel asked.

"You're both hellbent to get acclaim, as if that ever fills in the holes of *anyone's* heart."

"But isn't art a worthy quest?" Daniel had asked.

"You yourself wrote that it won't buy redemption. You are worthy of love even if you achieve no career distinction," Zalman had told him. "Two needy, immature narcissistic poets who lost parents in childhood cannot take care of each other."

"I offered to take care of her," Daniel argued. "I asked her to marry me!"

"You proposed last minute, in terror, like an arrogant, wounded man with no ears."

Daniel continued the argument with Zalman in his head, listing successful couples who shared both an artistic and a passionate connection: Elizabeth Barrett and Robert Browning. Donald Hall and Jane Kenyon. Sylvia Plath and Ted Hughes. Okay, not a good example. Now he was taking over Lila's adolescent Plath fetish.

He read over his new poem, wondering if it really was a breakthrough or just the manic high he always felt the rare times he completed something new. He needed to show it to someone but most of his fellow professors wouldn't be back until classes started in September.

He remembered calling Lila in the middle of the night, saying "I'm having trouble with a stanza." She'd rushed to his place, as if he had yelled, "Emergency. I need a blood transfusion." She'd anxiously comb over his every word and comma, making it her priority to fix his lines and ponder every dot of punctuation. Her notes soon became better than those of his older critics. Did he miss Lila more as an editor or a girlfriend?

"Going to finish your whole book before you pay me?" the waitress asked, smiling.

"It's just a poem," he said.

She touched his open notebook. "May I?"

"No, it's too rough."

"You'll publish for the world but won't show me?" she asked in a teasing lilt.

"How do you know my poems have seen print?" he wanted to know. And what would an Israeli food server make of an American man's poem of heartbreak and yearning anyway?

She held his gaze with her serious brown eyes, finger on the margin. "Haven't they?"

"Yes. I'll actually be teaching poetry at Hebrew University. That's why I'm here."

"So let me see if you're any good." She smirked.

He relented, deciding to play along. What did he have to lose? She sat down at his table. He watched as she read his twenty lines, her bangs falling in her eyes, looking rapt. She was small, maybe five inches shorter than Lila, petite and compact. Darker, with clipped chestnut brown short hair. Her bare arms were muscular. He'd noticed her before. She was not his type. The tall, soft Lila, all long flowing legs and light tresses—a Jewish shiksa Goddess—was more his style. But look where that had led him.

"Do you want criticism?" she asked.

He was taken aback by her presumptuousness, but said, "Sure."

"Pen?" she demanded.

He was amused. Intrigued. Was she a literature student? Bilingual translator? Editor?

Before he could hand it over, she took the silver Cross from his hand. She surprised him by making loopy circles and arrows, switching stanzas around with Lila's pen. What was she doing? When she was finished, he glanced at his page.

"There," she said.

Who was this foreign waitress to mark up his work? He grabbed back his page and studied her edits, annoyed. She'd switched the whole poem to past tense. That wrecked his conceit that the relationship was still happening, currently unfolding. Okay, maybe that was better, since it actually had already taken place and was finished now. Yes, that was more honest. She'd removed gaps in his rhythm to make it more melodic. She changed "I *can see* the joy of *your* passion" to "I *feared* the joy of *her* passion." *Fear* was a more surprising verb, stronger, he had to give her that. He looked at the waitress. Her oval-shaped brown eyes stared back. She had the longest lashes. They were quite lovely. Unlike Lila, she seemed astoundingly sure of herself, not at all insecure or neurotic.

Daniel flashed to a literary argument he'd had with Lila, when he'd argued that her work should be more gritty and literal-minded. He was trying to steer her away from emulating the vague surrealism of Baudelaire and Rimbaud. She disagreed and offered her theory that crafting poetry was the opposite of the TV quiz show, *The Match Game*. Instead of picking the most obvious and grounded word that came to mind, a poet should fill in the blank with the least likely. So if the question was, every morning John puts *blank* on his cereal, instead of "milk" or "bananas," the poet would say, "tears" or "sadness."

It was going to take a little more time to get Lila out of his head.

The waitress watched for his reaction. He read it over one more time. Her most significant amendment was to exchange "your" in the first line for "her," taking out the name "Lila." She'd deleted his direct address, using a pronoun instead. That gave the poem distance and perspective. If his theory that every poem was a letter was correct, perhaps it was too difficult and too soon to speak to Lila directly.

"It's true, I feared the joy of her passion," he read aloud the words the waitress had corrected aloud. He liked the past tense but not the third person. It seemed too distant.

"So? What do you think?" he asked the waitress, suddenly nervous for her assessment.

"Clever, though a bit sentimental for my taste." She stood up.

What was she talking about? He was an anti-sentimental realist. "You don't like it?"

"Linguistically sophisticated. But I find the content typically male and sexist."

Oh no, another one. Dr. Zalman said the smartest single women were feminists these days; it was unavoidable. "How could a goodbye poem be sexist?"

"In your mind, the man is naturally ambitious and gets love at the same time as he works. The woman's ambition is a deformity, like an extra finger," she said curtly, which made him laugh and like her. "But better now," she added, admiring her own handiwork.

"Ah, you're a poet too," he said. Now he understood. No wonder she'd been staring at him so intently all morning. He wondered if the book she'd been reading was poetry. At first she'd looked like a grad student. But staring at her face close up, he noticed crow's feet around her pretty eyes and lines on her forehead. Was she his age or younger? She was natural, no makeup, he liked that. New York women tried too hard. Lila wore high heels she couldn't walk in, too much perfume and paint, all that camouflage hiding her beauty. Funny that he might have stumbled into a sharp female critic to replace Lila while he was writing about her.

"Did you study poetry here?" he asked. "Or in the States?"

"I am no poet. I'm a waitress with a cheap American at my table who had two coffees in four hours," she said. She handed him the check, winking before she walked away.

Typical. Now that she'd hooked him, she was leaving. Daniel packed up his notebook, followed her to the cash register. "Really, tell me where you studied." He dug into his pockets but to his horror he noticed that he'd run out of shekels. "Can I pay with a Traveler's Check?"

"A big university professor doesn't have a dollar?" She looked at him skeptically.

He took out a check and signed the back. "I just moved into my apartment near the Jerusalem campus. I don't have a bank account yet. I can explain it to the manager."

"I am the manager," she informed him.

"You're a manager doubling as a waitress who just happens to be the female Maxwell Perkins?"

"I don't write or edit, I cook. And I own this place," she said. "If you want me to cash a twenty dollar check for your one dollar coffee, I'll need to see I.D."

As if he would rip her off for a few cups of joe.

"Unless your poem is your identification?" she asked.

She was clearly a poet, definitely toying with him. He hoped it was her way of flirting.

He pulled out his driver's license. "Not my most handsome picture." For a wordsmith, he sure was rusty with a come-on. Wait, was he coming onto her?

"Not too bad," she commented, reaching in the register and handing him change.

"Don't I get to see your work?" He tried again.

"This is my work," she snapped.

Daniel wondered if she was lying. Or being coy. Unless she was an editor? "Well, thank you for your help." He tipped her five dollars. "Can I see you again?"

"Maybe you'll come back to eat sometime. Since it is a restaurant," she said. "You've been here six times and ordered no food."

Ah, she'd noticed him here before. And counted.

"A shame since I am an excellent cook," she added.

He thought of how Lila had refused to prepare food for a man as the waitress took off her apron and hung it up, running her fingers through her dark hair. She was sturdy, her khaki shorts accenting her athletic thighs, her green halter top showing off sun-streaked shoulders and sculpted arms. Had she been a soldier? He would certainly want someone like her defending his country. He did not want her to leave.

"I won the Dorman Fellowship this year. That's why I'm here," he threw out. Oh God, how lame. That was the best he could come up with? He should bring her the extra copy of *Beyond Despair* in his suitcase. She was literary, she would be impressed with the back cover blurbs praising him as America's darkest and most exciting young poetic voice. But that was ten years ago. "A friend recommended my work to the editor of *Urban Review*," he said, catching how pathetic that sounded before he'd even finished the sentence.

"Who? The ambitious girl who hurt you?" she guessed.

He felt embarrassed that he'd already let the waitress know so much about his breakup with Lila, sacrilegious somehow. "Do you get the magazine here?" He changed the subject.

"Of course," she said. "We have a subscription."

The "we" was confusing. She wasn't wearing a ring. "Thank you again for those smart comments you made on my poem. We didn't officially meet," he said, holding out his hand. "I'm Daniel Wildman."

"I know, I saw your I.D."

"Do you have a name?" He knew Sabras were tough cookies but this one seemed impenetrable.

"Ronit Halev." She had a firm shake for someone with such a diminutive hand. He sensed she could beat him at arm wrestling.

Ronit—what a nice sound the two syllables had. He made a note to check what it translated to. "There's a brilliant poet with your last name, Ari Halev."

"You have good taste," she nodded.

"You've heard of him?" Daniel asked.

"Only because he's my brother," she said.

Ari Halev was her brother! Daniel laughed, recalling how he'd introduced Lila to all of Halev's work, reading his whole first collection to her aloud while they laid together on his green couch, her head resting on his shoulder.

Well, of course the waitress subscribed to *Urban Review*. Ari Halev's poems often appeared there. In May, in honor of Israel's thirty-fifth anniversary, the editors had run six consecutive pages, a controversial leftwing masterpiece called *Catastrophe Day*, the name the Palestinians had given the commemoration, about Israelis stealing Arab land. Daniel heard the magazine had paid Ari two dollars a word. He tried to add up how much money Ari made from that. Imagine getting rich from poetry. And with an unabashed political screed, at that.

"Out of all the gin joints in all the towns in all the world," he said, assuming she'd have no idea what he was talking about.

She inched closer to him and whispered, "And you walk into mine."

"It's my favorite movie," he said, still stunned at how excellent an editor she was. How amazing, that he could have the same eyes on his poems as Ari Halev had. It was a blessing, or a sign. "Can I meet him? Maybe he would sign his book. I brought two with me." Daniel felt like a starstruck teenager begging for an autograph from his rock star idol. She ignored his request and walked outside. Damn, he'd blown it by being too excited about her brother. But he couldn't help it.

"Wait," he followed her, desperate to explain. "You're really his sister? What a coincidence! He's my favorite living poet."

"He is the greatest living poet," she said.

"I could use some scrambled eggs if the offer is still good."

"One of the other girls can get it for you." She turned away from him, about to leave.

Emboldened by their *Casablanca* moment, he didn't want to give up. "Well, maybe we could have a cup of coffee together sometime?" he tried meekly.

"Haven't you had enough coffee for one trip?" she turned back to say.

"What's your hurry?" he asked.

"I have a date."

"Can I write down my name and number for you? Here." He reached into his briefcase, scrawled his new number on one of his old New York cards. But she wouldn't take it.

"We'll remember," she said, opening the fence and walking away.

We, as in Ronit Halev and the boyfriend she was going to meet? This short-haired spitfire and her famous brother Ari? Or the proverbial we? Daniel was dying to know which.

17
September 1982
LILA

"Early again. Don't you have a life?" Elaine asked as Lila walked into the editorial library on Friday.

"This *is* my life," Lila said, sitting down at her bright blue IBM Selectric typewriter amid the cluster of worn wooden desks in the center. She pulled out her can of Tab, opened it, and picked at her raisin bagel, not really hungry. Her boss Elaine –who also showed up before everyone else—was 68, with brown beauty-parlor hair, mauve lipstick and huge round glasses. She was wearing her usual staid librarian outfit: below-the-knee, pleated gray wool skirt and beige silk blouse with a bow buttoned to the neck.

Lila remembered how nervous she'd been for her first interview here that Friday afternoon in June, all dressed up in the conservative blue suit her mother had sent. To make it less formal, Lila had ripped out the shoulder pads and worn a bra-less camisole underneath but kept the blazer buttoned over it. She'd felt so sophisticated and daring.

"I want to be a writer," she'd confided to Elaine.

"Pretend you don't and you can start Monday," Elaine had said.

Excited out of her mind, Lila'd hopped a cab right to Daniel's place, to tell him the best news of her life. That was three months ago. The last time they'd spoken.

Now Lila looked around the hoary room, filled with dilapidated furniture that hadn't been replaced in half a century. Thousands of oversized scrapbooks were filed alphabetically in the floor-to-ceiling shelves. On her left was a poster of a unicorn on a unicycle under the words *Keep Trying* and an open box of Graham Crackers on top of the radiator. A morbid section of files and books towards the back was labeled *Dead Contributors*. It was the dingiest office Lila had ever seen. It suited her mood; she could hide here forever.

"So when do we get to see your dashing blond beau?" Elaine asked—again.

"He's just a friend," Lila reiterated. "He's finishing law school in Wisconsin."

"Law is a good field," Elaine said.

She'd been asking about Jeff ever since Lila made the mistake of letting him pick her up from work when he was in town. Since then Elaine kept saying how handsome he was. Though they'd slept together that week at the end of June and spoke on the phone often, Lila didn't know what she wanted from Jeff—except for him to turn into Daniel when he got out of bed.

As Elaine walked by, she shook her head at Lila's black jeans, black T-shirt and the black cowboy boots she'd found on sale at 8th Street Shoe Hop. "And I thought you were going to be my fashion plate," she said, shaking her head. "Well, open the window so we can smoke before Miss Priss comes."

Elaine lit a Pall Mall as Lila smoked a More Menthol. When the phone rang, Elaine picked it up. "Yes, James Thurber's first piece ran February 26, 1927," she recited off the top of her head.

"Did you ever meet Thurber?" Lila asked when she got off the phone.

Elaine nodded. "He used to call me and say, 'It's the blind old man of the mountain.'"

"Was he really a womanizer?" Lila asked, quizzing her for literary gossip. Lila loved how Elaine knew where all the ghosts were—and wasn't afraid to tell.

"The only one I ever saw him with was his mother," Elaine said. "She was this dear, elderly Midwestern lady who wanted to see her son's scrapbooks. I took them out. 'Do you mean to say you wrote all of this yourself, Jamie?' she asked him."

Lila had told her own mother that when she entered the magazine office, she felt like she'd walked into the Katherine Hepburn movie *Desk Set* that they'd watched together on TV. She'd called her mom long-distance for free, whispering when she'd caught a glimpse of Jackie O stubbing out her cigarette as she left the building yesterday. And Monday Charles Addams had showed up in the library—in a three piece suit—asking for the original of his first 1932 cover.

"Talk about a Romeo," Elaine had whispered to Lila. "He just married his third wife—in a pet cemetery." Lila called to tell her brother, who was impressed she'd met the man whose cartoons inspired *The Addam's Family*.

Since her "editorial research assistant" position paid only $13,000 a year, Lila took on typing, editing and transcription work for some of the magazine staff that she labored over until late every night, earning the extra money to pay her bills and $400 a month rent. She wasn't up for social life—or even her own writing anyway. It was worth scrimping to feel like part of this family of artistic misfits hiding in a haven where depression and oddness were not only allowed but celebrated.

"Subway problems," mumbled her preppy coworker Katrina as she slunk in, ten minutes late. She was tall and skinny with a blond bob, in beige khakis and a striped sweater.

Elaine divided up the page proofs for the "front of the book" section in the upcoming issue, as well as the long pieces they had to read and type up summaries of on little file cards.

"Anything interesting next week?" asked Katrina, who had a BA from Yale, an MFA in British fiction from Columbia and spoke three languages. At lunch, she'd eat ham sandwiches and type stories about an affair with a Spaniard she'd had during her junior year abroad in Madrid that Lila had read on the sly.

"Here's another tedious sixty-two page treatise on the staples of life."
Elaine handed Katrina the stack of pages, rolling her eyes. "This one is on
wheat."

Sipping Tab through her straw, Lila turned to the table of contents to see
who wrote next week's poems—the section she'd claimed the first day. She
couldn't write verse these days—the disaster with Daniel had dried up all
the poetry in her heart. When he'd abandoned her three months ago, she'd
felt scared and dead, a soulless corpse, the blood in her veins turning to ash.
But she still relished reading, analyzing and even indexing other people's poems, comforted by the proximity to her old passion, pretending not to be
distressed by her inability to make art anymore herself.

Past the nonfiction articles and short stories, this week's poems were listed. The first one was Richard Wilbur's "Pasture," the poet's name italicized.
Underneath Wilbur, in small type, was Daniel Wildman. Her Daniel? Lila
choked on her soda, spray fizzing up her nose. Next to it was the title "To An
Ambitious Young Woman." Was she the young woman? Her fingers quivered
as she quickly turned to page 55. Seeing his poem splayed out there made
her dizzy. Her heart was thumping. She read: "It is true, we cannot keep the
brilliance of this moment/that burns both of our flesh like sunlight…"

What was true? Which moment? Whose flesh? The ambitious young
woman was her! She'd been immortalized. Though sunlight burning seemed
obvious, what else would it do? But—more important—he wasn't over their
relationship either. Tears blurred her vision. She scanned the poem quickly,
searching for his meaning. She skated over lots of verbs: dreaming, laughing,
cajoling, desiring, knowing the body's grammar. For a gritty realist, these
lines were pretty ornate and cryptic, like he was trying to imitate Yeats' The
Second Coming. Still, he was speaking directly to her. He still loved her. Nobody had ever written her a poem before.

Lila grabbed a Kleenex, blew her nose, then rushed over to show it to
Elaine. "Read this and tell me what you think."

Her boss read. Grasping the importance, she read it again. "It's by
your older gent?" Elaine asked. Lila nodded. "Well, clearly he still has you

in his heart."

"Right?" Lila said. "That's what I thought."

"Who? Your old teacher?" Katrina asked and stood up to read the page proof over Elaine's shoulder. "Actually, it's reminiscing about the end of a relationship," she said in her annoying chirp. "Kind of purple. Reads like a goodbye letter."

"It does not! You only like fiction by prissy biddies named Elizabeth and Margaret. What do you know from American poetry?" Lila flared up, grabbing the page back. She reread the stanzas to see what Katrina saw. She thoroughly disagreed, though going over it a third time, Lila did have the urge to cut the floral line "think of how our flesh has been sweetened." It seemed cliché—and sugarcoated. Too much fleshiness for her taste, given their lack. But Daniel was no longer asking her to edit. He didn't need her help now. He was making a bold statement on his own. She just wasn't sure exactly what it was he was stating.

Lila read it over and over that day, holding it in front of her nose as she speed-walked the forty blocks home, going against the traffic light and almost crashing into a taxi. Running in the door, she showed Sari to get her take. ("Ambiguous" was her verdict.) Lila called to read it to her mother ("charming but misguided,") her brother Mark ("seems a little phony-baloney, if ya know what I mean"), her classmate Tarik ("muddled, neo-modern romanticism") and her enemy Judith (who thrilled Lila by saying she was jealous that Lila had inspired such a "masterly farewell creation.") So she agreed with Kartina. Even if his intent was vaguely regretful, Lila voted in Elaine's camp: He still clearly had Lila in his heart.

She picked at the shrimp mu shu Sari had ordered, trying to answer him. She used the silver Cross pen Daniel have given her to craft a poem that corresponded, syllable by syllable, to his. "It is a shame we cannot meet for coffee" she scrawled. Unlike him, she tried to tone it down, understate, be anti-romantic, like he'd taught her. Lila hadn't written a word in more than three months but suddenly she spent eight hours on twenty lines. Afterwards she crashed, exhausted, at 4 a.m. She woke up with the page next to her on the pillow.

"You're sleeping with the magazine now?" Sari asked Saturday morning, sparking a cig.

"What?" Lila asked, embarrassed she'd drooled on it. Luckily only the cartoon got wet. She realized she was sleeping with his poem instead of Daniel.

"Jeff called," Sari said, adding, "He's a good guy who wants you. And he can get it up for you. And he's in *this* country."

"We were just having fun before he went back to school," Lila explained for the hundredth time. "We're friends."

"You don't kick me out of the bedroom three nights in a row for your other friends," Sari taunted.

After two years without sex, it had been such a relief to be in bed with Jeff again. He felt so warm and easy. Lila had been trying to will herself back in love with him, to stop talking to Daniel in her head every day. But seeing her professor's poem in the magazine and trying to decode the meaning woke up her senses and sent her brain soaring. Lila reread her scrawled lines back to him, slowly and then more quickly, smoking a cigarette. "Not good enough!" she said aloud, finishing her soda, cracking open a second and stubbing out her smoke only to light another. She couldn't go to Israel to get Daniel back, or marry him, or live with anyone yet. She wasn't ready. She could barely take care of herself.

Her mother had once confided, "The Goodman women are witches," which Lila secretly believed. So she summoned up all her power to make a wish that Daniel would return to New York, where he belonged, so she could see him again. They needed to unravel what happened and mend their horrible miscommunication. She missed him, couldn't even read an impressive paragraph in a book without wondering what he would think.

"Don't let one poem throw you back into your Daniel depression," Sari said, sitting on the edge of Lila's futon.

"I'm not depressed anymore. But it's not just a poem. It's a message to me," Lila said. "I'm working on my response."

"Is that a good idea?" Sari looked worried.

"You don't understand! There's no choice."

"You want to show it to me?" Sari asked.

"Not yet. It's too rough."

"Well come on, let's get out of here. I have to feed my parents' cat while they're away," Sari said. "Will you come uptown with me or do you turn into a pumpkin above 14th Street?"

After they put out kitty food and litter, Sari insisted they stroll around the Central Park loop on Saturday morning Lila chain-smoked. The early copy of the magazine was under her arm, the page of her response tucked inside so her print was touching his.

"Come on, you have to admit this is a sign he feels the same way I do," Lila said. "Think about it. Daniel recommends me for my job. This is the fastest poem he ever finished, the only one of his they've published, and it's about me. At my interview I told Wentworth how great a poet Daniel was, he buys Daniel's submission and they wind up running it right away—which they never do. They once held a poem of Mark Strand's for fourteen years."

"No wonder so many poets kill themselves," Sari said.

"Yeah, they pay on acceptance, so they own it," Lila explained. She French-inhaled, blowing smoke rings the way Sari had shown her.

"That's pathetic." Sari puffed out competitive curlicues.

"Disgusting habit," hissed a jogger in an all-white sweat suit whizzing past them.

"Come on." Sari led Lila off the track to a hidden patch of grass, where they sat down.

"Listen, if you read Daniel's poem…" Lila said.

"I've read it!" Sari yelled. " Everyone you ever met in your whole life has now read it. We get it—the ambitious woman is you. But no matter how many interpretations you try, he's still not saying 'I'm sorry for proposing then psycho-ing out and leaving the country in a huff and I want you back.' He reiterated his take on why your relationship ended."

"But what about the third stanza where he says, 'Remember when I protested the difference in our age/And you argued that time does not make a man less fearful.'"

"Fearful. As in being so filled with fear he was immobilized," Sari countered.

"But what about the next stanza?" Lila recited it from memory: "'I feared the joy of your passion/which blossomed with such invention I was more admirer than teacher.'"

"Not *husband* or *lover*, but *admirer*. As in, from afar." Sari sighed, pulled out half a leftover joint from her cigarette pack and lit it. "Then he throws in his stupid theory that you chose ambition over him, as if he was your only shot for romance, and your job was this horrible two-headed monster you loved more than him. As in the decision was already made, it's over, done deal. Dead."

"But then he ends, 'Now you make a choice between love and ambition/ as if the heart was a prism in which each pleasure must be fractured.' That could be interpreted as saying the heart is NOT a prism and each pleasure does NOT have to be fractured," Lila argued. "Meaning that it can all cohere in the future."

"You just finished a twenty thousand dollar degree to spend the summer over-analyzing a few stanzas by a guy you never even slept with." Sari hit the joint twice, as if dealing with Lila's stubborn love-sickness required a double dose.

"That was my fault for getting stoned and acting like an idiot," Lila admitted. When Sari handed her the pot, Lila shook her head no. Daniel was right. She didn't need artificial highs getting in the way of her art. "Why would he craft a beautiful poem about me and get it printed at the magazine where I work if he wasn't sending me a message?"

"Because it's a top place to get published. This is about *his* ambition. Nothing to do with you. His title should be *From an Ambitious Old Coot*."

Lila stuck out her tongue. Daniel had never seemed old to her, until Jeff visited New York. Then, comparing them, she recalled the gray in Daniel's hair and the lines on his forehead. Even his lips were thinner and drier than Jeff's. "He always says 'Every poem is a letter.'" Lila couldn't let it go; the idea of being Daniel's muse was too romantic. "So he penned me a very public love letter. That proves he still cares and wants to be with me."

"A big, show-offy egomaniacal GOODBYE letter," Sari insisted. "To prove that his poetry dick is bigger than the real one and he can get into a prestigious magazine even though he couldn't get into your pants."

"Intriguing metaphor," Lila said, though she still found Sari's take on everything too overtly sexual. She felt justified learning that Daniel hadn't been able to erase her either; their love was still real and complicated and percolating in his blood.

"He should have blamed his sexism, not your ambition," Sari added.

"I'm almost done with my response."

After months of mourning him, and typing other people's work at the magazine, it felt so intense and exciting to finally see her own words resurfacing. She was hurt and enraged that he'd never responded to her messages or the letters she'd sent in June. She wouldn't call or write Daniel again. She refused to be pathetic and keep chasing him so he could keep rejecting her. Instead she would wait until she finished her poem and submit it for publication. Seeing it in print would be the way to deliver her lyrical missive, the way he'd sent his. Lila felt like he'd challenged her to a duel. But her poem wasn't in good enough shape to win. She needed his help. If only she could show it to him now, get his fingers on it, imagining the marks his pen would make to fix her words and make them more melodious.

"I'm calling it *From An Ambitious Young Woman*," she said.

"Original," Sari sneered.

"When I'm done, I could send it to Wentworth. What if my response to Daniel's poem is my first publication? That would be so symbolic –we'd be recreating each other in our poetry. A literary homage, à la Ted and Sylvia."

"After she wound up with her head in the oven, he deleted every negative word she wrote about him," Sari said. "And his second wife wound up with her head in the oven too."

"Yeah," Lila conceded. "But Assia was a copycat suicide cause she was jealous of Sylvia's poetry and all the awards *Ariel* won."

"I see your Daniel obsession hasn't put a damper on your Plath mania," Sari said.

"At least I haven't given up writing to work at Planned Parenthood," Lila said.

"I hate the whole bullshit, competitive publishing scene," Sari told her. "I want a normal life. I need to make a difference in the world."

It slaughtered Lila's heart to even consider Sari living without literature. It felt like she was leaving Lila as well. She refused to believe all her friend's ramblings about social work and normalcy. Who in New York would really rather be normal when you could be published?

"You want to hear the latest stanza of my rebuttal or not?" Lila asked, taking her draft out of the magazine where she'd tucked it for safety, unfolding it.

"Go for it," Sari said, crushing out the joint.

"Now I revise my résumé nightly as if achievement/were redemption and redemption/the one-bedroom in this neighborhood/I still can't afford."

"The real estate of love," Sari commented.

Lila nodded, folded the page back and carefully put it in her pocket. She felt calmer keeping it close, as if the page were her prayer and potion for Daniel's return, her best revenge, her medicine.

18

September 1982

DANIEL

"Well, what a nice coincidence, running into you again," Daniel told her.

"Yes, it must be fate, to find you back at my restaurant," Ronit said with a teasing lilt.

Never mind that he had walked by her Jerusalem café daily over the last two weeks looking for her, a copy of *New Urban Magazine* under his arm every time. He hoped her subscription had arrived and she had seen it on her own. Had she gone away with that lover she'd mentioned last time?

If he asked where she'd been for the last fourteen days, Ronit would know their meeting this Thursday evening was not accidental. Since it was raining, he came inside. She seemed happy to see him, smiling, offering him a center booth by the brick wall.

"*New Urban Magazine* published the poem you helped me with," he blurted out.

"Mazel tov," she said, nodding.

"Want to have a drink to celebrate?"

"I shouldn't drink," she said. "I'm working the late shift tonight."

"OJ?" he asked. "To toast my breakout."

"Sounds like you've been in prison," she said, untying her little white apron and walking towards the bar. She brought over two fresh orange juices, then sat down across from him. He imagined she'd squeezed the fruit herself, which meant she was impressed with his newfound success. Didn't it?

Imprisoned was not a bad metaphor for how he had felt, toiling away in solitude for more than a decade, gathering insults in New York, terse rejection letters filling his desk drawers. Then Lila, his only solace for the last two years, had rejected him too. But now here he was, with a prestigious foreign fellowship and a poem in the best publication in the world, restoring his dignity. And, he hoped, a new, special woman to start over with.

"Maybe you'll help me escape," he told Ronit, lifting his glass of pulpy juice. He left the page of the magazine open on the table between them. But she didn't pick it up.

"A serious poet can't do better than that?" she asked, clinking her glass against his.

Man, she was a tough audience. He stared at her. She looked lovely in her magenta blouse. Unlike Lila's morbidly black clothes, Ronit liked bright colors. Her tight top showed off her pert breasts. He imagined she'd worn the fiery fabric just for him. But then he realized she was not expecting Daniel to show up here tonight. So it was probably for the guy she was dating.

"Really, your editing was brilliant," he insisted. "It wouldn't have happened without your eyes." He was dying to know if she had already seen it or not.

"My eyes fixing the poem about your young girlfriend," Ronit reminded him.

"My ex-girlfriend," he clarified as she finally took the page to read.

He worried it was tacky and impolite to ask Ronit to celebrate the acclaim he was receiving for a goodbye poem to Lila. Some nights his failure with her haunted him like tinnitus, a hectoring noise his inner ear could not escape. He would lay awake and argue with her in his head, trying to explain how misguided her desperation for independence was. A low-level job at a magazine was not God or love or enough to wrap a life around. But other days Lila's youthful, ludicrously idealistic energy continued to inspire him, filling him with the confidence he'd lacked since he lost his mother.

All week he kept picturing Lila at work, opening the magazine, noticing his name and then reading the twenty lines he wrote to her. He knew she would be touched and impressed. He imagined her crying when she came to the cathartic, poignant ending and realized it was completely over between them. He still felt wounded that she didn't want to be his lover or his traveling companion or his wife. It stung every time he thought about their last night together. But at least he could control his words better than his pathetic feelings, fashioning his phrases and clauses into a coherent creation that gave him back power.

He hoped he wasn't trying to avenge her rejection, or worse, use his talent to win her back. For a second he pictured her rushing onto a midtown street, magazine tucked under her arm, hailing a taxi. She'd rush to board an El Al plane to find him here, taking him to bed, ripping off his clothes to finish what they'd started, begging him to let her stay.

But no, that would never happen. That was the problem. Lila worshipped at the false altar of Manhattan, her size ten feet stuck on New York cement. Her love for him was regional and conditional, only strong when he offered her a free twenty-four hour mentoring, reading and editing service in the Village. Daniel and Lila were finished. Though he was confused why speaking so intimately to her on the page had made his voice more lucid and lyrical.

"Better than the first draft," Ronit decreed at last.

"So you like it?"

She paused. "My brother said you might be the real deal," she finally offered.

Aha! So she had not only read it, she was impressed enough to show her brother. Daniel smiled, allowing himself to fantasize that Ronit had indeed known he was coming tonight and chose her shirt's sexy color, like a matador's cape, just for him.

"He really said those words? 'Real deal?' In English?" he asked. He sipped his juice like expensive Champagne, basking in this rare feeling of success. "Does this mean I get to meet him?" he asked too quickly. "I loved his new poems in *The New Urban* last month." Daniel didn't know which Halev he wanted to get to know more, the lovely woman sitting across from him or her acclaimed older brother.

"Yes, that's from his new book. It comes out next week. Are you free this Sunday?" Ronit asked.

"I'll always be free for you," Daniel said but even to him, his flirting sounded pathetic. Yet this moment felt destined, as if he had come to the Holy Land, without Lila, so that he could find a better voice and bearing, and both Halevs. He envisioned doing a reading with Ari and being accepted by their circle, embraced and welcomed into this new foreign family. Lila had moved to New York to study with Daniel. What if he was starting over as the adoring student of his own literary master? For a second he was afraid he was regressing, becoming an ambitious star struck acolyte, like Lila.

"Let's say Sunday at 5?" Ronit asked.

"Good. Should I meet you here?"

She nodded. Wait, was she expecting a romantic rendezvous? Or did she think he just wanted to meet Ari?

He had accused Lila of choosing ambition over love, of putting a prestigious job connection before him, which he felt was a terrible mistake. Daniel understood the thrill of meeting a literary idol. But he was not going to be a starfucker. He had toiled diligently for twenty years, the work was his compass and key, not a link to fame. Celebrity was superficial, the opposite of what a true poet would choose.

"Let's make it the two of us on Sunday," he declared. "You're the one I want to get to know."

"You aren't ready to meet my brother?" she asked.

He didn't know if he was actually ready for Ari or his sister—let alone the duo. Ronit was older, wiser, stronger. She liked cooking. She wasn't a student or protégée on any level. He told himself to slow down and be patient this time. His rush to travel abroad together and bring up marriage too soon had obviously overwhelmed Lila. Then again, it was probably better to find out now than two years from now that she was not really physically attracted to him, that he'd been in love alone.

When he had told Lila all about his romantic history, she'd called him "a serial monogamist." True, although it took him so long to get over breakups there was always an emotional overlap. Indeed, he often took longer than the relationship itself had lasted to really recuperate from the ending.

"Everything is too important to you," Zalman had once commented. He explained that Daniel found romantic separations so traumatizing because they made him relive his mother's abandonment, which he'd never completely recovered from. That was who Daniel was. The rare times he found love, he always cared too much. He was starting to understand that Lila could not return his passion and his scars would linger. "But you can be ambivalent and make a decision," Zalman taught him. Daniel did not want to waste any more years alone, or stuck in another adolescent courtship with someone who didn't want him.

"I'll be visiting Ari next Friday," Ronit said. "So maybe you'll come with me?"

"Will you introduce me as your friend or your date?" he asked Ronit, proud of himself. No nonsense, no games. Lila's rejection did not have to continue to be crippling. He could let go of her and move onto a woman who was more appropriate, who might be able to really love him.

"Do you care?" Ronit challenged.

"Yes, I do. What about that guy you mentioned?" Daniel asked. "Are you still seeing him?"

"It's a little premature to be possessive," Ronit said. "We've only met twice."

"Dante only met Beatrice twice," he told her.

"So you need another muse, now that the ambitious girl is gone?" she asked.

"That's finished. I'm starting over here," he answered, not backing down. "But you should know my heart is not good at casual."

"Another good line. You seem full of them today," Ronit said.

"Are you calling me full of it?" He laughed, feeling buoyed and taller since the magazine had come out. Imagine getting paid five hundred dollars for one poem, not to mention recasting the disaster with Lila in a better light, erasing his shame.

"For a famous poet you're pretty paranoid," she said.

He loved that she called him famous, catching of course that she was being facetious.

For some reason, he flashed to the night he'd read Lila *Lovesong*, Ted Hughes' immortalization of his legendary breakup. To counter Lila's endless fascination with Plath, he wanted her to study Hughes' masterpiece. But she had been outraged by Daniel's opinion that the male bard possessed the truer talent of that couple. Daniel related to the theme of how a fierce bond between two intense poets could backfire and twist the lovers inside out. He could still hear Lila's voice as they intoned: "Their heads fell apart into sleep like the two halves/Of a lopped melon, but love is hard to stop./In their entwined sleep they exchanged arms and legs/In their dreams their brains took each other hostage/In the morning they wore each other's face." Then they had repeated it all again, reading aloud in unison, like a prayer.

Lila said the best line was "But love is hard to stop." Was that because she thought it was his favorite? Those six words foreshadowed their demise. He wished he could see the look on her face, staring at his poem to her in the magazine. Surely she missed him too.

"Where did you go?" Ronit's voice startled him.

"Nowhere," he said, looking at her clearly. She was smaller, just his size, in flat sandals, so she would not tower over him. He admired her sinewy arms, her chestnut brown eyes staring at him, with no long windy hair or makeup getting in the way. "I'm right here. With you."

19

September 1982

LILA

On her way to Three Lives and Company to look for Ari Halev's new book on Sunday morning (which the Brentano's and Spring Street bookstores annoyingly didn't have yet), Lila saw Professor Fell sitting outside The Village Den. He was eating at a sidewalk table by himself, reading *The New York Times*. She bent her head down, intending to walk down Greenwich Avenue, passing him quickly. She hadn't seen him since her graduation in May. She hoped he wouldn't shun her, feeling like Hester Prynne in *The Scarlet Letter* though, as Sari kept telling her, she wasn't married and hadn't actually had an adulterous—or any kind of—affair with anybody. Still, she was paranoid that Daniel told everybody important what a young, callous bitch she was for choosing the magazine over him, imagining herself as the pariah of the old downtown poet brigade. As she rushed by, Professor Fell put his arm out to stop her.

"Hello, Lila," he said in his low voice, flashing what looked like a genuine smile.

At least he was still speaking to her. Yet it could be a trick to avenge her rejection of his best friend. She was dying to know what he'd heard from Israel.

"Professor Fell," she said, feeling a little self-conscious to be caught in her torn jeans, low-cut black mesh T-shirt and cowboy boots, her Village grunge mode.

"Howard," he insisted.

He always spoke sparingly and paused for so long between each word that she was never sure if he was finished with his thought or planned to continue. When she'd once asked about his book *Lithium Lullaby*, he'd confided that his mother had been on the medication to treat her manic depression when he was a baby. Maybe she'd gravitated toward confessional poets because their tragic pasts made hers feel more normal.

"How are you?"

"Fine," he said in a friendly warm tone.

"Good piece?" She pointed to his open *Book Review*.

"*Times* fawns over Harvard poets named John," he sniffed.

It was the kind of pissed-off, against-the-literary-establishment quip Daniel made. She recalled when they'd come here for brunch, sitting at a booth inside. Daniel had ordered them cheese omelets with bagels instead of toast. He drank coffee and kidded her about how many free refills of diet soda she sucked down. She could hear his loud voice bellow, "Why don't we hook you up to the machine intravenously?" as if he were still here. She wished he was.

Feeling awkward standing there, she said, "I was looking for Ari Halev's latest collection. Nobody has it yet." She didn't know if Professor Fell was as big a fan of Halev's work as Daniel was. Lila bet Daniel would want to get his new book right away. He might even look up Halev while he was in Jerusalem, or go to one of his readings. She was vaguely aware her desperate quest to buy the Israeli poet's new collection today had to do with Daniel, as if reading the same book around the same time meant at least their minds would be touching.

"How are you doing?" he asked.

Lila shrugged. She'd always been a little intimidated by Professor Fell.

He gestured to the empty chair across from him.

"I don't want to interrupt."

He pushed the chair out for her. "Sit."

He spoke like he wrote. Sparse. Haltingly.

"Thanks." She sat down, putting her black purse on the ground.

"Don't like your job?" Professor Fell asked.

"Are you kidding? I love the magazine," she said. "Such an incredible place to work."

"Tell."

He economized so much he couldn't even spare the word "me."

"My office is dingy and ancient, like nobody has redecorated since 1932," she said. "Updike came in last week to request a copy of everything he's published there—short stories, nonfiction, book reviews and poetry. My boss joked that he should try a cartoon so he can hit every genre."

"Another Harvard John. *Ode to Rot?*" He put his finger in his mouth in a gagging gesture.

"I read that poem. Totally sucked!" Lila agreed, laughing. Howard's comments on writers more famous than he was were as sarcastic and bitter as Daniel's. "Like we really need scientific rhyming light verse."

"Lots of crazies in and out of the office?" he asked.

She nodded, wondering if he was gathering a dossier on her to tell Daniel. Lila hoped so. "Yeah, there's this old staff writer who hasn't had anything in the magazine for forty years but nobody fires him. I hear he sleeps in his office." She paused to come up with more dirt, wanting Professor Fell—and Daniel— to think she was an important insider now, and not the broke peon typist she really was. "There's a Payne Whitney ward reserved for the magazine's staffers. Last year four editors got caught buying marijuana from a messenger who put the dime bags in interoffice mail." Then, feeling guilty for spreading malicious gossip, she added, "But everyone's been really nice to me."

"So what's wrong?"

"It's not work. I'm having a rough time."

"With what?"

"With Daniel, actually. Well, you know."

Professor Fell looked at her with a blank expression.

"Haven't you spoken to him lately?" she asked.

He shook his head. "You?"

"Daniel won't speak to me. He returned my letters unopened. You know we split?"

"You were together?"

"Seriously?" Lila looked at him, offended. "You didn't know?"

"Oh, maybe I heard something."

"Not from Daniel?" she said, too fast. How could he not know?

"From Faith." He took a bite of his eggs.

"Aren't you and Daniel close friends?"

"Not so close," he said. "I saw his big poem."

That seemed cagey. Or was it sarcastic? Was Howard jealous that Daniel got the magazine clip and fellowship? Daniel used to say academia was so cut-throat because there was so little to lose.

"Did you like it?" Lila asked. Surely he had to know it was about her.

"Typical Danny," was his verdict.

Hearing his despised nickname made Lila wince. When Cormick had once called him "Danny Boy," Daniel had stormed home, muttering profanities.

"I thought it was beautiful," she said. "Though I'm not exactly unbiased."

Indeed she was still carrying a copy in her purse, along with the response that she had been blocked from finishing. Whenever Lila was stuck she found the ritual of reciting Daniel's poem out loud soothing; maybe it was *her* lithium lullaby.

When the waiter walked by, Professor Fell stopped him and said, "Menu for the lady."

That sounded courtly. She missed being with an older guy. Howard was on the short side, like Daniel, and in his forties too. Yet in his gray khakis, green button down shirt and sneakers, Howard looked slimmer, more muscular. She'd liked his poem *Purple Belt*, about getting over being bullied as a kid in Baltimore by taking karate lessons. "Now I shield myself with tae kwon do,/ reverse-kicking color/ of schizophrenia."

She missed having a sharp critic to dissect poems with. Jeff was fun in bed but he was a law student with no interest in long-distance calls devoted to breaking down syllabic meters or analyzing line breaks. Nor did he care about minutiae from the magazine, which he'd nicknamed "Snobfest Central." In her journal she wrote letters to Daniel about work, her feelings, her poetry. She feared he'd ruined her for non-poets. Howard didn't fall under that category.

"So what happened with Danny?" Howard asked.

"We had a fight, then he just left me—and the country."

"Really?" He squinted. "*He* left *you*?"

"Well, it was confusing. He invited me to Israel. But I'd just taken the job. He thought I wouldn't travel abroad with a man who wasn't my husband, so he sort of proposed. When I didn't accept, we had a fight and he never called back." Lila couldn't call off her tears.

Professor Fell stopped eating his eggs mid-bite to hand her a napkin. "Sorry."

"No goodbye. Next thing I know he's on the other side of the world." She blew her nose. "Professor Fell, I didn't mean to break up with him."

"Howard," he repeated, putting his hand on hers. It was nice, how protective he was being, the same way Daniel used to treat her. Daniel had called his friend mousy, but there was something steely and determined in Howard's eyes Lila had never noticed before. She nervously took her hand back.

"Nothing against the Holy Land, but I was born to be here, at the magazine," she told him. "If I postponed, I could have blown my shot. But I didn't mean to hurt him so much."

He forked more food in his mouth, sipped his coffee, then said, "Don't take it personally."

"What do you mean?"

"Not your fault."

"I didn't handle things very well," she confessed. But she didn't mention their thwarted attempt to sleep together, which Daniel had obviously not shared with his friend. The thought of it still embarrassed her. "I fear I acted kind of weird and immature –even for twenty-one."

"Right." Howard was nodding, like he completely understood.

For every thirty-five words she uttered, Howard coughed up two. Still, his eyes were wide open, enrapt. Hanging out with Howard made her feel closer to Daniel.

"Have you spoken to him? Do you have his new number?" She worried it was tacky to take advantage of this meeting but couldn't help herself.

Howard shook his head no, then handed her the menu.

"Not hungry. But please, keep eating," she said. He took a tiny bite out of the edge of his toast, chewing for a long time. He ate as slowly as he talked. "I haven't had much appetite."

He looked her up and down, taking in her tight top and torn, 28-inch waist Levi's –which were a little loose on her—and said, "You look good."

She wondered if he noticed she'd lost thirteen pounds. Sari thought a hundred and twenty-three was too little for a five foot nine girl with big hands, feet and shoulders. And when Lila was in bed with Jeff, he'd whispered that she needed more meat on her bones.

"Don't worry about Danny," Howard said.

"How can I not? Doesn't it seem crazy that he'd propose and then leave town?"

He removed his wire-rimmed glasses, rubbed his eyes and said, "Not the first time."

"He's done this before?"

"Breakups make him insane." He spread a bit of strawberry jelly on the rest of his whole wheat toast. She recalled Daniel once calling Howard a health food freak.

"Define insane," Lila insisted.

"Since his mother offed herself," Howard said, "he's had this abandonment thing."

"Are you saying he's unstable?"

"He'll be fine," Howard said. "He's always fine." He finished his toast and added, "Then he gets another girlfriend."

"He does? Who? How long does that usually take?"

"Not long."

"Like a year?" Lila asked. "Or six months?"

"Less."

She was outraged at the thought that Daniel could replace her that quickly. Of course, she'd rebounded by leaping back into bed with Jeff. Yet in her book, a few rambunctious nights with your first love only counted as nostalgia. Jeff hadn't even added a number to her list of lovers; it was still technically stuck at one. Lila hated her lack of experience. Daniel, Sari, Jeff, and Mark all boasted double-digits of sex partners. She assumed Howard had enjoyed a whole bunch of romantic rendezvous too.

"Daniel told me he'd never proposed to anyone before. Are you saying he was lying?" she asked aghast, staring into Howard's gray-brown eyes to determine whether or not to believe him. He looked earnest. What motive could Howard possibly have to deceive her? "It's a pattern? Which part? The dating, marriage proposal, freak out, or taking off abruptly?"

"Whole shebang," he said.

What? So Lila was just one in a harem of women that Daniel threw away in his neurotic cycle of obsession? She was shattered to think she hadn't been special. What an idiot she'd been, mourning him for months. (When she hadn't been with Jeff. Or working. Or hanging out with Sari.) Even though they had broken up, she felt extremely hurt all over again. Then angry. Then outraged. Fuck Daniel!

"Who else did he want to marry? Faith? The redheaded actress?" she asked. "He did this before? How many other women?"

"Bunch," Howard confirmed, chewing.

She shook her head. "Professor Fell, you can't really be serious."

"Call me Howard," he said, which made her think of the first line to *Moby Dick*.

All of a sudden Lila felt hungry. She picked up the fork and tasted his eggs. "Too squishy."

He signaled the waiter. "She'll have a cheese omelet. Well done."

How did he know what she wanted?

"With bacon, fries and Diet Coke. Instead of toast, a bagel and cream cheese," she added. "I was worried he'd trash me to all the older, important writers he knows in the city. So everyone would blame me."

"Everyone knows Danny," he said.

"That he goes nuts after breakups?" she asked.

"Overreacts."

Lila envisioned Daniel's blurb on the back of Lithium Lullaby: "Howard Fell's honest, hauntingly harsh voice is hectoring, heartbreaking, thoroughly unforgettable." Thinking about it now, that wasn't exactly unadulterated praise. So there was animosity between them? In a poetry class, "hauntingly harsh" and "hectoring" could be interpreted as passive/aggressive.

When the food came, she poured salt on her eggs and bacon, ketchup on the fries, jellied the bagel and took a big bite. "At least I don't have to worry about him trashing me to the poetry bigwigs at the magazine."

"You met Wentworth?" he asked, looking fascinated, opening his right palm in a gesture that meant "tell me more."

"What an odd, out of time duck he is. Tall. In three-piece suits and bow-ties," Lila obliged. "He doesn't like my poems so far. But he gets back to me right away. It's cool to have the most influential poetry editor in the country taking your calls. You know, I was the one who first told Wentworth about Daniel's work."

"Ah. Interesting. I wonder if you would..."

"Submit your poems for you? Sure, no problem." She felt important and flattered he was asking. Barely out of school, she liked that she could already help her professors get published.

"Danny was lucky to have you," he said.

What a warm, empathetic guy Howard was turning out to be. With confessional poets, you could get right to the heart, no bullshit, no social pretense.

"Listen, I loved Danny to death." She accidentally picked up Howard's moniker. "But truthfully, sometimes he could be draining. If I wore baggy clothes, cut my hair or didn't cook, I was denying my femininity." She forked a chunk of her cheese omelet and a bacon bit onto her bagel and devoured it, feeling relieved and starving. "And we could only go to certain places where he wouldn't see anyone he knew," she continued with her mouth full of food.

"With me too," Howard jumped in.

"Who is he always trying to avoid?"

"Cormick. Other enemies. His past women," Howard listed.

"I do miss his editing though. I got addicted to his poetry critiques," she confessed. "I can't finish my new poem without his slashing my words. He says I had too many."

"I always liked your work," he said.

He did? Lila remembered Daniel said all the professors had read the submissions and voted on the students they wanted to accept. She was extremely flattered to think that Professor Fell must have fought for her too.

"I'll take a look at your poem," he offered.

"You will? Really?" Lila recalled Daniel's joke that Howard was such a good critic, if Daniel were gay he would have married him. "Cool. Thank you." She pulled a page from her briefcase. "What do you think of this one, it's called *From An Ambitious Young Woman.*"

"Rebuttal?" Howard smiled, taking it in his hand.

Rebuttal. That was a good word. "Yes, exactly," Lila said. "Sure you don't mind? You can mark it up." She pulled out the silver Cross pen from her purse.

She watched Howard read the twenty lines. Very slowly. When he starred the first two stanzas, her heart took an excited leap. But then he crossed out a bunch of words and drew an arrow indicating the order of the last two stanzas should be switched.

"Really?" she asked. "But the one bedroom is important. I can't afford a room of one's own. Get it?"

He pointed to the sixth stanza, insisting it end the poem. He crossed out the word "for" in the line "you composed *for* me." Then he intoned his revision aloud:"Ignoring sirens across the street I turn/to your page in bed, where my eyes read again/the last lyrical sonnet/ you composed me."

"Big change of meaning when you take out the word *for*," she said. She somehow felt even more determined to make the poem sing and publish it now, to spite Daniel. "You composed *for* me," she read it her way, arguing for the original.

Howard shook his head and said: "You composed me."

"Daniel says poetry's about what's left out, what's never said." She reread Howard's revision. She had to admit it was much better. When the waiter left the check on the table, Howard picked it up.

"On me." He took a twenty from his pocket.

That was so sweet of him. Almost like they were on a date.

"Thank you. So you want to give me your poems to submit to Went-worth?" she asked.

"Walk me home, I'll give you copies," he said, chivalrously helping her on with her jacket and opening the door for her. "My place is just two blocks from here."

20

September 1982

DANIEL

"Can I crash a Yom Kippur service next week or do I need a ticket?" Daniel asked.

He was sitting next to Ronit, holding her hand, on the crowded bus to Yemin Moshe, the exclusive Jerusalem neighborhood where her brother lived. In the Jewish state for the most religious holiday of the year, he felt a little homeless, with nowhere to pray.

"I'm a high holiday Jew singing Frank/ Sinatra on the saddest day of the year," she recited a line from Daniel's first collection.

He was flattered that Ronit had found his old poetry files in his closet and read them all, but wondered if she was avoiding his question. Maybe it was too soon for them to spend such a holy occasion together. He should slow down, let it happen naturally. But in the last three weeks, seeing each other almost every day and night, Ronit had revealed herself to be smart, feisty, a great cook, *and* she quoted his poetry. Plus she was hot and playful in bed, getting on top of him and taking charge the first time. Everything was easier with Ronit than it was with Lila, less confusion and pressure. This made him rush less and his rushing love had ruined enough relationships for one lifetime.

"You say every poem is a letter. So you write poetry to confess your atheism to the God you don't believe in?" she asked.

"My shrink says it's really to get hot chicks," he said, taking her hand. "The better the poem, the hotter the girl."

Ronit smelled of musk oil, drier than Lila's overpowering floral scent. She looked beautiful today, in her soft pink sundress showing off tan shoulders, high sandals, clear gloss on her lips. Normally she wore flats with no makeup or perfume. He wondered if she'd dolled up for him or her brother.

"You Americans, navel gazing with your shrinks," she said. "Ari's poetry is his therapy."

"'A way to transform deepest pain into beauty' is what he told the *Paris Review*," Daniel said, feeling as if her brother were already sitting between them. "You grew up here, in Yemin Moshe?"

She nodded. "When it was still dangerous. My dad was killed by Palestinian militants in '57, when I was seven. He was a Major General in the army. He saved his whole unit during a siege of our town."

"You were the youngest?" Daniel was still piecing together her family tree.

"A change of life baby. My mother was forty-three," Ronit explained. "Ari was already in the army."

No wonder she spoke of him like a father. Lila had lost her dad around the same age. Daniel feared Ronit would also want a heroic father-replacement he could not live up to.

If Ronit was seven in 1957, she was thirty-two now, a decade older than Lila. He knew he was better off with a grown woman. She knew who she was, never doubted herself. He liked how Ronit refused to be malleable, busting his balls, not letting him get away with anything. Zalman would be proud of him; she was the opposite of a student sycophant. As the sting of Lila's rejection receded, the breakup story he told himself put the blame on Lila's youth.

It seemed ridiculous that Ronit was considered an old maid here, especially since her age and self-assurance was what Daniel liked about her. In Manhattan, nobody he knew married in their twenties. Every date, he found something new to admire about Ronit's maturity. Unlike Lila, she enjoyed feeding him. She fawned over her nieces and nephews. He shocked himself by adding to her assets that she'd make a good mother. Not that he was ready to have children yet.

Howard used to label women who wore no makeup or perfume "earth-uglies," preferring the loud, done-up look. His best friend used to be jealous he was dating Roxanne—with her push-up bra, crisscross hose, makeup and big red hair. Since Roxy had a Marilyn Monroe-Arthur Miller fantasy, when they'd split Daniel almost slipped her number to Howard. But Dr. Zalman nixed the triangle, saying, "You have enough problems without courting Oedipus."

Ronit was Lila's opposite, but Daniel realized that all his girlfriends—including Roxy—had the premature death of a parent in common. He gravitated towards members of a mourning club, as if they were all so hurt by their early loss they needed extra years to catch up with normal people.

"My father was emotional, like you," Ronit added, "wearing his heart on his shirt."

"Heart on his sleeve," Daniel laughed, enjoying the way she sometimes botched American colloquialisms.

"He was the family cook. What an eater, with a huge round stomach. He used to say, Ronit, get your big fat *chazzer* Abba some pound cake," she said, patting Daniel's stomach.

"Are you calling me fat?" he asked, sucking in his gut.

"No, but I like a man with a good appetite."

Odd that she opened a restaurant when she could have been a great writer like her brother. Daniel used to think Lila's late father's job as an editor was why she was so drawn to the magazine. Maybe they both wanted to be closer to the first men they'd lost. Then again, part of the reason he'd come to Israel was to fulfill his mother's dream. So who was he to talk?

When the bus stopped, Ronit said "This is us." Daniel's stomach lurched. After weeks of eating onions, peppers, and spicy *hummus* and *tabouli* for breakfast at her restaurant every day, getting heartburn in the hopes of meeting Ari, Daniel was suddenly terrified. He had an urge to turn back, to be alone with Ronit. He didn't want to share her. He finally felt strong and successful; he feared fading in a greater man's shadow.

After getting off the bus he followed her down cobblestone streets. Although it was a nice, breezy day, he was perspiring, wishing he'd worn shorts and sneakers, not long pants and loafers with no traction. Ronit pointed to the huge windmill overlooking the Hinnom Valley on King David Street.

"We bolster our love, like building/ a white windmill in a city with no wind," Daniel quoted, amused it was a literal landmark Ari saw from his window, not a metaphor.

"It hasn't worked in decades," she said. "Want to see the museum? It's dedicated to the English Jew who build it in 1860."

The only Israeli monument on his mind was Ari Halev. Daniel felt like a disciple about to meet King David himself. As he climbed the steep hill of rickety steps carrying his briefcase and a bottle of Chivas, Daniel was dripping in sweat, like a pig. He prayed she didn't notice.

"Ah, here we are," Ronit said as they reached the black iron gate of this ancient castle.

The courtyard's floors were white stone, the high walls lush with green vines, punctuated with purple flowers. Ari stood waiting for them. He was bigger than Daniel expected, a huge bear of a guy, tall, tan, robust, bald, bespectacled. Majestic and ancient, like a Hebrew Buddha. He wore beige shorts, a T-shirt and rugged hiking sandals—how Daniel should have dressed.

"Ronity *sheli*," Ari said, kissing her on both cheeks.

That meant "My Ronity." He was calling her *mine*. Possessive already, Daniel thought.

Ari looked at him and said, "Just what the world needs, another Jewish poet."

"Yes, how original of me." Daniel fumbled with his briefcase and bottle to find his hand.

Ari shook it with an iron grip.

"Yemin Moshe is so picturesque," Daniel fawned, feeling desperate to win over this giant genius. Was it envy or awe that had him so tongue-tied?

"In this country your land and your children are your only legacy," Ari one-upped him.

"In Manhattan it's all location," Daniel said.

What did that inane real estate slogan mean? The brilliant commentary Daniel had rehearsed flew out of his mind. He recalled how Lila confessed to being so nervous to meet Daniel at orientation, she'd forgotten every word she'd rehearsed the second she saw him.

Daniel handed Ari the Chivas Regal Royal Salute, thinking the name had the proper gravitas for this meeting. His host barely noticed, putting it down on the counter.

"So how long has your family lived here?" Daniel ventured.

"Through five wars," Ari answered.

How could he compete with Ari's eloquence? As they ambled through the foyer, Ronit in between them, Daniel reached for Ronit just as Ari put his arm around his sister's waist, claiming her.

"Ronit said you fought in the last three?" Daniel asked.

"Yes. Not the business of a poet," he said. "You've never been to war?"

"I just missed the draft in Vietnam."

"Would you have fought?" Ari asked.

"No, I would have fled to Canada," Daniel admitted, immediately regretting his words, seeing himself through Ari's eyes: a cowardly American. Daniel told himself that poets were word warriors who didn't belong on the battlefield, and Vietnam was a war he didn't believe in. But now all the brave poets who had fought in wars they'd chronicled were flooding his mind, mocking him: Wilfred Owen. Rupert Brooke. Randall Jarrell. Anthony Hecht. James Dickey, Richard Hugo.

"Only the religious refuse to fight in my country," Ari commented.

"I'm not religious," Daniel said, making it worse.

"I wouldn't have gone to Vietnam either," Ari said.

Daniel relaxed a bit.

"You know, I teach my New York classes your poetry," he said.

"In Hebrew?" Ari tested.

"Unfortunately the English translation."

"Which translator?"

"I prefer Sarah Berger's from the *Norton Selected*," Daniel tried.

"Yes, Berger hears me."

"Chaim Segal has a tin ear," Daniel added.

"Yes, exactly." Ari nodded.

Daniel scored one!

"Not enough music," Ronit piped in, winking at him.

"Segal doesn't do your work justice. Because he's not really a poet himself." Daniel shared his theory. "Though the translators who are poets turn your work into theirs."

Ari nodded. "When Aton Pegis translates the Bible, the Bible becomes a Pegis treatise."

Daniel laughed. Too loudly.

"Here, let me show you around," Ronit offered, momentarily ending the inquisition, taking his hand and leading him down the steps to the sunken living room with high ceilings, a fireplace and gray stone walls.

"Gorgeous home." Could Daniel find anything more superficial to say?

"They've asked him to stay on at Hebrew University," Ronit said, then kissed Daniel on the lips. The gesture made Ari wince.

"You came to my country by yourself? " Ari wanted to know.

"Yes, all alone," Daniel confirmed.

"Never married?" Ari asked a question he obviously knew the answer to. "Why not?"

Israelis were the least subtle people on the planet. Ari was asking 'What's wrong with you? Tell me now so you don't waste my sister's time.' Just what Daniel didn't need was to feel bullied by the Hebrew Cormick.

"You're a great advocate of marriage," Daniel shot back. "With three divorces."

"Yes, what a ridiculous hypocrite I am. But I liked it so much I had three nice wedding buffets. You should try it sometime," Ari smiled slyly.

"Maybe I will," Daniel mustered up the courage to say, adding, "Let's have a drink."

"Should we open your fancy whiskey?" Ari threw out.

Aha, he had noticed the gift. There was not much he missed.

"We could all use a drink," Ronit agreed, taking the bottle, running her hand against Daniel's arm as she went to the kitchen. He immediately missed Ronit's presence in the room. He felt stronger beside her, calmer.

"So has time made the man any less fearful?" Ari attacked Daniel with his own line.

Daniel was overjoyed to hear a snatch of his poem coming from Ari's mouth, yet also embarrassed by what the poem revealed. "The breakup wasn't that long ago," he confessed.

"Yes, that young woman of ambition," Ari said. "They say a true intellectual has found something more interesting than sex."

He had no idea how loaded that line was. "All your wives were younger, no?" Daniel asked.

"That's why I have six children."

"The six anchors of time," Daniel said, citing a poem of Ari's.

"My Ronit has no time for fear. She's thirty-two," Ari said. "She was engaged at seventeen, to Shmulik. *Hazara betshuva.*"

Daniel didn't understand and shrugged.

"Returned to the faith," Ari translated. "He became religious. He wanted a traditional wife to stay home and give him children right away. Ronit wasn't ready."

"Yes, she told me," Daniel said.

"Changed his name to Shmuel, voting for wars he became too pious to fight."

Daniel tried to decipher whether Ari had contempt for any man who didn't fight, just poor Shmuel, or all of Ronit's boyfriends.

"That's why we have the mess in Lebanon now. A mess my son must fight but not Shmuel. He married a *frum* girl who already gave him four sons who won't go to war either."

Daniel was trying to follow. "Talk about hypocrisy," he said, actually pleased Shmuel was now occupying Ari's wrath instead of himself.

"When Ronit was in the army, she brought home Alon, her pro-Palestinian boyfriend. He gets himself released from military service for declaring his pacifism," Ari revealed. "That didn't get enough of a rise out of me. So while she's studying at Tel Aviv University, she plays peacenik and starts dating Baqi, a Palestinian professor. Romeo and Juliet's cliché," I told her.

"Oh. I didn't know about him," Daniel said, more interested in Baqi's age and career than their religious differences. So Ronit had dated an old professor, looking for a father figure, like Lila.

"Meanwhile Baqi lasted six months," Ari added. "Until she found out he was married with two kids in Jordan."

Daniel wondered whether Ari was sharing a list of Ronit's old boyfriends to scare him away. It wasn't working. They were all losers who made Daniel look good. All he'd have to do to win the contest was not be married, a public pacifist or a religious hypocrite.

"So Ronit says you're forty-two with no children?" Ari asked.

"Not even illegitimate ones," Daniel joked.

Ari pulled a cigarette from a box of Noblesse, offered one to Daniel. He didn't like cigarettes, but Daniel chuckled nervously and took one, wanting to hide behind the smoke.

"Don't you want children?" Ari lit the cigarette for Daniel. Another test.

Ari's penetrating stare made Daniel feel like he'd better decide. This minute.

"Yes," Daniel surprised himself by confessing. "I want kids. Very much."

"Well, we don't grow any younger," Ari commented.

"Here we go," Ronit sang, coming back with a tray holding the bottle and three glasses of whiskey. They each took one and held it up.

"Salut," Daniel said.

"To your future sons and daughters." Ari hit his glass against Daniel's. "*L'Chaim!*"

Ronit must have noted Daniel's pale expression because she asked, "What did I miss? Did he propose you marry and impregnate me by next week to avenge the loss of six million?"

As Daniel emptied his glass, Ronit poured more.

"Religious Arabs and Hasidic women are smart enough to have nine and ten children each," Ari said. "But overeducated secular Sabras are too busy getting PhD's to replenish the planet. A Jewish man without children is like a river with no water."

"A Jewish woman without children is like a dirty floor with no mop," Ronit mocked.

"You think it's funny to be childless?" Ari asked.

"A Jewish woman with no children is like a kangaroo with no pouch," Daniel tried.

"A Jewish woman without children is a jigsaw puzzle with no edge," Ronit went on.

"Go ahead, make fun," Ari said, pouring more booze. "But I have re-created my ugly DNA on the planet six times while Ronit has left nothing. Wasting your beautiful, smart, strong genes is a biological tragedy, my dear."

She waved her hand, as if to dismiss Ari's plea. "Daniel's joining us for Yom Kippur services on Monday," she said. Interesting, how she didn't ask either of them. She'd already decided though her brother clearly hadn't.

"Do you fast?" Ari wanted to know. Another exam question.

"Yes. Of course I do," Daniel lied.

"Not me. I like to eat shellfish," Ari said.

Daniel wasn't sure if this was a joke or a trap. Could the most acclaimed Bard of the Holy Land actually go for lobster on Yom Kippur?

"You'll come with us to temple and break fast here," Ari stated.

That meant, Daniel hoped, that he was starting to win him over. "There's nowhere else I'd rather be." He bowed his head before Ari, feeling honored, welcomed, as if he had to travel thousands of miles to find home.

"Want to get us food?" Ari asked his sister. "I'm hungry. Always hungry, like my father," he told Daniel. "It's a male Halev trait."

"What am I, your servant?" Ronit asked, nonetheless going back to the kitchen to fetch food for her men.

"To your beautiful sister," Daniel toasted, holding up his glass.

"If you hurt her, I'll drink your blood like Christ's," Ari said.

Daniel coughed up a little Scotch. "Good line," he conceded, pouring them both another glass.

21

December 1982

LILA

"No, Howard, I can't get your check early," Lila said. "I don't work in accounting. Stop calling me at the office." She hung up the phone, her hand shaking. What a horrible morning already. He was hounding her for payment for his poem—which she'd submitted for him—not knowing she'd just received a cold rejection for her own: "Sorry, not right for us." She reread the handwritten note on the magazine's small yellow stationary. Nothing like a triple rebuff—the editor accepted Howard's work, refused hers, and both happened right as she realized that he'd been using her for her connection to the magazine. She reached for a tissue to dry her eyes.

Howard had been acting bizarre and erratic ever since their one-nighter three months ago. The sex on his double bed wasn't bad. With his flat stomach and muscles, he didn't look so old—though she did find a gray chest hair. She'd liked how he kept repeating how gorgeous she was, but he wasn't much into kissing or cuddling. When he insisted she stay over at his place, she hoped he'd be a replacement for Daniel—except this time consummation was included, and he would be staying in the right city. Lila was proud of herself for adding a second name to her list of lovers. But it felt like an empty victory when he'd slept in a fetal position at the bed's edge, without touching her—and then didn't return her call for two weeks.

Just as she'd completely given up on him, he starting leaving incoherent messages on her answering machine at 3 a.m. When Lila asked what his problem was, he admitted he was off and on with his ex-girlfriend, his mother's illness freaked him out and his new anti-depressants' had bad side effects—night tremors, weight loss, and insomnia.

And she'd thought Daniel was a handful!

Lila knew she shouldn't have slept with Howard. By trying to erase Daniel, she wound up missing him even more.

"They need the page proof for the new full-page ad in checking," Christopher barked as he walked by. Bad enough that her boss Elaine had offered her up to the business department on the 20th floor while the assistant publisher's secretary was on maternity leave. But Lila had to give up the warmth, security and great literary gossip of the organized Elaine—her fantasy Jewish grandma—to try to decipher the needs of this cold, disorganized male WASP.

"I dropped the ad proof off hours ago," Lila told him, stashing the damp tissue in the waste basket. She was embarrassed to be caught crying in her temporary cubicle. She feared Howard's inappropriate calls and her own mood swings were now screwing up her job—the only thing in her life that was working.

"Well, make sure," Christopher ordered, marching into his office and shutting the door.

Five minutes later, he buzzed her to come in. She pulled a compact and makeup from her purse, brushing concealer under her eyes so she wouldn't look so red and blotchy. Lila worried she was going to be reprimanded and disgrace Elaine by being sent back down to the editorial library. Or she might even get axed altogether. Then she would have ended her relationship with Daniel for nothing. She shouldn't have been revising her own poems instead of working, not to mention all the calls and interoffice mail pushing to get Howard into the magazine.

"The message about the missing page proof must have been from this morning. I've had a chaotic day," Christopher said, in the robotic way he always spoke. He left the door open, then sat down, looking uncomfortable at his huge oak desk, his brown eyes peeking out over gold-rimmed glasses. At thirty-two, he still had a baby face. In his beige jacket and navy tie, he resembled a scrawny nerd playing dress-up. They'd stolen him from the publisher's office at *The Atlantic*, Elaine had told her. Lila thought someone overseeing the finances of a famous literary magazine would be artsy, but he came off like a Wall Street MBA. "I wanted to apologize," he added. "I didn't mean to upset you."

"You didn't upset me," Lila said.

"We don't want to lose you," he went on.

She was flattered, albeit confused. "You're not losing me." It wasn't like the world was banging down the door of a broke, doubly broken-hearted unpublished poet lately.

"Nevertheless, I should not have yelled." He gestured for her to sit down.

She sat on the edge of the rust-covered chair, dangling her legs, fidgety. What a suit this guy was, always so polite. He'd barely raised his voice. "I'm from a family of screaming Jews," she told him. "I thought you were just trying to make sure I heard you."

"And I'm sorry I've been making you traffic everything to the other departments."

"That's my favorite part," she said. "That way I get to meet other editors and artists."

"Good. I was worried I was turning you into a messenger. So why the tears?" He avoided her eyes, obviously a bit undone by her emotional display. In the three weeks she'd been filling in here, this was the longest conversation they'd had.

"It had nothing to do with you," she explained.

"That's good." He sounded relieved, but still curious. "Is someone else at the magazine pushing you around? Anyone I should beat up?"

That was kind of him, chivalrous. "No, you don't have to defend my honor."

"You sure you're okay?"

"I just got another rejection," she blurted out. "That's all."

"I see." He looked flummoxed by her admission. "What was rejected?"

Didn't he know she'd been submitting all her poems to the upstairs poetry editor, as all the underlings did? He probably also had no idea they were secretly sharing bags of marijuana through interoffice mail either. But surely he'd heard that another editorial assistant had recently sold a poem, a girl Lila's age had her humor piece taken, and another fellow peon had a front-of-the-book interview accepted—one with a dog psychiatrist. Lila wanted to know what they had that she didn't.

"Wentworth hates my poetry. I've tried him with eight batches. Everything I have," she spilled. "Last week he said, 'Almost,' so I rewrote the whole thing. But he was more curt today. It was totally a no-go. It had a 'never go' kind of vibe."

She'd had her heart set on sending a message to Daniel through publishing *From An Ambitious Young Woman*. It was frustrating because Wentworth's previous note had said: "Closer." That was all. She didn't know whether that meant she'd regressed, or should revise again or put it away for a while. Breaking into *The New Urban* might have summoned Daniel back—at least led him to congratulate her. Maybe Sari was right, it was over and this was a further sign that when it came to poetry and poets, Lila should hang it up. She was afraid she'd never again connect with a man intellectually. Unfortunately Howard didn't want to critique her work anymore which, she'd figured out too late, was how he'd lured her to bed.

"I had no idea you were submitting," Christopher said.

She battled back more dumb tears. The other low levels strove and suffered dejection in silence. She shouldn't broadcast her ambition. It was gauche to bring it up at this genteel place, let alone to cry in public. He pushed a box of tissues. She took one, blowing her nose.

"I didn't realize you wrote poems," he said.

"I have my MFA in poetry!" she told him. How could he not know? It was the first line of her résumé. Hadn't he looked at it before he trusted her with the details of his internal affairs for six weeks? She'd assumed being a straight A student and recent NCU grad was why they'd wanted her in his office. When Mark chided that her fast typing and big breasts would get her further than her MFA, she'd called her brother a raging asshole. But now she worried that the magazine wanted her for her clerical skills and looks, not her brain power.

"That's right. You just graduated." Christopher moved the Kleenex box back, trying to recover from his faux pas, but the damage was done.

"I graduated seven months ago, actually."

"Did Wentworth give you any indication how to improve your poems?" he asked with a perplexed expression, as if this were a math problem he could solve.

"No. My professor says a poetry editor has to fall in love with your work to take it."

"It's completely amorphous?" he asked. "There's no definite reason or standard?"

What part of falling in love didn't this guy get? She hid her frustration with a shrug.

"So the criteria is just a total mystery," he said.

"Well, once Wentworth wrote, 'No sky opening up, sorry.' I begged for more feedback, asking if there wasn't enough blood. He said, 'too much blood, not enough music.' Some say he prefers pretty air."

"I'm not following," Christopher said.

For someone so high up at the magazine, he was clueless when it came to literary colloquialisms. "His preference is for work that's technically proficient with no blood or soul backing it up. Didn't you ever take a poetry class?" she asked.

"I studied business."

The in-house bios claimed he'd been Phi Beta Kappa at Harvard and went to Wharton though, unlike other Ivy Leaguers in the office, he never rubbed it in. Then again, why rub in that his goal from 9th grade on was to be a boring materialist? "You don't write at all?"

"No. Never wanted to."

Since her days with Daniel, Lila had found non-artistic men staid and colorless. Last Sunday, when Jeff was in town, after a weekend between the covers, she'd invented an excuse to call Howard to get his pen on the latest revision of her poem. But Howard became enraged when she mentioned she'd gone back to her original "you composed *for* me" instead of his minimalist "you composed me" and said he was finished.

"Are there other editors you could send your poems to?" he asked, not getting what it felt like to work at the best magazine in the world, but not be good enough to get into its pages.

"I guess. Someone from the *Downtown Journal,* our grad school rag, wanted me to submit work there. But they don't pay and it's not really that professional." Sari had been pushing her to just get her damn response to Daniel's poem in there to get it over with, for closure. Nobody would ever see her rebuttal to Daniel but at least that would mean they were really over and she could move on.

"Well, I'm glad that the man who's upsetting you isn't me," Christopher said, then added, "Not that I want Wentworth to reject you."

"No. It isn't you," she reassured.

"Isn't there a story I should tell you about Hemingway losing a thousand-page manuscript in a suitcase on a train and then suggesting all young writers do the same?"

"Look, it hit me harder because Wentworth recently took poems from two of my professors." She left out that she'd been in love with one of those professors she'd never slept with, and had slept with the other, whom she didn't love.

"They're older than you," he said. "They've been doing it much longer."

"I know. But now they'll probably both get big book deals."

"What's a big book deal for poetry?" he asked.

She recalled Daniel saying what Knopf offered Cormick after he'd won the Pulitzer Prize. "A ten thousand dollar advance," she said. "That's top echelon."

"How long does it take to finish a collection?"

"My old professor has been working on his manuscript for almost ten years."

"Ten years!" Christopher looked aghast. "A thousand dollars a year?"

"Though he said having a critic as good as me helped speed him up."

"You're a good critic?"

"He said I gave the most incisive criticism in our program. I'd review all his work."

"That's your former suitor?" He raised his eyebrow.

The word suitor was so corny. Almost a decade younger than Daniel, Christopher was apparently even more old-fashioned. She guessed he'd overheard her on the phone. Then again, he'd have to be deaf to have missed Lila telling her office mates that she was the inspiration for The Poem. Even Fred, the janitor, agreed with Lila, that a guy wouldn't publish love poetry to a girl unless he still had feelings for her.

"Yes. Why? Have you heard anything about Daniel?" She couldn't help but pry.

"Wentworth said he was difficult to work with," Christopher coughed up. "Seven last-minute telephone calls questioning a comma change." That definitely sounded obsessive and Daniel-like.

"Then again," he said, "you'd have to be fanatical to make poetry your life's work. Who else would choose a field where it could take a decade to make ten thousand dollars?"

What a stupid, vapid, reductive thing to say. He should be working with cold-hearted Wall Streeters instead of promoting art and literature. "I suppose. If you wake up in the morning with the main goal of seeing how much money you have in the bank," she sniffed.

"I didn't mean to offend you." He took off his glasses, rubbed his eyes. She looked at him closely for the first time. His lashes and brows were light blond, like hers. His chin and cheek bones were sculpted; nose small and lean. When they'd had lunch and Sari caught a glimpse of Christopher, she'd called him "a tall drink of water" and thought he resembled the actor in *Brideshead Revisited*.

"I'm not into skinny British guys with chicken legs," Lila had snapped. He wasn't Lila's type. Daniel was. But look where that left her.

"I found Wildman's poem quite lovely," Christopher added, as if to redeem himself.

If she told him the ambitious woman was her, he'd think she'd slept her way into Daniel's poem. Though it might be worse for him to know that, after two years, she hadn't. That might mean she's a weird frigid tease or a scared virgin.

"Look, you're doing a great job," Christopher was saying. "You come early, stay late, catch typos and other mistakes everyone else misses. Would you consider staying on the business side?"

"No! I might not make it six more weeks," Lila said. "I want to write, not type."

"Oh." He seemed taken aback by her bluntness. "I can ask Kevin if you could do a review for the front section. I know we're trying to broaden the magazine's demographic."

"Wow. Really? That would be awesome. I could review a poetry book!" Lila said. "I think the new Sharon Olds is her best."

"He said we're a bit overloaded with book reviewers. What about opera?"

"I've never been to the opera," she said. "You know, ninety percent of the magazine's book critics are men. Updike, Amis. Arthur Krystal. It's like you need a penis to break in."

He looked alarmed. Was it the accusation of sexism or the anatomical reference?

"I heard they sent a batch of fiction to Joyce Carol Oates and Ursula Le Guinn," he argued.

"I could try film or theater?"

"Books, film and theater are the most crowded," he told her.

"How about television?" she threw out.

"The top brass thinks it's too lowbrow for us to cover." He folded his arms.

"But this is what could broaden the national demographic. In *Hill Street Blues* and *St. Elsewhere*, the writing's darker and more sophisticated than you'd expect," she said, trying to make TV sound higher brow. "It's the new literate television. These one-hour dramas are smarter than cinema because they're controlled by the writers, not by actors, directors or producers. Twenty hours a season is the equivalent of ten movies."

"Do you have expertise in this area?" he questioned.

"Yes, I actually do."

After Daniel deserted her and Sari started commuting to Wisconsin to see Mark on weekends, Lila had spent most nights alone in her apartment, getting stoned and zombie-watching TV for hours on end, falling asleep with the set still on. Daniel would say she was wasting her brain but she found it addictive and soothing. It made her feel less lonely. Plus *Hill Street Blues* hero Daniel Travanti looked a bit like Daniel Wildman. She'd over-identified with Veronica Hamel's hard-hitting public defender secretly sleeping with the captain. They'd break up and get back together every episode, which fueled Lila's hope for resurrecting the romance with her Daniel.

"Tell me more about these new shows," Christopher said.

"The hand-held camera gives *St. Elsewhere* a gritty documentary feel," Lila said, winging it, psyched. She could tell she was wearing him down. "It's perfect for brainiac film buffs who underestimate the boob tube." She played with the alliteration as if it was a poem, picturing her words—like Daniel's and Howard's—printed on the pages of the magazine.

He rubbed his chin. "That could make a sharp opener to introduce a roundup piece."

He thought she was sharp!

"I could put in *Cagney and Lacy* too," she threw in. "It's not just male doctors, lawyers and cops. There's another show, *Kate & Allie*, about working girls. It's an important cultural trend mirroring the feministic socio-political landscape."

"Good. If you get me a paragraph next week, I promise to take a look."

"What do you pay for those, anyway?"

"Two dollars a word. Though the reviews are short, two hundred and fifty words."

That was five hundred dollars for a double-spaced typed page. Lila calculated that number of words was the same length as the critiques of poetry books Daniel had assigned in class. She jumped up. "Fantastic. I can get you something in an hour."

"Don't rush," he laughed, standing up. "And make sure to change 'working girls' to 'working women.'"

As he walked her to the door, Lila looked up at him, just now noticing how tall he was. He must have been six foot three, way taller than Daniel. She could wear higher heels without fearing she'd dwarf him.

PART FIVE: 1983

22

August 1983

DANIEL

"A Knopf hardcover. *Boychick*, you've really made it now," Daniel said, greeting his friend outside The Village Den, their old hangout, draping his arm around Howard's shoulder.

"Have I?" Howard asked, looking bemused. He broke free of Daniel's grip and headed inside, to their usual booth in the corner, as if this were any normal Sunday and not the last time they might be meeting here.

The clatter of dishes and greasy aroma of burned fries hadn't changed, but an older waitress Daniel didn't know plopped down water and menus. He looked around for familiar faces but didn't recognize anyone. It was more spacious than the Tel Aviv dives he'd frequented.

"I miss this hellhole. You still come here a lot?" Daniel asked, bursting to spill all of his good news to his pal whom—he just realized—he'd really missed.

Howard nodded, then said, "I saw Lila here."

"You did? When?" Not what Daniel had wanted to hear. That odd tangent made his back hairs stand on end.

"Right after you skipped town," Howard said.

Daniel imagined Lila coming back to this place, looking for him. He felt guilty. She must have been so disappointed to find only his friend here instead.

"Hard to believe it's been a year already," he said.

"Fifteen months since you split," Howard corrected. "You put on some weight?"

"Ronit's a dangerous cook," Daniel said, running his hands over his beard, which she hated but he felt it gave him gravitas. He hoped his tan counteracted the fifteen pounds he'd put on from her cooking. "You put on a few pounds yourself too."

"All muscle." Howard made a fist to show off his enhanced biceps.

"So that means you're still karate chopping?"

"Why can't you remember it's tae kwon do? Brown belt." Howard took a sip of water.

"Well you look good," Daniel said. "Sad about your mother. Did you get my card?"

"In March," Howard told him.

"Jeez. Sorry it took so long. International mail," Daniel said. "She was 82, right?"

"What's that mean?" Howard asked.

"Nothing. Nothing. I lost my mother when I was a kid, that's all." Daniel opened the menu. "Just think you were lucky to have her so long."

"She was a paranoid schizophrenic in and out of hospitals her whole life." Howard waved over the waitress.

"Of course. You had it rough," Daniel said, thinking he'd had it rougher. He'd rather have a crazy mother for decades longer than a nurturing mother who killed herself in grade school. What were they playing now—dueling dead mothers?

"Did I do something wrong?"

"You weren't here," Howard said. "My last relative. Buried her alone. Cemetery. Shiva. You didn't call."

Oh, that was it. Of course. Daniel felt bad for him. "I didn't know until I got your letter. But I should have called you, buddy. Sent a tray. If I had the money, I would have flown in."

Howard nodded, hiding his eyes behind the menu.

"Well, despite your horrible loss, I think you're wearing your success well," Daniel said, feeling simpatico with his longtime comrade. They were both mother-less now. They both had finally found some hard-won happiness. He scanned the oversized green menu he knew by heart, bursting to share all his good news. But he decided to wait a bit. The guy was mourning his mother. And Howard's new book deserved the spotlight, before Daniel's marriage. "Hey, I'm impressed you managed to nail the best publisher in the world."

"Thanks," Howard said.

When the waitress returned, Daniel asked for an omelet with extra onions and peppers, the way Ronit made it, along with fries and a bagel and cream cheese. He felt hungrier than he thought. Howard ordered eggs Florentine and a whole wheat muffin.

"Are you training for a marathon?"

"Healthier," Howard mumbled.

"Listen, I know it's a little late, but I want to host another book party for you," Daniel offered. "We can invite the whole gang."

"Kind thought, Danny."

Howard knew he preferred to be called Daniel. Hearing Cormick's infantilizing nickname coming out of his friend's mouth was jarring. Daniel had the urge to retaliate with *Howie* but he stopped himself from alienating the one true New York comrade he had left. "My sublettor's gone, so we can use my place." He pictured a crazy final blowout—like old times in Iowa.

"Faith's daughter sublet, right?" Howard asked.

Daniel had forgotten how everybody here knew his business. Greenwich Village was more incestuous than an Israeli kibbutz. "Luckily she's a neatnik. There's no damage at all. We can fit fifty people."

Howard didn't respond. The waiter poured coffee and threw down a bread basket that Howard pushed toward Daniel, who took a sesame roll, breaking it in two.

"Is your publisher already throwing you a launch?" Daniel asked.

Howard sipped his coffee. "Cormick."

Nothing like a kick in the gut. "I bet he wants credit for your book," Daniel said, forcing a chuckle, trying not to look pissed off that the Irish showoff was hosting the soiree. Daniel's was a last-second idea. After a year away, he couldn't expect the city to have stayed the same without him.

"Cormick was here. He offered," Howard said. "You left."

"Sounds like you think I abandoned you," Daniel said. "I didn't mean to. I was a wreck when I left. Rejections coming out of my ears. No money. The disaster with Lila. I was drowning. The fellowship was like someone throwing me a life raft. That's what it felt like."

Howard caught his eye for the first time. "You never told me."

"I was ashamed. I ran away like an idiot," Daniel admitted.

"Party's next Thursday night, the sixth." Howard changed the subject, seeming embarrassed by his friend's sudden vulnerability. "You coming back to NCU?"

"Why, you want my job?" Daniel joked, then saw that Howard might. "No, I'm not. I took an English professorship at the University of Vermont. Full benefits. Tenure track."

"Burlington. That's something." Howard nodded. "When do you start?"

"The tenth. The Monday after Labor Day."

"You'll stay for my book party." Howard's voice was louder, unusually adamant.

"I'll try," Daniel said. "But I'm picking Ronit up at JFK the next morning."

"Your Israeli chef is coming here?"

"Yes." Daniel suppressed the urge to add *for good.* "You'll have to meet her."

"Halev's sister. What's he like?"

"He's tough, droll and majestic," Daniel said. "The kind of guy you'd want to be."

"Only you could walk out of El Al right into the Halevs' home. Amazing coincidence."

Daniel sensed a sinister subtext. "What does that mean?"

"Ambition," Howard said.

Daniel was offended by his friend's accusation. "You think I'm *that* ambitious?"

"You don't?"

"No, My father was the striver. He went from being a poor Cleveland Jewish kid to a millionaire banker. My brother has his drive. I could never keep up."

"You kept up," Howard said. "Just in a different arena."

Daniel did not think of himself as ambitious. Confessional poetry and teaching were an escape from his father's macho, cut-throat business world. Were there any fields that paid less?

"You're lucky as ever," Howard mumbled.

"What? I had no luck at all until I got the fellowship."

"You always did. Teaching. Publishing. Women." Howard listed on his fingers.

"You're crazy," Daniel said, though doing better than Howard with women wasn't saying much.

The waiter brought the food and Daniel spread cream cheese on his bagel and took a bite. He wished he was wearing his wedding ring so everybody in New York would know the truth already. But Ronit insisted they wait to announce the news together. She was bringing the rings she'd had engraved by her sister, the jeweler, in Haifa. Most men whom Daniel knew didn't wear wedding bands. In fact, he couldn't think of many male writers who were married and monogamous—but he intended to be.

"What about Thanksgiving in Iowa?" Howard asked.

"I remember that vodka turkey we made," Daniel said, recalling how they'd drunkenly recited each other's poetry to seduce girls.

"Gorgeous Gabrielle," said Howard, sprinkling pepper on his eggs, taking a bite. Daniel forgot how slowly he ate, even more slowly than he spoke.

"Ah yes, the busty blonde from British Lit," Daniel said, immediately flashing to her huge breasts heaving over him in bed that long weekend he'd spent with her.

"I wanted her," Howard admitted.

"Who didn't?" Daniel asked. "Though I thought you slept with her roommate."

"I liked Gabrielle," Howard said.

The free love sixties was lifetimes ago. Daniel tasted his omelet. Too loose. He wanted it well done, the way Ronit made it.

"Gabrielle Robson." Howard said her name as if there were something significant that Daniel should understand. Had his friend held a grudge about this all these years?

"I'm sorry if I muscled you out there. With all the booze, dope and LSD, I was not at my best." Daniel took a bite of his home fries.

"No. You weren't," Howard spit out. "Myopic. Self-involved."

Did he expect his friend to apologize for his whole life today? "You wrote that you were seeing someone too?" Daniel asked.

"Betsy," Howard said. "The photographer."

"How's that going?"

"Better than a writer," Howard said. "Who needs another rival?"

What female scribe had Howard ever dated? Daniel wondered, focusing on the word "another."

"Yes, Dr. Zalman thinks women writers can be too difficult," Daniel said. He couldn't wait to tell Zalman he had tied the knot with a brilliant, beautiful, age-appropriate chef at their appointment tomorrow.

"Betsy moved in with me last week," Howard told him.

Ironic that Howard accused Daniel of ambition when he had Daniel's old job, a live-in lady, a big Knopf hardcover and Cormick throwing him a book party at his fancy carriage house.

"Ronit and I eloped," Daniel blurted out. "Two weeks ago."

"Kudos."

When he didn't say anything else, Daniel feared his news had taken Howard's thunder. "So you had more luck with *The New Urban*. That's five poems of yours they've taken?"

"Six," Howard said.

"Wentworth only bought two of mine," Daniel lamented. "One about Lila, the latest one about Ronit."

"Actually, Lila submitted my poems to Wentworth," Howard tossed out.

"She did?"

Another karate chop. Lila's talking Daniel up at her interview had helped Daniel break in—but they'd been in love at the time. Howard barely knew her! Had he mailed her his poems, or dropped them off at the magazine? Howard had crossed a line, clearly using Lila. She probably only put herself out because Howard was connected to him. Daniel felt betrayed.

The waitress refilled their water glasses and slapped the bill down on the table.

"Why are you just mentioning your Lila connection now?" Daniel asked.

"Didn't think you'd care. With Ronit and all," Howard said. "Why open old wounds?"

Why indeed? All of a sudden Daniel flashed to a therapy session two years before.

"Howard thinks Lila's a good apple," he'd reported to Zalman.

"The blind leading the blind into oncoming traffic," Zalman had said. "He is what you would call the classic unreliable narrator."

"What are you talking about?" Daniel asked. "He's my buddy. He's grateful for all my help with jobs and editors over the years."

"There's a Yiddish expression, 'What are you mad at me for? *I* never helped you,'" Zalman had shared.

"It's not a wound. Lila was too young," Daniel told Howard now. "She said I had a *Pygmalion* fantasy. She might be right." He shrugged. "Is she still at the job I got her?"

"You got her the interview. But she's making her own way," Howard said. "She does reviews now."

Daniel put the last bite of his bagel down. That was alarming news. "Lila's reviewing books?" he asked, his voice rising. When did this happen? He'd only missed a few issues when he and Ronit had gone to Haifa for their honeymoon. Why didn't he know about this?

"Television."

"Oh." Daniel sighed, relieved and finished eating. He was almost ready to submit his new collection and didn't need an ex-girlfriend to be in charge of the prestigious book section. He felt guilty for running away, without saying goodbye. Then again, he hoped his poem let her know he was sorry and still had kind feelings for her. After he and Faith split, she'd pushed his poems into *Ploughshares*. Sometimes it seemed that the entire poetry biz was a big bordello of people who either screwed you or screwed you over.

He didn't even know they'd bothered to review the boob tube. "News shows or something?" Daniel asked.

"Hour dramas," Howard said. "So come to my book launch. In Washington Mews."

Howard didn't have to rub the address in. Daniel had always envied Cormick's sprawling four-bedroom duplex that NCU footed the bill for. His only solace was knowing that Cormick had to keep teaching to live there—the minute he stopped, they'd revoke his free lease. But he'd probably be tottering to classes –and coming onto the undergraduates—as a centenarian.

"Cormick might be pissed I left him in the lurch with the fellowship. The one honor Cormick was never offered. No need for Irish Catholics in Jerusalem," Daniel cracked.

"Does he know about Vermont?"

"I dropped off a letter of resignation Friday." The office was quiet at the end of August. Even half-empty, it was hard for Daniel to return to the English building where he once was at home. He stopped by to see the secretary and felt slighted when she didn't recognize him for a minute.

"Some of your mail was in my box." Howard reached into his worn brown leather briefcase and pulled out a few folders and fliers.

"Ten years teaching at the place," Daniel said. As he looked through the mail, a thick wave of nostalgia hit. "To tell you the truth, a decade didn't add up to much."

"Sorry." Howard checked his watch.

"You got places to go and people to see?" Daniel felt miffed that Howard was in a rush.

"Meeting Betsy," he said, sliding out of the booth.

"Wait." Daniel touched Howard's arm to stop him. "I'm sorry about Gabrielle in Iowa. I didn't realize it hurt you. Inebriated or not, you don't do that to a friend."

Howard nodded. Then he said, "Oh, almost forgot" and pulled out something else—an issue of *Downtown Journal,* with a sketch of Washington Square Park on the cover.

Daniel stared at the NCU student rag and his mail, disappointed. He wanted so much more –an award for all of his hard work, a letter from the dean begging him to reconsider leaving—something that would make his decade of teaching important. Howard took the bill. Good, it was about time he picked up a check.

Walking outside, his comrade waved goodbye through the window, rushing, as if he couldn't wait to get away.

Signaling the waiter for more coffee, Daniel flipped through last year's graduate rag. He stopped at the title *From An Ambitious Young Woman.* Lila's byline. A response to his poem. Did Howard know it was here? The title sounded vengeful. Was this his friend's way of saying fuck you? It was in Howard's briefcase when he came, before he knew Daniel was married. Maybe he meant it as a gift, to let him know that Lila hadn't rejected his ardor and proposal and thrown him away so easily. Who else had read it? What would Ronit think?

Daniel's heart burned in his chest as he read: "It's a shame we can't meet for coffee/recite Lowell and Rich and Roethke the way we did/when I was a Midwest refugee in love/with your city." It was consciously anti-romantic, sarcastic even, parodying Daniel's exalted first stanza. He read it again intently. So that was her excuse for not going overseas—she was more in love with Manhattan than him. Her next lines played off his theme of ambition, adding the twist of revising her résumé nightly. Nice metaphor for her desperate need for validation. "One bedroom" alluded to Virginia Woolf's *A*

Room of One's Own. Lila was implying she couldn't yet afford love. How cold and curt, like saying "Sorry, couldn't do it."

But in her final stanza, he was stunned when she confessed: "Ignoring sirens across the street I turn/to your page in bed, where my eyes read again/the last lyrical sonnet/you composed me." Instead of "you composed FOR me," Lila had created a raw double entendre that proved she had learned Daniel's most important lesson: poetry was about what you left out, that you had to trust readers to read between the words. She *had* been listening.

His throat throbbed, his blood tangling up in his veins as he reread "you composed me." He found those three words blinding. Lila was admitting he'd made her what she was. She'd been irrevocably altered by him—artistically, emotionally, eternally. What a terrible time to realize that she really had loved him, after all.

23

September 1983

LILA

"It's our last party together. You can't really be cancelling?" Lila pleaded, her voice cracking.

"I have morning sickness. Want me to puke on all of your big-shot poets?" Sari asked.

"Why the fuck do they call it morning sickness if you get it at eight at night?" Lila stared with dismay at her roommate—who looked tubby and peaked as she drank ginger tea and ate saltines on the gray futon in the living room. "Well, then I'm not going either," Lila said.

"You have to go. But not in that." Sari pointed to the knee-length denim skirt Lila had on. She went to her closet and pulled out a black leather miniskirt and tight Spandex halter.

"You can't control my clothes if you're leaving me." Lila said it in a light tone but she'd felt betrayed ever since Sari broke the horrible news in May. She couldn't fathom how her hippest friend, who'd taught her how to smoke, toke, dress downtown and never let men mold her into a Barbie doll, got knocked up -while working at Planned Parenthood, no less. Then she decided to give up Manhattan and minimalist fiction to be a wife and mommy! Worse: the inseminator was Lila's brother, who was kidnapping Sari to Wisconsin next week, for good. Lila was losing them both—to each other. She glared at the bulge that had replaced Sari's once flat abdomen.

"I know, everyone says how big I'm getting. I'm seeing the doctor Monday."

If she was this bloated and lethargic after four months, Lila couldn't imagine what she'd be like by her due date. She wished she could talk her out of it, get the old Sari back.

"Why do you keep staring at my stomach?"

"Still in shock," Lila admitted. Only the religious girls from home had husbands and babies this young; nobody Lila knew from Manhattan did. She was jealous that Sari and Mark's passion was blossoming into marriage and motherhood while her sexless romance with Daniel ended in desertion. Who would she be in New York without Daniel and Sari?

Lila tried on the sexy outfit, panicked at the thought of showing up alone at the party. She'd felt flattered getting the invitation to Howard's big book launch. But they'd barely forged a friendship after their twisted one-nighter. He'd be fawning over his new live-in photographer girlfriend amid the magazine and Knopf brigade, pretending they'd never slept together.

"What are you so shocked about?" Sari tied a black scarf around the middle of Lila's skirt to cinch her waist. "I told you Mark and I were serious."

Looking at Sari's blue stretch pants and loose flowered top, Lila flashed to the cool Sari, chain smoking, wearing a miniskirt, ripped fishnet hose and halter the first time they'd met.

"How can you want to be a Jewish housewife in Hicksville?"

"You know, there's a real town called Hicksville." Sari plopped back down on Lila's futon, shoving more crackers into her mouth, getting crumbs on the striped pillows.

"The boonies. Hinterlands. Cow country," Lila listed. "Podunk."

"Growing up with Park Avenue bullshit wasn't such a dream," Sari said.

"You were the one who turned me on to the downtown scene." Lila tightened the belt on the skirt that Sari no longer fit into. Lila was at her lightest—as if to spite Sari, their appetites and worlds suddenly veering in different directions.

"Are you kidding? Getting laid by guys who never called again?" Sari asked. "Or only called months later for a drug connection? It was demeaning." She took off her slippers, rubbing her feet. "Being with a gentleman who listens, takes me seriously and treats me well is liberating."

"Mark? Are we talking about the same person?" Lila tried on different shoes, picturing the collection of foreign condoms, beer steins, porn tapes and *Penthouse* magazines lining her brother's frat-boy apartment in Baraboo. He'd barely let Lila visit but now Sari was moving in.

"We'll be moving to Madison."

"Right, the big city," Lila said. "Consisting of two malls, the college, football stadium and state capitol. First two capitols burned down so they keep rebuilding them uglier."

Sari nixed the flat black sandals. Lila tried the five-inch spikes she couldn't walk in.

"You've become an East Coast snob," Sari sniffed. "Why stay in the apartment alone for eight hundred dollars a month? You'll spend your whole paycheck to live in 400 square feet."

"I got a raise. So rent will only be three weeks' salary. And when I look out my window, I won't see Wisconsin," Lila shot back. "Think Middle America can handle an Armenian Goth-girl married to a frat boy Jew?"

"I'm more worried about my relatives. Yesterday Grandma Varteni and my twin aunts were chanting *Aman. Akcghh Marium Astvudtz.* That means, 'Oh my God, Mother of Christ.'"

Lila was intrigued that Sari's Christian relatives were as taken aback by this turn of events as the Lerner tribe was. "I thought they weren't religious?"

"When I told her, my Manhattan mother regressed back to Armenia, saying *tse tse tse*, shaking her head back and forth." Sari imitated her mother's Old World gesture.

"Sounds like my mom's *Oy vey.* Is your mom freaking because you're pregnant and not married? Or because Mark is Jewish?" Lila asked. She grabbed a blazer to cover her bare shoulders, checking herself in the full-length mirror. Sari shook her head: *no*.

"My whole life, my parents insisted the father determines a child's religion."

"In Judaism it's the mother," Lila explained, taking off the blazer.

"I know. My dad just changed the rules and says my baby will be Armenian because I am."

"He knows you never liked Armenian guys, doesn't he?"

"You mean that I've screwed the United Nations?" Sari quipped. "The only Armenian I dated was Sarkis Abadijian in high school, who was half-black. But he had the 'ian' last name and spoke Armenian so my father was stumped. He finally said, 'There's only one black Armenian in North America and you had to find him.'" Sari handed Lila a black mesh wrap.

"Bet he'd prefer Sari Abadijian to Sari Lerner," Lila said. "You have to keep Sari Dare as your last name. Don't give up that great byline." Sari was right, the sheer wrap was better.

"Mark insists that I take his name. He found a reform rabbi who might convert me."

Nobody told Lila these plans! It pissed her off. "So you're going from one patriarchal sexist culture to another," Lila snapped. "Your parents can handle you converting?"

"They're glad I picked someone getting a law degree and not an MFA. My dad said Jewish men make good husbands. And they really like Mark."

Wait! When had her parents met Mark? Last time he visited? Lila was hurt she wasn't invited. In her old circles, the *shadchan* who introduced the couple was honored. But a mixed marriage was a *shanda*. Sari's pregnancy was summoning up all this ancient Yiddish idiocy.

"How will your mother handle it?" Sari asked.

"She's in shock too. Nobody pictured Mark married or being a father so young."

"He was the one who insisted I have the baby," Sari said. "That's why he flew in with the ring. It was heroic. He's quite virile, you know."

Yuck! Lila couldn't bear boy talk when the boy being bandied about was her little brother. Her feminist mentor being swept off her feet like Cinderella was screwing up her whole worldview.

"He looks a little like you," Sari said. "He has your thin lips, you know."

"Sorry you've been nauseated," Lila tried. "Now I am too."

"Morning sickness, nicotine and pot withdrawal. Not a good time," Sari said, missing the joke.

When the phone rang, Sari started getting up. Lila stopped her, gesturing to the machine.

"Oh, I forgot to tell you Judith Bay called," Sari said. "She wants you to review books for *The Journal*."

"I get three hundred dollars for a television review for the magazine."

"But there's no byline. This way your name would get out there," Sari said.

"Forget it. I'm not writing for a grad school rag for free. For Judith."

"You let them publish your poem," Sari said.

" I just needed *From a Young Ambitious Woman* to see print. Not that anybody reads *Downtown Journal*. I'm not even sure I should review for *New Urban*. Daniel used to say a poet doing criticism is like a eunuch at an orgy."

"Ironic, coming from the guy who couldn't nail you in two years," Sari said.

Lila didn't mind Sari trashing her ex anymore. Arguing about him revived the sardonic Sari and kept Daniel close, as if he wasn't in the Holy Land, lost forever.

"Reviewing isn't real writing," Lila fretted. "It's commenting on someone else's art."

"Unlike navel-gazing confessional poems, reviews help filter through pop culture crap and guide people to what's smart out there." Sari chomped on more saltines.

"Come with me tonight. Please," Lila begged, sounding pathetic and needy.

"I'm having dinner with my parents. You don't need me, you're NCU's emissary now," Sari said. "No wonder they help students get jobs. Then you owe them for eternity."

"I owe Daniel. When Christopher was out, I sneaked into his files and found Daniel's recommendation. He said I was the most intelligent, diligent, impressive student he'd ever had."

"So Wildman was good for something." Sari handed Lila red lipstick.

She lined her lips, kissing a Kleenex to test the fire engine hue. She put her hair in a ponytail. "What if I karmically ruined any future chance with Daniel by sleeping with Howard?"

"He left you and the country. In that last poem in *New Urban,* he picked up a hot Sabra who cooks for him. Bet he publishes a poem each time they screw."

Lila winced at the mention of his new muse, with "the brown-eyed smile that left door-to-door salesman speechless." When she'd read it at the magazine, she decided he'd plagiarized Van Morrison's "Brown Eyed Girl" and tore it up. But she was surrounded by tons of copies. She told herself it was just a foreign fling. But Lila was dying to know what Daniel's brown eyed girl looked like. Luckily they were five thousand miles away so she couldn't stalk her.

"Do you think Howard told Daniel what happened?" Lila asked as Sari pushed the miniskirt down lower on her hips.

Sari nodded. "You both did it to spite him. You were pissed he left. Howard was sticking it to his longtime rival by sticking it to you. And to get his poem in the magazine."

"Not true. Howard wouldn't do that. He's not a bad guy," Lila argued, defensively, regretting their fling. "He's had a lot of *tsuris.* Having a schizophrenic mother doesn't make it easy to connect. And Howard and Daniel really love each other." She went to get a diet soda, jonesing for a cigarette. But she'd quit when Sari did, in sympathy.

"Yeah, that's why Howard wormed his way into your pants and your magazine connections when his supposed best friend left the country," Sari said. "Daniel couldn't get in there, so Howard took his place." Sari smirked. "Might not even be about you. It's homoerotic."

"Fuck you. Future mothers shouldn't be so risqué," Lila said. She uncapped a Tab, stuck in a straw and took a long sip. It wasn't fair that Sari was poaching the Middle American past that Lila couldn't wait to leave, becoming the daughter her mother always wanted. Lila felt edged out; Sari had taken her place. "I just don't know how I'm going to live without you."

"Stop being so self-involved," Sari said.

"Me? I'm not the one ransacking *your* childhood."

"Don't you want me to be happy?" Sari asked. "This is what I want. I'm not dying!"

"But that's what it feels like!" Lila was enraged she couldn't see how quasi-incestuous it was.

"You're not losing me, you're gaining a sister-in-law. My baby will have your blood," Sari tried to explain. "You'll be an aunt. We'll all be related."

"You sound like the Armenian Mary Poppins, justifying your abandonment."

"You can move home anytime you want," Sari sang, like a sick nursery rhyme.

"So now you're morphing into my Jewish mother?" Lila asked.

"*Es mayn kindella*," Sari imitated Hannah's Yiddish, holding up the final saltine.

Lila was stunned to see her mother's diamond chip engagement band on Sari's chubby finger. It was the most important piece of jewelry in her family, bought by her late father. Lila always assumed it would be hers some day. She was hurt that her mother gave it away without consulting her. But Sari was having her first grandchild and moving back to the Midwest, while Lila was a big disappointment, single and staying in New York.

"You're really gonna go through with this?" she blurted out.

Sari's mouth opened. "Wait, are you telling me to get rid of the baby?"

"It's not too late. You worked at Abortion Central, for God's sake."

"I can't believe you just said that!" Sari yelled, her eyes tearing up.

In three years, Lila had never once seen her cry. She felt horrible and guilty and knew she should apologize. But even if it was immature and selfish, she wanted Sari to stay and take care of *her*, not her brother in her old life and the kid they didn't ask Lila's permission to have.

"Well, I can't believe you're stealing my family."

Sari stood up, wiping crumbs off her lap, waddling to her room. "I'm trying to grow up and have my own family here. This is real life!" she yelled. "It's not a goddamn love poem."

24

September 1983

DANIEL

"Good to see you, Daniel. Impressive work in *The New Urban*," Cormick said the minute he walked in, offering a strong handshake, looking him in the eye.

"Thanks, Conor . Coming from you, that means a lot." Daniel nodded, returning his shake, feeling powerful. Exonerated from past sins. He should have left a long time ago. Taking off had obviously earned Cormick's respect.

"Let me take your coat."

As Cormick took Daniel's raincoat to the back room, Howard greeted him with a big shake and backslapping, as if they were all comrades now playing together on the winning team. "Let's get drinks." Howard led him to the makeshift bar on the marble island by the kitchen.

Daniel asked for a Heineken from the bartender, who poured it into a long glass. Cans of Bud apparently wouldn't do tonight.

"Come on man, have a shot of whiskey with us," Cormick said when he returned.

"Jack Daniels Black Gold," Howard pointed out.

"Better not, on an empty stomach." Daniel shook his head. He wasn't adjusted to the time change. He hadn't been sleeping or eating well without

Ronit. He looked at his watch. She was due in at six. He'd planned to pick her up at the airport and bring her to the party to show off his new bride. But a flurry of messages said her flight was cancelled and she was catching the next one. According to the CNN channel he'd checked, a storm in the Middle East caused a mess of flight delays. Daniel decided to go to Cormick's bedroom to call the airport again.

As he turned, he saw Lila walk in the living room. He couldn't breathe.

Her long, lovely dirty blond hair was now shoulder-length. She removed a black gauzy wrap from her shoulders that Howard took. Under it was a low-cut top, a short black leather skirt, spiky high heels and red lipstick. She looked older, slimmer, more sexed up than the innocent Midwest girl in his memory. Stuck at Cormick's sprawling abode, with Ronit's flight from Tel Aviv delayed six hours, Daniel suddenly felt vulnerable, untethered, all the work and love failures he associated with Lila slamming back into his brain. He was enraged that Howard hadn't warned him she would be here.

Daniel ducked back into Cormick's kitchen, spying on her, hiding behind the pillar so she couldn't see him. From the side, her all black silhouette looked too skeletal. He liked his version of her better—more curvaceous, disheveled, clashing in the bright colors of the tacky Baraboo tops her mother sent her. With those scary spikes on her feet, Lila would really tower over him now. He made a mental note to write that down, for a poem.

"Daniel dear, come get something to eat. They have hummus for you," Faith said.

He smiled while staring at Lila, just ten feet away. Had she seen him too? He couldn't tell. He made a beeline for Howard, standing by the table where an assistant was selling stacks of Howard's new book. There must have been fifty copies. All hardcover.

"Could we speak alone for a minute?" he asked quietly, not wanting to cause a scene.

Howard led him into the bedroom, where coats were piled high on the bed and chairs. "Why didn't you tell me Lila would be here?" Daniel demanded.

"Didn't I mention it?" Howard asked.

Daniel finished his beer, craving something stronger.

"This isn't high school. Go say hello," Howard urged.

"But I haven't seen her since we split."

"You're married to Ronit. Why does it matter?"

"Why does it matter that my best friend doesn't let me know he invited my ex to his book party? After I rushed across the world to celebrate with him?"

"You're in town to get rid of your apartment and ship all your stuff to Vermont," Howard said.

"But I switched my travel plans to be here tonight," Daniel lied. "Why do you need former students here anyway? You didn't have to send an open invitation to the alumni."

"I didn't," Howard said. "I invited Lila myself."

"Why?" Daniel asked. "She wasn't your student. She was *my* student and *my* advisee. Not to mention *my* girlfriend." Daniel glared at the man of the hour, uncharacteristically dressed up in classy gray slacks and a dark tweed blazer.

"She did me a favor by giving my poems to Wentworth," Howard reminded him.

"After we split up, you asked *my* ex to submit your work to the editor at the magazine job *I* got her," Daniel said through clenched teeth. "Don't you think that's exploitive?"

"No. I think you're being weirdly proprietary for a newlywed," Howard answered.

Was it Daniel's imagination or was Howard speaking more than usual? The Knopf gold star on his forehead had emboldened his quiet friend. Daniel put the beer bottle on the counter. He felt suspicious, something was wrong. If Lila's name had helped him get in there, and Howard too, something else was up. Lila must be screwing Wentworth! But if she were sleeping with the poetry editor, he would have surely taken at least one of *her* poems too.

"And you were the one who left," Howard added. "You took off for your big foreign fellowship."

"That's not an excuse for you to move in and use Lila as a go-between," Daniel said.

When the doorbell rang, Howard said, "I have to greet my guests."

Daniel followed him back out to the living room, wondering where Lila went. He looked around, trying to reason with himself. Having her submit Howard's poetry for him wasn't the same as asking her out. He pictured Howard stopping by the magazine to see her, taking her to lunch. Or had he gone over to her place to drop them off? Just as Daniel was going to force him to clarify what had gone on between them, someone touched the sleeve of his jacket. He caught a glimpse of blond hair and turned around, nervous it was Lila. But it was only another student.

"Professor Wildman, welcome back," she said. "I loved your poems in *New Urban.*"

Good, everyone here had seen that he, too, had impressive bylines, not just Howard and Cormick. "Thank you." He shook her hand and smiled, trying to recall her name.

"I'm Judith Bay. From your Intro to Post Modernism."

"Ah, yes, of course." Daniel nodded, recalling the lengthy, overwrought rhyming verse she'd written on her Protestant American lineage.

"Did you hear Daniel's leaving us for good?" Cormick said, jumping between them—God forbid Daniel should be getting any female attention the lecher wasn't in on. Some things never changed. "I have to say I'm surprised you're deserting us for the Green Mountain State. You know, I read there with Frost in '58. Spent a whole week at his log cabin in Ripton."

"You actually read with Robert Frost?" Judith asked. "Was he the Poet Laureate then?"

Cormick nodded wistfully. "They called him the Poet Laureate of the Human Soul."

Before Daniel could gag, he slinked away, heading back to the kitchen for another drink. Where had Lila gone? Had she left already? Howard stopped him, pointing at the door, where three men were walking in. "Look."

There was a stir as everyone watched *New Urban Magazine's* poetry editor, Charles Wentworth, walk through the door with Frederick Elliot, the infamously reclusive imp-like editor-in-chief and Christopher Penn, the new publisher. The extremely rare appearance by this trio caused a palpable hum. Howard and Daniel looked at each other, knowing that this book party had just become legendary.

"Boy, you must be a big shot if the Three Musketeers turn out," Daniel mused, in awe.

"I'll drink to that," Howard said, standing taller, pleased with himself. He reached for a fancy bottle of whiskey on the table and poured two shots.

"If I didn't hate you so much for showing me up, I would be very proud of you right now," Daniel joked, patting him on the back.

"Thank you for being envious," Howard said. "You just made my night."

"If I'm seething with jealousy, does that make your week?" Daniel asked.

"Yes." Howard held up his glass. "Couldn't have done it without you, my friend."

"Salut," Daniel said.

They downed their drinks, then Howard poured another. "For courage," he said.

The alcohol was clearly working for him; Daniel watched as his once-mousy comrade strode through all the guests, cut straight over to Wentworth and the other two *New Urban Magazine* editors and shook their hands. Cormick cut in. They chatted away, like they were all close pals who owned the city. Daniel had also been published in the magazine, though it was a year ago. He pushed himself to not be intimidated and make his way over to the big shot brigade.

But then Lila reappeared, joining the alpha males in the center of the room. She pulled out a cigarette that Cormick lit. Daniel slunk to the kitchen, reaching for the whiskey. He poured himself another glass full that he finished fast. On his way to drunk, mesmerized, he spied on her from behind the pillar. She was drinking too while showing off her body in that miniskirt, all long tan legs and cleavage and hot flesh. As she smoked, the set of silver bracelets on her wrists jingled. She was sipping her drink, laughing, life of the party. The other men obviously liked her. She had Wentworth on one side, that tall WASPy-looking business guy on the other. Which one was she sleeping with? Could it be both? She didn't even notice Daniel. Howard held up his glass and clinked it against hers. Since when was she so flirty with Howard?

Daniel poured himself another shot and guzzled it down. Lila used to be in love with him. He wanted to steal her back from Howard and Cormick and the other old lechers fawning all over her. Daniel came up with the excuse of buying a copy of Howard's book in the living room. He rustled for twenty bucks in his wallet to pay. Even though Howard had used Daniel's old blurb on the back and should have given him a copy for free. He inched closer to Lila but she was still drinking and smoking with the guest of honor and *New Urban Magazine* crew, talking casually; she was one of them now and he wasn't. She'd replaced him.

Feeling inconsolable, he needed to leave this party—memorable as it was, in mid-swing. This was not his scene anymore; he no longer belonged. He had to get back to his place to call Ronit to find out what was going on with her damn flight anyway. Why wasn't she here like she was supposed to be? He staggered to Cormick's stately blue bedroom and found his raincoat on the bed. He spied it from under a pile of fancier jackets and furs.

"Daniel. When did you get back?"

When he heard her voice, he spun quickly and all of a sudden she was beside him, in Cormick's bedroom.

"Lila. Yes. Last week. I am. Um, back here. In New York. For now, I mean." He was dizzy, stammering like a high school idiot, dropping his coat back on the bed.

"I saw you in the kitchen. I waved but you um, didn't see me," she said, sounding tipsy, inching closer. Was she lying?"I had too much to drink. These events make me nervous," she whispered, biting her lower lip. Was she always so much taller? Daniel stood up straighter. "So, how was your Holy Land?"

"Good. Really good." He pulled himself together to sound cheerful, puffing his chest out, smiling. Man, she looked beautiful. Definitely older and thinner. Still too much of that horrible perfume.

"I better leave too. A bit dizzy." She reached over and claimed her gauze wrap, threw it around her lovely shoulders. Her legs were bare, tan, no hose. "How's everything been?" she asked, looking at him with those big endless round blue eyes he feared he could still fall through.

"Everything's been good," he said. Shit! An acclaimed poet couldn't find a better word to keep saying than *good*? "I hear everything is good with you." Damn, what did that even mean? That he'd been checking up? Or stalking her? He tried not to teeter, putting his hand on the regal bedpost to steady himself.

"Your poem blew me away," she said.

"Good." Damn, he was stuck on the fucking word. He couldn't say anything else.

"It is true, we cannot keep the brilliance of this moment/that burns both of our flesh like sunlight…" she shut her eyes, reciting.

He was ashamed by what he'd confessed in the poem, as if he was admitting he still had feelings for her now. He was caught in a mixed up time maze.

"I wrote it in Jerusalem," he finally was able to muster.

"I thought you were staying there?"

"Did you want me to stay there?" He was vaguely aware he was too drunk and that his question had just sounded louder and meaner than he'd meant it to.

"What? I never wanted you to leave." She seemed confused, as shell-shocked to be this close to him as he was.

"I have to go," he said, turning to grab his coat. He had to get home to find out when Ronit's plane was coming. She might be landing any minute. She may have already landed and he'd miss her.

"It's hard to see you," Lila told him. "I didn't know you'd be here."

"Busy with your new friends, I see," he murmured idiotically, turning back to her. "When did you and Howard become such good buddies?"

"Oh God, I'm sorry. I never meant to hurt you," she said, starting to cry. Her tears stunned Daniel. What did she mean?

"I didn't either." He flashed to her graduation night, when she came to his apartment to stay over for the first time.

"It was about you," she was saying.

What was about him?

"I was missing you," she cooed in his ear. "That's all it was about."

All what was about? He smelled smoke and vodka on her breath.

"I was missing you too," he admitted. "When I wrote the poem."

"You did? I never got over our fight or the way you left," she said. "I never recovered."

"You didn't?" He longed to run his fingers through her long soft blond strands, as he was doing in his bedroom that warm night they were supposed to sleep together.

"It was my fault," she was saying. "For getting stoned. I ruined everything because I was scared. I'm sorry I was such a young pathetic idiot."

She leaned against him, tears flowing, her breathing jagged, her head collapsing on his shoulder. "No, you weren't. You're my favorite student." He was in the wrong tense, out of sequence, away from his body, lost, as he wrapped his arms around her back. "Don't cry, Lila. I'm sorry. I screwed it up. It was my fault."

"You did?" She sniffled.

He patted her soft hair; he just wanted to get her to stop crying. "I never stopped loving you, Lila," spilled from his stupid mouth.

She turned and surprised him by kissing his ears, his neck, his face. Within seconds she was pushing him down, fumbling on top of him as they fell on Cormick's king size bed. She was kissing him harder, confessing, "I always wanted to be with you too."

Before Daniel could think or stop himself, they were making out on top of the coats, landing on a white rabbit jacket, the room a Tilt-a-Whirl of colors. She reached her left arm to turn off the lamp, rubbing herself against him. He was soaring through the past, to the summer night in his bed, almost two years before. She kissed his lips, gauze coverup falling from her shoulders, shoes dropping, leather inching up, legs wrapping around his waist.

"I was just afraid," she sang.

"I was afraid too," he was telling her when the door burst open, harsh light invading the room.

"Daniel, your wife is on the phone." It was Howard's voice.

"Your *wife*?" Lila shrieked, sitting up. Lipstick stained her cheek, mascara smudged under her eyes like a raccoon. "What? You're married?" She was screaming, pushing Daniel.

He fell to the floor, smashing his elbow. The bright angry bulb blasted his eyes. He felt caught in the wrong bed, the wrong city, the wrong train, the wrong direction. What was he doing here, dizzy on the plush carpet of Cormick's bedroom, the white rabbit jacket and striped fox tumbling on top of him? From upside down, he spotted Cormick and the *New Urban Magazine* crew crowding the doorway to see what the commotion was. They stared inside as Lila rushed past them all in tears, spiky shoes in her hands. Daniel was going to throw up.

"Oh," Howard said. "Sorry to interrupt."

25

September 1983

LILA

Lightheaded and muzzy, dashing down the brownstone's regal steps that seemed to mock her, Lila could barely find her breath. She straightened her skirt, covering her thighs with Sari's wrap, feeling overexposed, in shock that Daniel had finally come back—married! To the brown-eyed girl from his poem. She couldn't believe she'd found and lost him and ruined her reputation as a serious career woman by getting caught on Cormick's bed, screwing around with someone else's husband. Horrified, she pictured the faces peering in, seeing her drunk, half-naked, making out with him: the poetry editor, her enemy Judith, the professors she idolized. Worse—her boss Christopher. She was terrified she'd be fired, blacklisted in her literary world for being an immoral slut.

When she was in third grade, her mom muttered *navka* every time they'd spotted Risa, the bleached blond secretary who'd dated the rabbi before he was divorced. Lila asked what the Yiddish word meant and her mom said, "a tart." For years when Lila saw Risa she'd picture a *hamantaschen*.

She hobbled past Waverly Place, lowering her eyes to avoid imagined stares, sure everyone knew. Lila looked for a dime to call Sari. She found a pay phone on the corner but the dial tone was broken. The old Sari would say, "Fuck those pretentious coots. You don't need male approval to be worthy." Yet her ballsy feminist friend was deserting her for a baby, leaving Lila alone in the city. Maybe jobless. How could she have idiotically screwed up the best gig in the universe? She'd ruined it with Daniel, Sari, the magazine she loved.

Unsteady on her silly stilts, Lila stumbled east, sobbing, seeking to hail a taxi that never came. She stopped on University Place, addled, nauseous, forgetting she'd left the dorm. She'd morphed into the kind of boozed-up freshman she hated. She wanted to fall into Sari's arms but feared she'd be angry that Lila kissed Daniel. She flashed to the moment she'd seen him in the kitchen. She'd lost her breath and balance, downing three vodka and Tabs, then hiding in the bathroom for a half hour so he wouldn't see her. She'd pulled herself together to stand by Howard and Cormick in the living room, self-conscious that Daniel was watching her. He didn't even say hello. Heartbroken, she rushed to grab her wrap and escape when she was stunned to bump into him in the bedroom. The next second she was kissing him on the white rabbit.

A gypsy cab drove her home at last, charging ten bucks for six blocks. Sari wasn't back yet. Lila peeled off her skirt and changed into sweats, and put on Sari's torn Black Sabbath T-shirt from the box she'd packed. She wiped off the mascara streaked under her eyes with baby oil, staring at herself in the bathroom mirror. Daniel's wife must be smaller and skinnier, she imagined, with a perfect tan face prettier than hers. What if she found out and told Lila's relatives in Israel? Oh God, even her mother's cousin the rabbi would hear: Hannah's little girl screwed around with the wrong old poet and became a jobless *navka*.

In Sari's bedroom, Lila rifled through the drawer, looking for the last of her "Gonzo Ganja." She found a thick joint, took it to the living room, opened the window and lit it, blowing out smoke so she wouldn't smell up the apartment. Lila hadn't been drunk or high in four months, since Sari became pregnant, in solidarity. The buzz hit fast. She kept inhaling, hoping to get obliterated. It was trippy, stronger than the stuff from the ruined sex night with Daniel, their breakup a terrifying, out-of-control rollercoaster ride she couldn't get off.

Why would he kiss her if he was married? Did he want revenge? It was the first time she'd seen Howard and Daniel together since graduation. Howard probably told his friend about their tryst. She stared out the window at the apartment across from hers where a guy was watching a big television screen. She toked faster, paranoid, ashes falling on her sweats. She pictured Daniel's rage when he learned she'd slept with Howard, imagining him plotting this vengeful act to take away the prestigious gig he got her, along with her dignity.

Without work, Lila would wind up back in Baraboo. Even Jeff—mad she hadn't visited over Labor Day—wouldn't want her on the rebound again. She picked up Jeff's recent card on the dresser, ran her fingers over his scrawled "I miss you." Had she fucked up that relationship too? Sucking in the final hit, Lila burned her upper lip. She ran to get Tab and ice in the kitchen. Seeing Sari's unopened Absolut in the freezer, Lila sipped from the bottle. It made her shiver, the liquid numbing her going down. She took a big swig, her living room upside down.

Lila touched the dried Korean deli tulips in Sari's vase. Cradling the cold vodka, she put her worn *Lady Sings The Blues* tape in Sari's boom box, pressing play, slow dancing by herself to "Good Morning Heartache." Her father had listened to Billie Holiday. What would he say if he saw her tumbling off Cormick's bed tonight? He would be ashamed. Is that why her dad had left? Everyone was leaving her.

She stumbled to her desk. Lila touched the picture of her handsome father behind the glass, Marlboro dangling from his lips. She sparked a cigarette, smoking like him, disappearing into his photograph. She recalled the afternoon she came home from elementary school and heard this song playing, her parents slow dancing, barefoot on the olive green carpet. As she'd rushed in, her history book fell to the floor. "Come here, my little Lila-head," Daddy said, crouching to pick it up for her, whispering, "If you drop a book, kiss it, sacred like the Torah."

"Stop haunting me now/Can't shake you no how..." Lila kept swaying to the heartache song her father used to play. He was the one who first taught her poems, in first grade. Yeats was his favorite. He pounded his fist and sang the line "I spit into the face of time." She yelled in the empty room. "That has transfigured me!"

Did she make up the memory?

After the rebuttal to Daniel, Lila had abandoned poetry. She'd dried up without his praise. Poetry was all his now. She put a piece of paper through her typewriter's roller. Each poem is a letter, he'd told her. She typed *Last Words*, the final poem she'd ever write, to Daniel: "In dreams you're overdosing like my dead father/sleeping with Aunt Francine who you never met/ exiled to the Holy Land where I scrawl you desperate poems on purple paper..." Not enough music, he would say. Wrong number of syllables. Mixing metaphors.

"Plath mixed metaphors!" Lila shouted, as if he were here, in front of her. She pulled out *Daddy* from the shelf, reading it aloud the way she and Daniel used to, reciting the part about the black man "who bit my pretty red heart in two."

"Color, heart, burial, suicide, bones, glue. See?" Lila argued, pointing to the page. "Plath takes a different metaphoric leap in each line. I didn't sleep with Howard out of spite. He was the closest I could find to you."

She typed: "I slow dance to Daddy's heartache in the mirror/holding dry flowers, homesick in my own room."

No, too disjointed, superficial. "Dig deeper," he'd yell. Be more naked. She wasn't good enough. Daniel was gone forever, like her father. He would never put his pen to her poems again. Nor would Howard. Or Christopher, who would axe her. She'd end up stuck at a rinky-dink newspaper like her dad, fixing other people's copy.

Lila's head was throbbing, tension tightening her brows. In the bathroom medicine chest there was no aspirin, just Tylenol. She took a blue capsule, washed it down with vodka but the pounding kept getting louder. To make the noise go away she took a handful more, stumbling on a good last line: *All my fathers are dead now.*

When Lila opened her eyes, Sari was standing by the side of her bed, in a ratty blue sweater and gray sweats.

"Thank God." Sari took her hand.

Where was she? Wait, this wasn't her place. She scanned the tiny windowless room, divided by a curtain. Were there other people behind there? The blue walls had ugly flower paper framing the top. It smelled like cleaning solution. She was in a light pink gown. No bra, but she could feel her underwear and socks were still on. Her nose was sore, her throat burning.

"You're at St. Vincent's Hospital. I found you on the floor last night and called an ambulance. Can you understand what I'm saying?" Sari was speaking very slowly. "Can you talk?"

"I'm not retarded." Lila's voice came out scratchy. She sat up, hung over. Frightened. She felt battered, like she'd lost a boxing match, her left rib aching.

"What the hell happened?" Sari looked worried and exhausted, like she hadn't slept.

Lila turned from her stare, foggy. She remembered the heartache song her father used to play and how it got tangled with Daniel leaving her again. Her shoulder hurt too. She checked her watch. It wasn't on her wrist.

"It's noon," Sari told her. "On Friday."

Lila touched the Band-Aid over a sore spot on her hand.

"From the I.V." Sari poured water from the pink pitcher on the nightstand and handed her a paper cup full. "They pumped your stomach."

"Why?" It hurt to drink. "I just took aspirin."

"The doctor said you chased a fistful of Extra Strength Tylenol with dope and vodka. Why would you do that?"

It was fuzzy but Lila remembered a man tying her down to a gurney. "I was upset. Daniel didn't tell me..."

"You're staring this shit again! It's been over for more than a year! He's in Israel!" Sari shouted.

"No, he's in New York. Really." She flashed to: Daniel's head falling on the fur coat on Cormick's bed. The heel of her shoe wobbling as she ran down Cormick's stairs. "We kissed. At Howard's party." She flinched at the thought. "But he married the Sabra. From his poem." Lila realized how screwed up she sounded. She sipped water. "You didn't call my mom?"

"Nobody answered," Sari said.

A short blond nurse in light green scrubs marched in and handed Lila a stack of yellow papers on a clipboard with a pen taped to it. "Fill these out," she barked before she left.

"What's her problem?" Lila asked.

"You yelled at her when you came in. You called her a *navka* and some other Yiddish words. Then you blacked out again," Sari said. "Mark's on his way."

"I don't want to see Mark."

"Tough." Sari sat down on the bed.

"Don't tell my mom." Lila gripped both of Sari's hands, pleading.

"I have to, Lila. I know what you were doing. I saw your poem in the typewriter."

The line jumped into Lila's mind and she recited: "'*In dreams you're overdosing like my dead father.*' What do you think?"

"Are you actually asking if I like your suicide poem?" Sari snapped.

"I wasn't killing myself." Lila shook her head no, adamantly. "I was killing my poetry. I'm a much better critic. Really."

"Come on. Who are you talking to? *Last Words*?" Sari took her hands back.

"My last words to Daniel. The last poem I'll write." She almost choked at the thought.

"You're scaring me," Sari said. "He left last year. He never even returned your calls."

"He kissed me last night. In the flesh. I swear." Lila couldn't have imagined it, could she? "Don't tell my mom. She'll make me leave New York. You can't do this to me."

"I can't do this to *you*? You almost died. What the fuck is wrong with you? I'm pregnant and puking ten times a day and had to ride with the paramedics rushing you to the emergency room at midnight since you almost offed yourself." She was breathing heavy, heaving, her belly rising and falling.

"I didn't. I wouldn't. Come on, Sari, you know me."

"You were reading *Ariel*!"

"I always read *Ariel*."

"The doctor said you need a psych consult. They're recommending a therapist."

"Daniel was always trying to push me into therapy. Now that I'll never speak to him again, he'll get his wish. Isn't that funny?"

"Yeah, hilarious," Sari said. "Stop with fucking Daniel! You have to do therapy. And get it together. Seriously."

"You're not my mother." Lila tried to fill out the first form, but her hand was shaking.

"When I went home to get your insurance card this morning," Sari said, "the phone rang and ...I couldn't stop him from coming." "Wait, so Daniel knows?"

"Daniel? This is a sickness!" Sari looked exasperated. "You are never allowed to mention his name again."

"Then who phoned?" Lila was confused.

"Christopher. From the magazine. He called to see why you weren't at work this morning. You missed some big meeting. When I told him where you were, he insisted on coming down."

"He's here now? Jesus! You told Christopher!" Lila recalled talking to her boss at the party. Damn, that meant he saw everything. "Tell him to leave now. He can't see me like this."

"He's been waiting two hours."

"Fuck." Lila pulled down the edge of the flimsy gown. "This is the most horrible moment of my life."

"My worst moment was coming home last night and thinking you were dead."

Lila leaned closer, grabbing the sleeve of her worn sweater that smelled like a mix of honey and puke. "I'm sorry. And I didn't mean to say you shouldn't have the baby."

Sari sat down on the bed next to her. "I would never get rid of a child. My parents discussed the Armenian massacres at breakfast every morning. You're not the only one with a genocide. Half our relatives were wiped out. I always knew I'd have kids."

"I never meant it. Listen, I want you and Mark to be a family." Lila put her hand on Sari's stomach and kissed it. "I just can't believe you're moving away. Ever since my Dad died, saying goodbye freaks me out…"

"It's okay. We're okay. We're not saying goodbye. You'll never get rid of me. I'm your family now," Sari said, hugging Lila tightly. "You're stuck with me forever."

Lila spied Sari's purse on the ugly orange chair. "Do you have your compact mirror?"

"Oh, now you're going to be vain?"

"He's my boss. If I look like a loon, he'll fire me."

"You should've thought of that before guzzling booze and so many pills they had to stick a tube down your throat to get out. That was really attractive." Sari tossed a mirror and hairbrush on the bed, then left.

Lila looked at her hungover, pale, makeup-less face in Sari's compact, wincing, terrified. She had to fix herself, to stay away from him forever. She realized for the first time: her feelings were way off, distorted, twisted out of control. The wrong love could kill you.

"We were worried about you," Christopher said, looking down at Lila, seeming extremely tall and stately.

Who was we? Other magazine bigwigs? She hoped they didn't know. Did

Daniel? Did she want him to? "It was an accident." Lila avoided his eyes, knowing she'd never looked worse. "Last night, when I came home, I had a migraine. I didn't know that he was…"

Christopher cut her off. "Of course you didn't. What your professor did was unspeakable. He should be shot. Thankfully, he left town," he said. Then he stood there, awkwardly looking around the room, finally adding, "Nobody blames you, Lila."

What? Daniel was gone already? How many times did she have to lose him? He must have gone back to Israel with his wife. Even though he was married, hearing that he left town shocked her, took something else away.

"Don't ever do anything like this again," Christopher was saying.

"I'm sorry I screwed up and made an idiot of myself and missed work. Please don't fire me," Lila begged. " I'll make it up to you."

Christopher stared at her, nodding. "I won't let you go. I promise."

PART SIX: 2010

26

April 2010

DANIEL

"Hey, Dad, the *Free Press* says two hundred people came to your Barnes & Noble gig in New York." His daughter Galia scrolled to an article on her iPhone. "More like two hundred and sixty-three. They lied."

"They approximated," said Sam, his firstborn, the MBA math brain. "Hey your picture's all over Twitter."

"I'll link it to your website," offered Baruch, his second boy, typing on his iPad.

Even his children liked him better since the award. As they'd tumbled into the house after their long drive back to Vermont, Daniel realized that instead of rushing to check their instant messages or Jon Stewart clips for what they considered news, they were Googling their father. At the end of his sixth decade, he'd gone viral.

As they all headed to their rooms upstairs, Daniel grabbed some Heinekens in the kitchen, thinking of last Thursday, when the award was announced. He'd caught Galia—wearing ripped black leather like her idol Lady Gaga—sitting on her bed, uploading articles into a Tumblr album she titled "My Dad's Big Prize." Samuel, who was "Sam White" on Facebook, (so nobody would know he had his business degree from the school where his father taught) switched back to Wildman. Baruch posted an old picture on his Facebook wall of himself, his brother, and Daniel, holding up a largemouth bass they caught on a fishing trip last summer. Daniel had finally infiltrated all their technology, not by snooping, but by winning.

"Thirsty?" He uncapped a beer, handing it to Ronit.

"Thanks," she said, taking a long drink.

Intellectually he knew that achievement was not redemption, of course. He waited for the festivities and adulation to taper off, expecting to crash with disappointment. Yet so far the recognition had made him feel lighter and more loved, as if the world was fair, after all. As he pulled up his driveway, the fall colors surrounding his farmhouse seemed richer, the family jokes funnier. He could not think of another serious poet his age who had managed to avoid mental breakdowns, multiple divorces, alcoholism and poverty. He should get a prize for that.

Leaning against the counter, sipping his drink, he pictured the crowd at the bookstore. Then he flashed to the shock on Lila's face as he'd asked her name. Twenty-four hours later he remained rattled by her.

"Hungry?" his wife asked.

"Starving."

"Think I have nothing better to do than cook for everyone?" She smiled, grabbing peppers and scallions from the fridge. "Chicken couscous for my prizewinner?"

"Perfect. How often does the whole family eat together anymore?"

"Let's hope they're not all moving back in," she joked but he wouldn't mind if they did. When their youngest Galia left for Yale in September, Daniel had slept in her room, on her twin bed, for three nights, with a worse case of empty nest syndrome than Ronit.

"I couldn't have done anything without you." He nuzzled her warm nape.

"You're in for it later," she whispered, brushing against the crease in his corduroys.

At the hotel, they'd made love three times in five days. Not bad for an old man. But he worried he'd need to take one of the little blue pills his doctor prescribed to get it up again tonight.

"You were nervous for nothing," she said. "Your book event was standing room only. Nobody wanted to leave."

Daniel still didn't understand why he'd panicked when Lila showed up at the bookstore. He knew he should tell Ronit already. It was only one dumb kiss decades ago.

"Did you see my old student Lila Lerner stopped by the reading?" he asked.

"The young woman of ambition," Ronit said, putting the name with the poem too fast. "Why didn't you introduce us?"

"Oh, maybe we were getting coffee. She couldn't stay long."

"Afraid for us to meet?"

"No. Why?"

He was about to share the difficult details he'd left out long ago when his wife said, "You two were very important to each other."

The statement was so Ronit –raw, generous, no bullshit. But her dark eyes looked away from his. He wrapped his arms tightly around her waist.

"You are my life," he whispered in her ear.

Daniel recalled showing Ronit the poem he'd made of his Lila anguish when they first met, deluding himself into thinking that a few lyrical stanzas could finish off their relationship. Yet, as Zalman warned, "Good art does not redeem bad love." Indeed, Daniel had never admitted to himself how he'd run away from his ex-city and his ex-girlfriend like a coward—no sex, no compassion, no closure. That unfinished longing must have poured out during their last inappropriate drunken kiss when—just for those fleeting seconds—he'd forgotten he was married. If he confessed to Ronit now, he'd wind up disclosing that he and Lila had never consummated their affair. That secret shamed him worse. Not that they didn't have sex –but that, all ths time, he'd let his wife think they had. The thought still embarrassed him, made him feel less of a man.

"I need to just check in with my publisher," he told Ronit. "Yell when dinner's ready." He would wait until later, when the kids were out. He would tell her then.

In his office Daniel shut the door and turned on his new 30-inch large font monitor. Who would have thought a Luddite like him would craft his best poetry on computer? In the days he'd been gone, three hundred emails had accumulated. Daniel read a note from his editor, asking him to pre-tape an NPR interview and commit to a charity benefit for the Fletcher Library. Over half a century immersed in the poetry world, he'd barely spoken to publicity people. This week he'd been assigned two publicist of his own, phoning and emailing daily.

He accepted both offers. In a burst of gratitude, he decided to shed old grudges and past bitterness. He'd forgive the editors who rejected him, along with Cormick who, in his nineties, could no longer bang undergrads from his room in the nursing home. And Howard, twice divorced and broke, whose success he'd once begrudged. Daniel was glad he'd taken Ronit's advice to thank Cormick and Howard in the *Losers Like Me* acknowledgments, before the prize ensured that anybody would read to the end.

He should have thanked Lila too. He wanted to make peace with everyone he'd ever crossed words or swords with, especially her. He suddenly needed to know what was in her damn envelope.

Sitting on his worn brown leather desk chair, he Googled "Lila Penn." Her website popped up: very jazzy, with different colors and bars for her bio, columns, radio and TV appearances. He clicked on the link that said "The Charlie Rose Show." Suddenly he was watching her discuss her book on national TV, blond hair falling over her shoulders, her eyes still that intense dark blue. She was wearing the same tight black dress as yesterday. Ah, so it wasn't bought for him but for Charlie and the television cameras.

He listened to Lila's lightning fast, familiar voice discuss how dope dealer Mary Louise Parker on *Weeds* screwed her way through the drug world, Holly Hunter's alcoholic policewoman in *Saving Grace* had an adulterous affair with her partner, and Kyra Sedgwick's sugar-freak deputy chief on the *Closer* bedded both her married boss and her FBI liaison.

"So in current pop culture, a female can be successful if she's a gorgeous size four substance addict who sleeps with multiple colleagues to get ahead," Lila said.

"What about all the female surgeons on *Grey's Anatomy*?" Rose challenged.

"How many of *your* physicians are blond, five-foot-ten, and put themselves through med school as lingerie models?" Lila asked. "And sleep with a straight doctor, a gay doctor, a heart patient and his ghost—all in the same season?"

Touché! Lila was so much more confident now. Charlie Rose read a review of her collection, *Sirens Of the Small Screen*, calling her "The Pauline Kael of television criticism." Daniel had enjoyed Lila's witty, acerbic weekly column in the magazine. The first time he saw her byline, he felt proud, since he was the one who'd taught her to be an incisive critic. She admitted his influence in that moving poem she'd published in the grad school rag. In his *Selected Poems*, she was forever "the tall blond Jewess from Baraboo." He *had* composed her.

When Daniel first saw her slender book in the store a month ago, he'd grabbed it, hoping it was poems. Yet it was a hardcover compilation of reviews. Turning to the back, he read that she lived in Tribeca with her husband, with no mention of children, which disappointed him. If they'd stayed together, maybe she would have had kids and he would have had Manhattan, he couldn't help but think. When he'd found nothing in her bio about her poetry background, he was surprised how slighted he felt—as if she'd completely edited him out of her life. He was sad that she'd ended up wasting her buoyant literary brain, merely commenting on other people's pop culture *dreck*. How could she desert her own talent?

Looking back, with his daughter now the age Lila was, he realized how young she'd been when they'd met. The thought of a college professor touching his baby, Galia, made him wince. As a mentor, he'd failed Lila. Daniel should have kept his promise never to fall for a student. Although he'd technically waited until she'd graduated, there was an imbalance of power that he now regretted. He suddenly worried that all the angst with Lila was his fault.

He hoped the romantic headaches he'd caused hadn't gotten in the way of her art. "Go back to your poems," he wished he could tell her.

He did understand her impatience to get fast bylines and why she'd settled for an easier genre. He could never handle rejection well either. He was almost in his seventh decade before being rewarded for his poetry. When she'd first taken the magazine job, he'd overreacted, mistaking Lila's motivation to mean she was choosing her career over him, as if she were selling him out for a steady paycheck and health insurance. How ridiculous he'd been. He could now see that it was a smart decision for a young woman to make, especially someone who'd grown up without a father.

"You can afford to be a suffering artist," Lila had once told him. "For you it's chic."

He replayed her Charlie Rose interview. Talk about chic. While he'd gained weight, lost most of his hair, suffered from disc problems and weaker vision, Lila had barely aged. The benefit of being childless? No wonder she was shocked to think he didn't recognize her. She'd turned into an elegant, successful, married Manhattan magazine writer plugging her bestseller on national television. Yet still, she came to see him. Nothing was forgotten.

He typed in her married name and found a photo of her and her husband at a Met gala. Funny how his Jewish poetess had fallen for a *shaygetz* named Christopher. A *Business Week* article said he'd gone from *New Urban's* publisher to president of their magazine group. That was a long cry from Lila's early days in the Village, when he'd assign only paperbacks in class because he knew she couldn't afford hardcovers.

Daniel remembered being in the bedroom with her at Howard's calamitous book bash. The very next evening, Howard, flat on his back, intravenous tubes in his arm, confessed their tryst. Fascinating what someone will tell you after open-heart surgery. It was as if the success of Howard's book almost killed him. When Daniel rushed uptown to Mt. Sinai, Howard had offered a deathbed confession. Then the bastard had the nerve to live.

He recalled it was that Sabbath, right after sundown on a hot night in September, 1983. Ronit had just lit the candles and served chicken and couscous for him and her Israeli cousins who'd moved to Park Slope. Daniel left them, hopping the subway to the hospital, praying his best friend would pull through. In the waiting room for six hours with the Jewish poet brigade, he heard the gossip: at Howard's party, Lila's boss Christopher from the magazine had trashed Daniel, calling him a scumbag. It became clear to Daniel that the tall WASP businessman string bean was sleeping with Lila. She'd gone for his complete opposite, which stung. Calculating the time frame, he'd figured out that was why Lila had kissed him the night before—to make her two other lovers at the party jealous.

At his final therapy session the next day, before Dr. Zalman's fatal stroke, Daniel ranted, "Lila screwed everybody but me!"

"Your best friend almost died and this is what you need an emergency session for?" Zalman was incredulous. "You're twice Lila's age. You're an adult. You two were incompatible. You married your *beshert*. Let this go or you'll ruin your life!" His therapist's last words to Daniel were: "The heart is half a prophet. Now be a man and use your head.'"

Sage advice. Ronit held him close that night, confessing she was pregnant. God's way of saying: start over in Burlington, where his professorship was waiting. He'd never visited New York again. Until yesterday.

Last night in Tribeca, one look at Lila catapulted him back to being a married lecher on the floor of Cormick's bedroom. Everybody was sneering at him, his sweet student sobbing as she fled Howard's party. Drenched in guilt, Daniel had chased Lila outside to apologize. But she'd already disappeared down the street. The memory of standing alone out there, puking on the steps of Cormick's Washington Mews stoop, made him ill. What caused his nausea was the feeling that he'd married the wrong woman.

Now he thanked God every day for Ronit. So when Lila handed him his book to sign at the reading, he should have just said hello casually, like a normal person. But even in his triumphant hour, he couldn't handle seeing the one lover he'd wanted but never really had. Staring up at her, he was terrified, paralyzed. He tried to rectify his tiny betrayal of Ronit, to revise his ending with Lila so *he* was the one who didn't want *her*. So he'd regressed to being the same idiotic buffoon all over again.

When he heard Lila's voice crack in hurt as she said her maiden name, he wished he would have relented and told her: "I am so sorry for the way I acted. I was such a foolish clown back then." Or "In fifty years of teaching you were the only student I ever loved." Daniel shut his eyes, reliving the spring night at his rickety apartment on Horatio Street right after Lila's graduation. He'd finally taken off her clothes. He was holding her naked in his bed, thinking, I can't believe this young, long-legged, gorgeous creature is in love with a loser like me. He scrawled *loser like me* on a Kleenex box by his bed right after she fled.

"Dan, the phone," Ronit called, walking into his office without knocking.

He clicked back to mail before his wife would see his former flame on the screen. If he confessed his long ago half-sin, surely Ronit would exonerate him. But why burden her with his old shame?

"It's my brother in Tel Aviv. He wants to congratulate you."

Mr. Big Shot Israeli Poet, who'd won a Nobel Prize a decade earlier, hadn't returned his calls in a month. "I have three hundred emails. Everybody and their cousin's crawling out of the woodwork," he told Ronit.

"You'll call him back?" She stood there, waiting for his answer.

"It's like Gogol's *Dead Souls* in here. Who'll be next—my mother returning from her grave?" Daniel asked. No, he would never tell his wife the end of the Lila story. He was lucky to live here with her, his last love, far from the superficial, ugly, noisy city.

"Just say hello," Ronit said. "Be nice."

27

April 2010

LILA

He kissed her quickly at the door, missing her lips. "I tried to reach you."

"So glad you're home." Lila hugged him, hoping he didn't notice how tired she was. She'd barely slept, still ashamed and wounded by the Daniel debacle. She broke away, carrying her husband's garment bag inside, overwhelmed with guilt that she'd gone to the reading.

Christopher dropped his briefcase on the floor, watching her. "Your hair's different."

She detected an accusatory lilt in his tone. Did he know? "Just a touch up," she said, hoping he didn't suspect she'd dolled up to see Daniel, not him. "So how did your meeting go?"

"Same idiots trumpeting the magazine's prestige while ruining it by plastering pop-up crap on the website, shoving tacky advertorials down my throat," he said. "Why didn't you call me back? I waited an hour last night." He sounded upset.

She couldn't tell him she'd been demolished by a rejection from a man he'd forbidden her from seeing twenty-seven years ago. "I got home late."

"L.A. is three hours behind," he said. "What's going on?"

"I must have fallen asleep. I've been so inundated with work. Gin and tonic?" she offered though she was hungover; the thought of alcohol made her nauseous.

"No thanks," he said as she led him to the leather couch. Lila stared at the Chagall lithograph "Red Poppies" over their fireplace: a man and half-naked woman floating above a world of flowers. She loved the picture and the airiness of this room, the edge of Manhattan skyscrapers gracing the wraparound floor-to-ceiling windows, the skyline the true work of art. "Tight deadline?" She felt interrogated as they sat down.

"How TV vampire series steal shamelessly from authors without credit. Leading with Sookie Stackhouse, Bram Stoker and Anne Rice. Titled: *Blood Suckers or Book Suckers*."

"I'm sure they'll change it," he said.

"Remember when they switched *Whacking Off to Mary Louise Parker* to *Weeding Out The Virgin Mary*? You'll take a look at it later?" she asked, glad her alibi worked.

But he didn't answer. She needed him to read –and help edit—her review. She wished she could show him the envelope in her purse too. But her old poetry was too juvenile and revealing. She'd given it up anyway, after the hospital stay decades ago. "Oh, Mom asked if we would have the second Seder at her place."

"Anything Hannah wants," he said, preoccupied, going to the bedroom to unpack.

Since Christopher and Sari converted, they did Jewish holidays better than Hannah's own kids. Christopher's late mom was a rich divorced WASP who preferred booze to food. So he relished how Hannah fed and fussed over him. In the kitchen, Lila anxiously unloaded the dishwasher, recalling how overbearing Daniel had found her mother. What he'd viewed as a liability, her husband treasured. Christopher even bought Hannah a nearby Gramercy Park pied-à-terre after she was widowed again. Daniel would never have done that. Her husband was probably overcompensating for being a workaholic who travelled too much. But now that he was back she felt protected, everybody essential nearby.

Well, not everyone. As she returned the forks, knives and spoons to their home in the silverware drawer, the digital picture frame on the wall flashed Sari and Mark at their twin girls' law school graduation. In another shot, happy Midwest housewife Sari was in sneakers and a U of W sweatshirt, gardening: her new passion. Lila put the crystal wine stems in the cabinet.

The next photo showed Lila's close friend Judith Bay, her husband Jeff, and their kids. Ironic that her two sophisticated New York classmates married Midwestern guys she'd introduced them to. The people in her life flashed around her. They all had broods, like Daniel. If Lila had married him, maybe she'd have had children too. Christopher didn't want any. Lila never had a strong maternal urge. Yet seeing Daniel's kids last night made her feel empty.

"For a Jewish woman, being childless is a tragedy," Hannah had once accused.

"You have three grandkids because of me! My best friend's your womb," Lila had yelled back. She'd read her mom an Orthodox rabbi's interpretation of Genesis, where G-d blessed Noah and his sons and told them to "Be fruitful and multiply," the first *mitzvah* in the Torah. But technically, multiplying was only mandatory for men. When a woman had a child, she merely shared her husband's *mitzvah*. It didn't even count as *her* accomplishment.

"You're my family. We're enough," Christopher had often claimed. Being a good person, wife and daughter was sufficient, she'd decided. So why couldn't she stop thinking of Daniel's big family? She kept picturing his daughter, who looked Lila's age in grad school.

Her therapist had insisted Lila's overdose back then wasn't an accident. A breakup could feel like death. Dr. Ness said Daniel's desertion had ignited an unconscious wish to join her father. Lila was skeptical, but last night—at four a.m.—she'd sobbed over the Franz Wright poem in the magazine about *his* father: "Since you left me at eight/I have always been lonely/Star-far from the person right next to me, but/closer to me than my bones you/you are there." Was she crying because it captured how she felt or because that was the poem she should have written, instead of a life of television commentary?

Christopher came out of the bedroom and stared at her. "Did you see Daniel last night?"

Startled, she dropped the glass she was holding in the sink. The side chipped a little but it didn't break. Her neck felt damp as she clicked off the video montage. She didn't want to keep important words from him anymore. "I did go to hear Daniel read," she confessed, trying to sound nonchalant. "Right around the corner at Barnes & Noble. Decent crowd. For poetry."

He poured himself the gin he hadn't wanted, no tonic. She hated that he wouldn't yell when enraged or raise his voice. He'd pretend nothing was wrong, drinking instead of shouting. But Mr. Moderation always stopped after a few, never getting inebriated. She sometimes fantasized about soaking his brisket in vodka, just to see him get sloppy drunk for once.

"He doesn't party. He won't get sloshed. He doesn't do any drugs—ever," Lila had complained to Dr. Ness when she'd first started dating Christopher.

"You're listing his assets, right?" her therapist had said, smiling.

Now Christopher opened the bar's freezer, grabbed a fork and chopped at the block of ice that had formed. "You left it too cold," he snapped, adding a few chips to his drink. Then he turned to her with a clenched jaw. "Did something happen between you two?"

Lila hesitated. She screwed open a diet soda bottle and took a sip, not wanting to make it worse by letting him know she'd been tanked the night before. "Seeing him was hard."

"Why?"

Her eyes teared up as she refilled his glass. "He acted weird."

"What happened?" her husband asked.

She felt stupid, vain and embarrassed as she uttered: "He didn't even recognize me."

"You can't be serious," Christopher said, then burst out laughing.

"Don't make fun of me." She hit his arm. "It flipped me out."

"That old schmuck knew exactly who you were," he insisted. "Come on. You look the same as you did the day he sent you to the magazine."

"No, he didn't. Really."

"Lila, your book was a bestseller, you were on national TV, your photo was in *The Times*. Think he doesn't read or watch television? He probably sits around in his pee-stained underwear, Googling you all day."

She loved that he remembered the underpants reference from a poem she'd read him, Gregory Corso's *Marriage*. Showing him other people's poems was safer than sharing hers.

"He couldn't spell my last name," Lila admitted.

"Oh, that's priceless." He scoffed. "Has anyone from your past ever not recognized you before? He's such a liar."

"You think so?" She tried to hide the relief in her voice. "But why would he act like he didn't know me?"

"Maybe he never got over your affair."

Lila broke away and put the chipped glass back on the shelf, thrown by the word *affair*. While Sari had concealed all the hot sex she'd had before she wed, Lila had hidden her and Daniel's *lack* of physical passion. Early on, telling Christopher of her two years with Daniel, she'd deleted one fact: they'd never made love. She wouldn't undermine their romance in Christopher's eyes. After her hospital crisis, she worried he'd find her insane to lose it over a guy she'd never had sex with. Or was she more afraid it confirmed how deeply she'd loved Daniel, with her head and heart, though not her flesh?

"You're so gullible," Christopher said. "It was his petty way of getting back at you."

"Why would he want to?"

He shut the cabinet, standing in front of her. "Because you're so much happier with me."

Lila nodded, not finished unraveling the ancient mystery. If Howard had confessed to Daniel she'd slept with him, that could explain why he'd pretended not to know her at the bookstore. If Daniel was still distressed decades later, it proved that their feelings had been mutual. Her chest felt lighter. She was buoyant, almost giddy.

Christopher pulled her close, kissing her neck, which tingled. "Still love me?"

"You know I adore you," Lila told him, breaking away. "I'm just having some kind of a career crisis. I'm thinking I should teach that seminar in cultural criticism at Columbia."

"Now you want to be a teacher, like Daniel?" he asked. He plopped the glass down on the counter without a coaster, splashing gin as if trying to stain their granite. "Better it's not poetry. All those neurotic poets you hung out with were so infantile."

Astounding genius justified a few personality quirks, she didn't say. So he *was* pissed off! Or was he jealous? MBAs didn't win the Pulitzer. "Did you eat on the plane?" She wiped away his spill with a blue sponge. "Want to order in?"

"No, I'm fine," Christopher said.

They were not fine. She'd defied his longstanding mandate. She hated that her husband knew she'd lost it, seeing Daniel again. Was he thinking of her at the psych ward? Lila had always worried that was why he'd fallen for her. So utterly taken—and demolished—by Daniel, she was ambivalent about Christopher then. *Will you take me like I am?* Joni Mitchell sang. *Strung out on some other man.* She bet he found her more alluring that way. He played the crusading knight, saving the damsel from an unfaithful cad, like he'd done for his mother. Christopher had never been the object of her obsession. He'd sidestepped Lila's mania which continued swirling elsewhere, concealed.

"Don't be angry I went."

"I'm angry you lied to me," he said.

She'd rarely deceived him outright, pretending that years of sly omissions didn't count.

"Were you impressed with his new book?" he asked, not letting Daniel go either. Her old boyfriend had been their unspoken shield, their buffer.

"It wasn't bad," she said, reaching for another soda. He grabbed her wrist, stopping her.

"Do you think he deserved the award?" he asked directly, his voice cracking a little.

She was touched by her husband's vulnerability. "Well, it's the old failure shtick he's playing around with. Nothing he hasn't done before." She didn't share her real assessment—that each poem was like an arm, a finger, a toe—and this time it all fit together to form a complete body. Daniel's new collection was majestic, a triumphant feat, deserving every award. Although she hadn't been in his life for decades, Lila was proud of him. She flashed to the Roethke poem he'd once read her, *Elegy For Jane* (*My Student Thrown by a Horse*), which ended: "I, with no rights in this matter/neither father nor lover." No rights. Nor lover.

These damn poems kept intruding; Daniel had brought them back. Christopher let go of her, poured himself another shot he downed. Two minutes seeing her ex was driving them both to drink.

"Do you wish you'd wound up with a famous writer?"

"Don't be ridiculous." She tried not to compare Daniel, a messy, jagged artist with Christopher, a practical, private man, who made everything cleaner, calmer, less chaotic. She did think longingly of the mania that she and Daniel once shared, reciting transcendent lines at midnight, certain that an idiosyncratic couplet would solve the riddle of the universe, or a fresh stanza could heal their childhood traumas.

Daniel should have kept his promise to never get involved with a student. But he wasn't a Svengali taking advantage of an innocent girl. She'd reduced him to a paternal figure, an unrequited fantasy in her head, not her bed. He might have been more scarred by their split than she was. After all, when she'd refused his proposal, he'd fled Manhattan forever. He couldn't even say hello to her twenty-seven years later.

At the reading, Lila had stared at Ronit, his compact wife with regal brown eyes. She had a kind face and the erect posture of a devoted mother and founder of an international charity. They'd won the Gandhi award, the womb lottery, not to mention last week's Pulitzer. Ronit clearly took care of it all: Daniel, their offspring, as well as poor Palestinian and Israel kids too.

For so long Lila had selfishly wished she could have kept Daniel as a mentor *and* stolen his talent. Late last night, unable to let go of *Losers Like Me*, she tried to pinpoint where his seamless rhythms and magic multiple meanings came from, how he learned to spin such lyricism from his neurosis and pain, while she'd just given up poetry altogether.

"No regrets?" Christopher asked.

She'd been hurting her husband over a phantom, a lingering father-delusion. But suddenly it seemed Daniel's sole purpose was to lead Lila to the career where she'd found success and authentic love.

"You know, if Daniel hadn't pushed me for the job, I wouldn't have met you." She took her husband's hand and squeezed his long, elegant fingers.

"Not one regret at all?"

"Not about marrying you." She kissed him hard, on the lips.

When she'd first told her therapist she wasn't sure if she could find happiness with Christopher, Dr. Ness had said: "Love doesn't make you happy. Make yourself happy."

Daniel had been right when he'd pegged her heart as a prism where each pleasure must be fractured. But the choice haunting her was between her ambitions. She'd been too weak to withstand rejection, impatient, wooed by the validation of seeing her name in print that she was paid for. She wished she hadn't stopped struggling with her own messy art to merely weigh in on what others were creating. Becoming a TV critic, she'd conceded defeat, filing away her youthful attempts at free verse. It wasn't Daniel she'd missed so badly, but sharing the dark confessions he'd embraced, following his brave mission to live the least secretive life.

"Hungry?" Christopher asked. "I'll sit with you if want. Spicy salmon from Nobu?

Her favorite. That meant he'd forgiven her. But the thought of fish made her ill.

"No, let's stay in," she said. She found her purse and pulled out the envelope she'd brought to the reading. "Going through my files, I found the last poem I wrote."

"Did you show it to Daniel?"

"No. He didn't ever see this one." If she gave it to Christopher, he'd know all her deceptions: She'd never slept with Daniel. She hadn't recovered from losing her father. It wasn't an accidental overdose; she'd wanted to join him, to become his loss. Had Lila kept her secrets hidden here, for safekeeping, until she was ready to remember?

She took out the graying sheet, nervously skimming the type. She now knew: *All my fathers are dead now* wasn't the end. She'd use it as the beginning too, in the first *and* the last stanza, like the repetition in Elizabeth Bishop's *Letter to New York*.

"Maybe it's not as horrible as I thought."

"Do I get to see?" Christopher asked.

"Let's fool around," she said into his collar, pushing against his body instead.

"Show it to me first," he insisted.

She offered him the frayed page, her hand trembling. Lila wondered who she was really rescuing her lost poetry for—her old teacher, her husband, or the lonely schoolgirl she used to be. Leaning against his shoulder, she felt a mad rush of fear and fire as she took her words back to read aloud herself.

About the Author

Susan Shapiro, an award-winning writing professor, freelances for the *New York Times, Washington Post, Wall Street Journal, Los Angeles Times, Newsweek, Tablet, The Forward, Jerusalem Post, Marie Claire, Glamour, Cosmopolitan* and *More* magazines. She's a *New York Times* bestselling author of ten books, including *Unhooked, The Bosnia List, Lighting Up, Five Men Who Broke My Heart,* and the comic novels *Overexposed* and *Speed Shrinking.* A proud Michigan native, she now lives in Manhattan with her husband, a TV/film writer, and teaches her own popular "instant gratification takes too long" method at The New School, New York University, and in private classes and seminars. You can visit her at www.susanshapiro.net and follow her on Twitter @Susanshapironet.

CPSIA information can be obtained
at www.ICGtesting.com
Printed in the USA
LVOW03*1319031215
465209LV00007B/22/P